Presents

Patrick Augustus'

Baby Father

Published by THE X PRESS, 55 BROADWAY MARKET,
LONDON E8 4PH. TEL: 081 985 0797

Distributed by Turnaround, 27 Horsell Road, London N5 1XL
Tel: 071 609 7836

Printed and bound in Great Britain by
BPC Paperbacks Ltd
A Member of
The British Printing Company Ltd

The Men

Gussie Pottinger
Beres Dunkley
Johnny 'Dollar' Lindo
Linvall Henry

SAY IT WITH DIAMONDS

Diamonds are a girl's best friend. It's amazing how many men I meet who don't understand that yet. Buy a woman a diamond and you buy happiness, beauty and eternal gratitude. With that sparkle in her eye, the worst indiscretion is forgiven and the most blatant disrespect forgotten. Simple. Especially on Valentine's Day. Buy your woman chocolates come Valentine's and she'll suspect you of trying to make her fat on purpose. Buy her a teddy bear and she'll cuss you for thinking her a child. Women expect more than flowers, and tacky cards with crude rhymes. Nowadays, if you're not 'saying it with diamonds' you're not saying anything. You say it with diamonds when you need to make your "sorry" count — for forgetting her birthday, for disrespecting her or simply to say "I love you." A diamond can smooth over the rough edges of any relationship. Most definitely. Last year I sold £80,000 worth of diamonds to the Valentine's crowd and this year I'm hoping to do better.

I won't be giving diamonds on Valentine's and I say that not because I'm mean or can't afford it. When it comes to impressing women, few men can test me. But I'm a thirty-four-year-old eligible bachelor, still looking for Miss Right. I thought I found her a couple of times, but I was wrong. That's why I date so many women, because I know my dream woman is out there somewhere it's just a question of 'seek and you shall find'. I'm so used to seeking that I can tell within five minutes whether a woman is the wife I'm looking for and I end up having to tell them that "this is just a sex thing, I don't want a wedding and I don't want babies." When you tell women straight what the deal is, they're cool. I give them a good time, no expenses spared and then we go back to her place or mine. It's over the next morning. Once you explain what the deal is and that you're only out for a good time, they either say 'yes' or they say 'no', but they never try and get inside your head and mess up your mind on the pretext of love and how "honest" you've got to be with each other, well that's what I tell myself, anyway.

I'd rather be married with kids and a family than single, but there's too much at stake for me to take the matter lightly and make the wrong choice of wife. For one thing, only suitable women need apply and only the right *type* of woman need apply. Awaiting the successful candidate is a ring with a diamond so big it'll make Elizabeth Taylor blush with envy.

Since flamboyant 100 metre runner Greg Owen — 'the fastest man on earth' — chose a diamond from my collection for his bride-to-be, there's been a steady flow of new customers at our Mighty Diamond shop. Apart from Anthony Gee, there aren't any other black diamond merchants that I know of in London. Greg came in, bought a diamond and The Voice did a follow-up feature and the rest is history. Now I'm being asked to turn out everything from ragga jewellry to £100,000 jewel-studded belts for supermodel Fabiana. It's a very sexy business to be in, diamonds. And Hatton Garden is the sexiest address in the business. Most definitely. There's a lot of sexiness in my life but I'm good and ready to give it all up for real love and a couple of kids.

If it was just a question of getting any woman, it wouldn't be a problem. As a single man, I'm all too familiar with the 'get man by any means necessary posse'. But I'm not down with that. I've got an exact idea about the kind of woman I want and anything short of that seems like a pale comparison. I refuse to lower my standards for any woman. I'm looking for a relationship made in heaven so that me and my woman can reach the skies together. I know I'm not perfect and I've made some mistakes, but I'm ready to settle down now and I'm seeking a like minded, laid back, female.

And things would be easier if I didn't think marriage was fundamental to having kids. So many of my friends are baby fathers for one reason or another and yeah, *sometimes* I feel left out and feel like asking the first woman I meet "Do you want to be my baby mother?", but my head keeps insisting that it's a question of finding a woman who I want to spend the rest of my life with and build a home with and have kids with. She's got to be good looking. When I say good looking, I mean the business, Miss Ten out of Ten, good face and good body. That's what people expect of me. One time I took out this girl who wasn't too pretty in her face, but I liked her still. We didn't get too far before I started hearing people calling out "your woman's so ugly it's a shame!" And she's got to be able to match me intellectually. I may not be the greatest brains in the world, but I don't intend to marry a bimbo. I know what I'm worth. I'm young, I'm black and I run a successful jewellry business. I'm one in a million. Show me the woman who can match those odds and she'll have my diamond on her wedding finger. Most definitely.

My sister Evelyn says it's because I don't consider how important the small things like romance are to a woman, that I'm still single. Like it was a big deal that a man is thirty-four-years-old yet free and single. But no, she's figured my 'predicament' down to a science and she's been choosing my clothes, fixing me up with dates and organising my social calender for the last three years to ensure I don't waste my potential. Now she's got it into her mind that I've been disrespecting her business partner Caroline by standing her up and then not calling her when I said I would and she intends to make sure that I do things right come Valentine's. There's nothing worse than a younger sister who's trying to marry you off to her best friend. My own sister has to keep asking me whether I'm sure there isn't a kid somewhere in the world who knows me as 'Daddy'. Can you believe that? I'm sure Evelyn can't handle the fact that I haven't been trapped by some woman, somewhere because when it comes to 'diss the black man time', I'm living proof that we're not all baby fathers with kids littered around the place.

Initially the Old Man was cool about having a twentysomething bachelor son, after all he had always encouraged me to take my time, saying "don't rush into things" and "test the water before you jump in." But over the last couple of years, he's been noticeably impatient and started punctuating his lectures on 'family values' with the words, "you have to tek your bucket go ah well before the well runs dry," directed at me. Yet this handsome, well-toned, six-foot two, Lennox Lewis lookalike, creative, articulate conversationalist, with no kids anywhere, and who loves badminton, cinema and eating out, has still not found the sweet, attractive female — that genuine relationship — he's been looking for. Money can buy you many things but it can't buy you love, not true love.

Evelyn says I'm too fussy when it comes to women because the slightest thing wrong puts me off, whether it's a mole in the wrong place, or teeth that need straightening, or if they speak with cockney accents. She says I shouldn't spend my time looking for Miss Right with the perfect body and the perfect mind, when really I should be looking for a woman who will suffice, who I can be happy with, a woman to be my best friend, someone who I will be happy waking up beside for the next fifty years. I still reckon she's got to be perfect to be worth it. Evelyn can't understand that a tall man doesn't want a short woman. If a man loves tall women, it's unlikely

3

that he's going to start looking for redeeming features in a short woman. No way, he just doesn't like them short. Evelyn nevertheless fixed me up with her old college friend Winsome, who was pretty and intelligent and could have been a contender, but I decided straight away that there couldn't be any serious stuff, because she was too short. If I had known she was five foot nothing, I would have told Evelyn not to bother. I got to the dinner at Evelyn's house an hour late, to find this petite thirty-year-old sitting expectantly and seductively next to the vacant seat reserved for me. One thing I will say about a lot of short girls, they make up for it in other ways. Winsome was no exception and that night I found myself admiring the body that launched a billion coca-cola bottles. Most definitely.

No, I don't want to father a midget Frankenstein. If my kids are going to end up looking like my partner, there's no way I'm going to choose an ugly person over Miss Jamaica. Evelyn's always saying "beauty is only skin deep," so I decided to test it out and started to check this rich older woman, Lavinia Crawford. Yeah, she was rich, but too darn ugly, no wonder her ex-husband was always away on 'business'. But that's the way it goes sometimes. The world is full of handsome paupers and wealthy ogres. What's more, Lavinia couldn't dress. All the money in the world couldn't make her look good in a new dress. What made it worse was she didn't know how to keep her clothes looking fresh either. After a single wear, a £2,000 designer dress would look like it was picked up at the Oxfam shop for a fiver. And everybody could see it, except for Lavinia. For crissakes, she was still wearing leather overcoats. That relationship was getting so embarrassing it had to end.

Being the only one of my friends who isn't a baby father, I sometimes feel left out when they talk proudly of their children. I've been seeing a lot of Beres, Linvall and Johnny lately on account of our success in the football championships. In the last three years, Brixton Massive FC — the team we devote our blood, sweat and guts to for ninety minutes most Sunday mornings — has gone from being an informal social club to being the hottest little amateur team in South London. The deciding match between us and the Harlesden Ruffnecks for the the London Amateur League Championship takes place on Valentine's Day. We were all supposed to go out and rave to celebrate afterwards, but I talked myself into a date with Caroline and now I don't know how to juggle it.

Evelyn says I still have a lot to learn about women and I

4

guess she's right about that. She's the pride and joy of the family. When I was younger, I was the apple of my father's eye. We used to be so close. I remember how he used to take a big interest in my athletics when I used to run for the County and whenever he was at home we'd go out for a road run and he'd time me and give me tips to improve. But we started to grow apart when I was about thirteen. I was going through a rough time with my teachers and not doing too well at school. I fell out of favour and Evelyn replaced me in his affections. It was like every time he looked at me I caused him pain, while Evelyn was exactly the daughter he had dreamt of. Time only proved to confirm his beliefs. While I spent my time drifting from one course to another, Evelyn came out of school with straight A's and went to read Law at Oxford. That's where she met Beckford — 'the backward barrister' as I call him — whom she later married. Of course everybody loves him and thinks he's a perfect husband and father. The Old Man is always asking, "Why can't you be just like Beckford?" Because he's a snivelling pussy, that's why. Not only did Evelyn marry the perfect husband and have the perfect child with the perfect father, she's also become the perfect career woman. She joined a reputable practice when she finished her articles and quickly became a reputable solicitor. Then three months ago, she declared just how ambitious she was by opening her own practice, in partnership with Caroline. Evelyn has done everything right. Meanwhile her elder brother merely runs the family business and still hasn't found a woman to settle down and start a family with. That sort of thing is important with Jamaican parents.

Right now, I wish I didn't ever say I'd go out with Caroline in the first place. Johnny's right when he says "Sometimes a man must endure celibacy to maintain his dignity." Evelyn can't stand him because of his attitude to women, but I'm telling you, that guy makes sense to me most of the time. But it's easier to talk about "celibacy" when you've got a permanent woman and guaranteed your rights every evening. There's no guarantees when you're single. When you're single you don't know when you'll next get a grind, it could be weeks so I always make contingency plans. That's why I agreed to take Caroline out in the first place. Evelyn was full of big talk that she was just my type — tall, intelligent, fit, attractive, thirty-years-old, single and conscious. She flattered me when I called to arrange the date, saying she had heard all sorts of wonderful things about me. We chatted about small things, birth signs, favourite films favourite clubs and so on.

5

She had a way of talking which made me feel good, like I was the most interesting person she had ever spoken to. Everything I said was met with a 'Oh that sounds really interesting!' response. Two-twos I started thinking 'this woman sounds like a bit of alright'. I suggested we go to a New Year's Eve party at The Roof Garden that the upwardly mobile contact club Excel were having.

"Oh that would be just fabulous!" she replied. "I've heard of Excel, apparently they organise really great events."

I arranged to meet her outside the venue at eleven-thirty. I had already had too much drink to drive and spent an hour trying to book a cab but it was New Year's Eve so every available driver was out earning some dollars. I decided to trek down to Clapham High Street to catch a black cab, something I never do on account of how many rocks I've felt like flinging through their windows when they've refused to stop for a black man at night. It was pissing down with rain, but I knew I had to make the effort. It's bad style not to show up when you agree to meet a woman, so I always make the effort. There weren't any cabs to be had. The tube was closed because of a bomb scare and every bus heading towards Town hurtled past the bus stops packed to bursting point with unsober suburbians making the most of the free ride for the night. I ended up walking all the way to Vauxhall Bridge before I saw a cab with its yellow light on. It stopped only momentarily at the traffic lights, but soaked to the skin and already half an hour late, I wasn't giving the driver a chance to refuse. I jumped in, even as the traffic lights turned to green and was met with a grunt from the fat-bottomed guy at the wheel. By the time the cab had crawled its way to Kensington, through the 'Happy New Year!' crowd tooting their car horns merrily, I was an hour late. There was no woman in a black dress suit at the entrance steps as I had agreed with Caroline however. I went inside and spent the whole evening looking in every corner of the venue, hopeful that I might find her. Then I asked the master of ceremonies to make an announcement for Caroline to come to the front entrance to meet Gussie. The guy couldn't resist going over the top and announcing through the microphone, "Caroline, are you in the house? If the beautiful, exquisite, sensitive, loving and irresistible Caroline is in the house, a young man by the name of Gussie, is dying to meet you. He says that he's your blind date for the night and doesn't know what you look like. So Caroline, please, if you have eyes to see, come out to the reception and see him, 'cause his New Year's going to be filled with loneliness otherwise."

I knew the woman would be vexed that we didn't meet, but I wasn't expecting the response I got. I returned home that night to find an icy message on my answering machine. "This is a message for Gussie. Gussie, this is Caroline. I waited almost an hour for you... I hope you've got a bloody good excuse. You know my number, so call me..." The message chilled me, it was just a date after all. For the next three weeks, I laid low, screening every call. But Caroline didn't call again. Finally, Evelyn called up and before I could say anything, launched into a full frontal assault.

"So what happened between you and Caroline, Gus? Didn't I tell you not to disrespect the sister?"

"Oh please," I answered defensively, "what have I done now?"

"Well for starters, you arrange to meet her and you don't show up? What kind of behaviour is that? You keep her waiting in the rain for an hour, on New Year's Eve! And then you don't even return her calls."

"Call, not calls. She called once. I haven't got round to..."

"Oh don't give me that, Gus. It's been three weeks..."

I remembered how much women love to chat gossip with each other too much. Evelyn obviously had a full account of the facts. I had to take what was coming to me, take it like a man.

"...I've never seen her like this before, every time I mention your name, she gives me this vicious stare and says, 'I thought he had disappeared off the face of the earth'. Gus, she's my good friend and my business partner and you're treating her wrong, man. She doesn't deserve that, she deserves better. What's wrong with you?"

"Alright, alright. It was out of order, I should have called her."

"Damn right!"

"What d'you suggest I do, Sis?"

"Well, the first thing is you've got to call. Not tomorrow or the day after, you've got to call her now. She's in the office, you've got the number." Evelyn wasn't playing, she meant business. "You go on about not being able to find the right woman. Then I set you up with a woman I know would be perfect for you, but you just want to play games. You're thirty-four, Gus. You've got to stop playing small boys' games with women."

She slammed the phone down. I reluctantly called Caroline. That was my next big mistake. After playing it decisively cool at first, Caroline suddenly became warm towards me and suggested that we rearrange things and this time she choose the time and the place.

"This time, I'm taking *you* out," she insisted.

"Well that's fine by me. When do you want to make it, it's up to you, I'm free whenever."

She suggested that we should go out that same night. "Some friends of mine are holding an event down at a nice, little hotel out in the countryside. It should be a romantic evening and we can spend the night there. The treat's on me."

When a woman invites you for a dirty weekend in the countryside, you don't spend much time deliberating. She insisted on driving down in her car.

Caroline picked me up around seven in her immaculate, red Triumph Stag convertible.

"Finally, we get to meet," she said spreading her arms wide to embrace me, "I hope you don't keep all your women running after you like this."

I don't know what I expected Caroline Simmons to be like, but she was the mirror-image of Evelyn, a typical ambitious female solicitor with above average looks, a tightly-toned body in a navy dress suit, and hair trimmed into a neat little bob. The only thing that seemed out of place was the sunglasses. She apologised that she was still dressed in her office clothes. She had only had time to pick up a travel case and a change of clothing. I told her jokingly that I could overlook that minor detail. I also overlooked the fact that she was probably a couple of inches below my minimum height requirement. She looked good enough for me to live with that. As I squeezed into the front passenger seat of the Triumph, I wished I also was a couple of inches shorter.

After a two hour drive West down the M4, we arrived at a hotel overlooking the Malvern Hills. From the number of luxury cars parked in the driveway, it was clear that the buppie clientele mingling in the hallway really had money.

"A friend of mine runs this dating line called RSVP," Caroline explained enthusiastically. "They hold these exclusive events for upwardly mobile romantics like myself to get together for the weekend, away from it all. This one's like a pre-Valentine's night."

"Yeah, I heard of RSVP, I didn't think that a successful and attractive solicitor like you would use a date line."

"Get real, Gus. This is the modern world; working women like myself haven't got time to hunt around for men. We're far too busy making money. A dating line like RSVP is a fast and efficient way of meeting the right person."

I carried her travel bag into the reception area, where to my delight I discovered that because she had booked so late, they only had a twin room available. I insisted that it didn't bother me any which way and Caroline laughed that it didn't bother her if it didn't bother me. 'Yes', I told myself, 'a result!'

It was a traditional country house hotel with excellent leisure facilities: indoor swimming pool, sauna, health club and solarium for those who wanted to get romantic and keep fit at the same time. I offered to make a contribution to the bill, but Caroline kept saying, "I said I was taking you out, so that means I'm paying. Relax." I didn't ask how much it all cost, but I knew it wasn't cheap.

Like the other couples, we were given a special aphrodisiac 'loving cup' and a complimentary red rose on arrival. The place was stuffed full like a meat pattie with lawyers and accountants and one or two TV newsreaders I recognised, everybody drinking cupid cocktails at the candle-lit dinner and dance. Some couples smooched away on the dancefloor to the sounds of Barry White, while other couples looked lovingly into each other's eyes. The white staff looked on, bemused, unable to understand how there could be so many black people in Britain who earned more in a week than they did in a month.

A table had been reserved for Caroline and myself by the French windows. Unfortunately, the couple next to us were engaged in a heated argument, which made me feel uncomfortable. My man was your typical buppie wannabee and his woman, the original black browning with her nose stuck way up in the air.

"All I'm saying is that I forgot to bring my credit cards with me," Wannabee explained, "I didn't know that this night out would be so expensive. If you could make a small donation towards the costs, I would be very grateful..."

"Well I'm sorry, Dale," the browning declared unsympathetically, "I don't go dutch, I just don't do that. When a man takes me out, I expect him to pay for everything. Do you know how many men wanted to take me out tonight? But I chose you over all of them and now you're asking me to pay for myself as well. What a cheek!"

"Give me a break now baby..."

Considering the financial arrangement between Caroline and myself, it wasn't the kind of dispute I wanted flaring up on the table next to me.

"Evelyn says that you're quite smart, but that you try not to use your intelligence too much," Caroline offered.

"Yeah, Evelyn talks a lot about me. That's the problem with having a sister..."

"Oh come on now, don't get defensive. Men gossip amongst themselves as well."

"Not like women they don't. So what else has Evelyn told you about me?"

"Well, she said that you're every woman's dream — you're handsome, single and you have potential to make a lot of money."

I was embarrassed. Why is it that the first thing women want to talk about, regarding men, is how much money they've got?

"And what else did she tell you about me?"

"She said you're getting a bit old to still be single, but she thinks you're afraid of women."

"That's because there are too many money-hungry women out there ready to take a man for fool..."

"Well most men are fools aren't they?" Caroline cut in with a wide smile on her face. Maybe she was teasing, maybe she wasn't. "I must say, I can't blame those women. I like beautiful things myself and money's the only way you can get them. If you've got money for diamonds, then get diamonds and I don't see what the point in squeezing yourself into a hatchback is when you can afford a luxury car. When I meet a man that I like and he wants to get me beautiful things, it flatters me."

The waiter brought our champagne and we toasted each other. There was something about this woman, I don't know exactly, maybe a twinkle in her eye, that made me curious. She relished a battle of the sexes, yet she didn't seem to be taking the debate as seriously as I was.

"So what about you, Caroline? I know you're a high-powered lawyer with the world at your feet, but tell me about the real Caroline Simmons?"

She laughed again. "Well, I suppose I'm fiercely independent and that's why most men end up running as far away from me as they can. But that's just the way I am. Do you like going out raving?" She changed the subject as she often did. "I used to love it so much I never thought I'd stop. But nowadays, I can't find the time. A legal business is like any other business, it only succeeds as a result of a lot of hard work. So I've had to abstain from the raving scene for a while. At least until Evelyn and I can afford to pay other people to

10

do a lot of the mundane work we're having to do at the moment... I found this great place where I go to whenever I need to really chill out. It's in West London and it's called the Factory. Have you heard of it? Oh, we should go there together. You'd love it, I'm sure you would. It's this huge warehouse-type gallery with a collection of paintings of black heroes — Marcus Garvey, Mary Seacole, Malcolm X, Martin Luther King... I go there to relax and I always end up coming out with a sense of pride in black cultural heritage and the fact that these individuals, long dead but not forgotten, are being rediscovered. Paul Robeson's face is sadly missing. It's a pity that in these days of black consciousness that no one remembers old Paul Robeson. Do you know that in Russia there's a mountain named after him, in Berlin a museum, in Pennysylvania a film festival and in Poland a street bears his name."

I had begun to take a keener interest in Caroline. My ears had perked up and I was tripping about having a conscious intellect as my companion. A conscious black woman with intelligence always makes me horny. Dinner was served. While Caroline picked away at her avocado salad, I dived into my steam fish, ignoring the potatoes.

"So do you have any heroes?" she asked .

"Not any more. I used to when I was younger, but I got disillusioned with them all. Your heroes have a tendency of letting you down when you start finding out more about them. Christopher Columbus for example, turned out to be a damn liar... I always wanted to be an explorer because of him. Then when I was thirteen, I got to know that he didn't discover Jamaica at all, but that there were Arawak Indians and even a few black men and women there long before Columbus."

"I know exactly what you mean. That's why I'm so glad we have black private schools now. It's the only way to get a balanced education. That's why I work so hard, so that when I have kids I can afford to send them to a good black private school."

"Well don't work too hard, or you might miss your chance to have kids."

"Oh, is that some kind of proposal?" Caroline laughed.

"No...uhm...no of course not..." Suddenly I felt embarrassed. "So, are you planning to have kids?" I needed to know. When you're planning on getting off with a woman, it's important to know what her state of mind is regarding babies, *before* sleeping with her. My spar Johnny Dollar's always

11

saying that, and I know he's most definitely right.

"Not before the quality of the men on offer seriously improves. I'm not kidding," she laughed again, "I've been meeting some seriously low forms of life out there recently."

"Maybe your demands are too high," I said defensively.

"No, it's not that... it's definitely not that," Caroline continued thoughtfully, "I just don't seem to meet men who are prepared to take a minute out to really know what I'm about. You know, what I want from the relationship, what I want out of life. It's a challenge to all men. I bet they can't put up anything in defence. If men made sure they understood their women to the max, I wouldn't see so many cases of acrimonious divorces coming to our offices every week. Understand your woman, Gussie, that's the secret."

I was determined not to get involved in a 'diss the black man' session, partly because it was an argument I couldn't win and partly because something was telling me not to fall out with this woman. She was a woman I could definitely do business with.

I let out a sigh of gratitude as a lover's track finally came through the speakers, sublime and sultry. It was the only reggae the deejay had spun all night and it was time to celebrate.

"You wanna dance?" I asked, pushing my empty plate aside and offering Caroline my hand. With my arm around her waist as we inched our way lightfootedly between the other couples onto the dancefloor, I realised for the first time how incredibly fit Caroline was. And she could dance, also. She bumped her waist teasingly between my two outstretched arms and made me feel like I was in heaven: my eyes and thoughts fixed on her. I felt like the luckiest man in the place, with the most attractive woman in my arms. I wanted her bad and hoped deep down inside that she wanted me too. I had a lot of love to give her that night.

She decided to turn in first.

"Caroline, you must be reading my mind," I said with a twinkle in my eye. She simply smiled. In a few minutes, we were inside our twin room, but I didn't have sleep on my mind. Caroline took off her jacket and excused herself to go to the bathroom. I didn't waste any time. Within seconds, I had pushed the twin beds together, stripped myself naked in a flash and lay across the beds waiting. Caroline burst out laughing uncontrollably when she came out of the bathroom.

"Gussie... what are you doing naked on the bed?" she spluttered between bouts of giggling. I played it cool.

"Take off your clothes too," I said calmly, "take off your clothes so I can spin you around and see how beautiful you are."

She started to undress slowly.

"Look we better get one thing clear, Gus. I don't intend to make love to you tonight. If I wanted to make love to you, you'd know it already. I don't waste any time in letting a man know my desires. Trust me. If I wanted to make love to you, I'd be walking all over you already."

She continued stripping down to her black silk knickers and her bleached white blouse. I admired her in all her blessed beauty. Her skin soft and black and shiny, the way I like my women. Her breasts... her neck, her shoulders, her legs... her round, pert, firm behind. She was more than sweetness. I wasn't going to give up easily, because I had to have this woman tonight.

"Come on Caroline," I insisted, "don't tell me there's been a mix up that we've got to straighten out. I've wanted you all night and you've wanted me too, I know it."

She laughed. "Gus, don't flatter yourself. I want nothing from you tonight. And if you want anything from me you'll have to work harder than you've been working so far."

My mind told me to cool it. My desires were mostly lustful and physical. Every man knows just what I'm getting at — I had to have that woman before morning. However, she gave me a definite kiss off.

I don't remember my exact words, but it was the usual stuff. You know, "Did anyone ever tell you that you've got heaven in your eyes?" and then, "Something strange is happening, to me... I can't understand why I can't resist you." It ended up with me pleading to the back of her head as she hit the light switch, "There's no easy way to say this, but I think I'm falling head over heels in love with you..."

I couldn't sleep a wink that night; I had to control myself. A gorgeous girl, who I desperately wanted to make love to, lay just inches away in the same bed, so near and yet so far away. I didn't just want to sex her however, I would have been happy to just hold her there all night long, but I had already played my cards. My desire for Caroline increased, I was determined to have her somehow, somewhere, sometime. I spent every hour, every minute, every second of that sleepless night planning how I would do that. When we got up at midday, a champagne brunch awaited us. Between glasses of bubbly and chit chat, I promised to take her out on St Valentine's Day.

13

NO WOMAN NO CRY

Virgo — Make the most of your opportunities today. If you're single, a new friend or admirer could pop up. If you're married, plan that holiday or break to somewhere lovely you've been thinking about. Money matters will improve and nostalgic thoughts are apt to cruise back to you.'

Beres was thinking of cancelling the rest of his appointments to fetch his daughter from school. The child minder had just called on his mobile to say she couldn't collect Lara. It was an emergency, but that was a moment ago. His thoughts had since been distracted they were was every week day afternoon by the sight of the most attractive woman in town. The woman looked perfect: tall, slim, elegant and confident. He supposed that she must be a secretary working in one of the office buildings around the Square. As always, her charm and beauty held Beres transfixed. He had thought about her every day and every night for weeks and seeing her now sent chills up his spine. He liked the way she did her hair and the stylish clothes she wore. If only... if only he could muster up the courage to talk to her. That's all he had wanted since the very first time he blessed his eyes on her, but when you're looking for more than sex, friendship and socialising, you have to take it slow. Beres was looking to find a mother for his daughter, but he had lost the courage to make a move.

"Boy!" he said to himself, as he peered out through the plate glass window. Maybe his prolonged celibacy was playing tricks on him, but he thought he had never seen a body look so very good and a face as fresh. It was the same thing every day. At 2pm sharp, this black Cleopatra would make her way to the north side of Berkeley Square, while Beres admired her through the well polished plate glass windows of the showroom. In an area with very few black women, she was one of the few distractions in his working day. She looked like the kind of woman who liked the finer things in life and he wanted to give them to her. He could take her on a romantic weekend to Paris, he considered. He would get her to wear that red dress and high heels and he'd buy her some sweet perfume... So why didn't he make his move? He who in his earlier years had been such a smooth operator, such a sweet talker, hadn't bothered to have his confidence serviced during his married years. He didn't need to, he had a woman at home that he loved and felt he no longer needed the boost an affair would give to his ego. When Sonia walked out of their home after seven years of marriage, he went searching for that confidence and found it crumpled in the attic, decaying and trampled underfoot.

By rights he should have made his play today if he was ever going to succeed with the black velvet princess across the road. He had studied his horoscope before leaving for work, a habit he had formed since Sonia left. He was looking for good news and as always the Virgo chart didn't fail to deliver: 'Make the most of your opportunities today. If you're single, a new friend or admirer could pop up. If you're married, plan that holiday or break to somewhere lovely you've been thinking about. Money matters will improve and nostalgic thoughts are apt to cruise back to you.'

"Mr Dunkley?" The voice was low, suggesting authority.

Beres spun around to be greeted confidently by a short, white man of about thirty with a friendly, if slightly impatient smile. Dressed in a striped blazer and hooped cricket cap, he presented himself as a man with a sense of humour and a healthy cash flow. For a moment it didn't register, Beres' mind was still on the beautiful woman across the road. "Yes, that's right," he answered. "How can I help you?"

The man cast an impressed eye over the young black man in the Armani suit and sporting a heavyweight Rolex watch, yet managed to maintain an air of higher status.

"I'm Declan Galloway-Smith. I spoke to you on the phone yesterday. To test drive the Lotus Esprit."

"Oh yes, I beg your pardon, Sir. How do you do? I wasn't expecting you quite so soon."

"Well you know how it is, I had to do some shopping in Fortnum & Mason's so I thought I might just jolly well come over early. Is that alright?"

Beres looked Declan up and down. He recognised the type: the landed gentry with private income and a mansion in the countryside — all inherited of course — and a sporting affinity for cricket and fast cars. In this business, you got a pretty good insight into the lives of the rich and famous. And it was this insight or maybe intuition that told him there was something that didn't quite fit about Declan Galloway-Smith.

Tender thoughts, love-warmed hearts and a mellow mood, were some of the familiar images that filled Beres' mind, whenever he thought about his wife. Yet she had left him alone and now, with only two weeks to go before Valentine's, he remembered that he was still missing the essential ingredient for the day — a loving woman. He had the soothing candlelight to set the mood, but he lacked the partner to deliver an abundance of loving compliments or just a card, a present, words of love and dinner for two at some upmarket restaurant. He'd get a babysitter for Lara and borrow one of the luxury cars in the showroom, if he could get a woman to date him on Valentine's.

Beres was tired of feeling lonely. He hadn't planned to bring his daughter up alone, but that's the way it had turned out. Lara needed a mother, he knew that. That's why he was only interested in something serious, a one-to-one relationship with someone who was caring. He didn't even mind a divorcee with her own children as long as she filled all the other requirements, most important of which was that Lara approved and secondly that it was a woman who could bring up his daughter as her own child. One thing for sure, he couldn't sit back and wait for things to happen. Tomorrow he would walk right across the square and ask the woman out.

In the three months he had been employed at Dan Oliver's luxury car showroom in Berkeley Square, Beres had risen to become the top salesman. It was a remarkable achievement. While other salesmen had felt their commissions squeezed during the recession, Beres was suave and sophisticated under pressure and knew how to make a sale. The others had been in the game longer and thought they knew their art better. While they would bend over backwards to say the things they thought their client wanted to hear, Beres would be straight. He'd tell the prospective customer the good sides and the bad sides of the car and he would be honest about whether he thought the car suited the person in question. His boss almost collapsed and died when he overheard the young black salesman dissuading a customer about to write out a £134,000 cheque for an Aston Martin Virage, insisting "this car just doesn't suit you." However, the boss quickly revived when he saw the customer write out a £168,000 cheque for a Bentley Continental R instead. Beres understood that money was the bottom line with Dan Oliver, who had given him only three months to prove that he could pull good custom. Dan Oliver would rather not have had a black salesperson in his exclusive showroom, but he had to admit that Beres' face seemed to attract more Arabs and rich Africans — who seemed to have an unlimited supply of cash and were always looking for a big car to export home. Somehow the boy usually did good. The only reason Beres got the job in the first place was that he brought three firm sales with him — Arab oil tycoons he had got to know while selling fax machines in the Gulf countries. Otherwise Dan Oliver's was a totally white environment. That didn't bother Beres, he needed the money, not the company. When he left South London every morning, he turned his back on one world and entered into another. Berkeley Square was a long way away from Streatham, and few of his customers had ventured further South than the Elephant and Castle. They had only seen places like Brixton on television and from their general conclusions, Beres thought it better to say he lived in Islington if they got chatting. He enjoyed his job nevertheless. It was glamourous. One moment he would be driving through Berkeley Square at the wheel of a £70,000 Mercedes and the next he would be showing a client the joys of driving a Ferrari Mondial through Richmond.

Beres was so tired of being on his own, he prayed to God to send a little sunshine his way and soon. When Sonia left him he had tried sleeping around at first but quickly decided that it was not for him. For one thing he would rather be safe than sorry, though it was tougher resisting the urge than taking the chances. Johnny, Gussie and Linvall slept with whoever they pleased but Beres had no interest in jumping from one woman's bed to another. He had tasted that and it was nothing special. All he got for his troubles was a hot, rough banging with women who wanted nothing but a good grind to satisfy them. The women he was meeting had not learned that a man is not a toy. After all the hurt he had been through, fifty-fifty loving was no good to him, he wanted one hundred percent of strong loving. That's why he was looking for a mother for his daughter as well as a wife who wouldn't cause him pain and strife, but would give him love and affection.

Beres Dunkley was a typical buppie. He had had a good upbringing and his teacher parents opted to send their only son to Millfields — an average public school in North London. There, Beres got the benefit of a good education, but most importantly he learned that confidence, which some call arrogance, that distinguishes a public school boy. He had so much confidence in fact that he couldn't see the point of university when there was money to be made out there and no time to lose. So with three A levels in his back pocket, he

17

pounded the streets at the age of eighteen, from office to office leasing photocopiers. A chance meeting with an old school friend put him on to facsimile machines at a time when nobody knew what they were. Within a year, Beres was earning more in a day than his parents made in a week, selling the joys of a fax. The market was soon flooded and a drop in profits followed. Another old school friend, Femi Adefemi, had returned from his home in Nigeria and arranged to go for a drink with Beres in Covent Garden. Femi convinced his old school chum that Africa needed fax machines.

"All we've got out there is telegram and that's so expensive. Sell your facsimile machines in Nigeria and I guarantee you'll put telegrams out of business in Africa as they are everywhere else."

Within a month, Beres was on a plane to West Africa with Femi's sister's Lagos address in his wallet, a demonstration fax machine in his luggage and the confidence of his public school days in his heart. Few salesmen had branched outside Europe at this point. Beres' several trips to West Africa and the Gulf states kept his income high for a few years, but it was hard work.

Beres was thinking about picking Lara up from school, but also thinking of the gorgeous woman with no name who was the current object of his desires. His confidence had been so badly damaged in the last six months, he no longer knew what to do. He turned his mind to the cars he was now selling and in particular to Declan Galloway-Smith. There was something troubling him about the short man in the striped cricket cap.

"If you'll follow me, Sir." Beres ushered courteously. They walked over to the gleaming black Lotus on the far side of the showroom. It was a beautiful machine through and through Beres thought, and from the orgasmic look on his face, so did Declan.

"I take it Sir's the sporting type?" Beres asked nodding at the striped cricket cap.

"Yes that's right," Declan replied enthusiastically. "I just like to get down to the old nets every now and then for a spot of batting and bowling, nothing more."

Beres smiled to himself. A spot of batting and bowling was as it may be, there was still something that didn't quite make sense about Declan. But he'd get there in the end.

"So, are we all ready for the test drive?" Declan changed

18

the subject. It was then that Beres remembered that he had intended to cancel the rest of the day's appointments so he could pick up his daughter. Damn. Now the customer was here, it wouldn't do to pass him on to another salesman. Especially as it would mean passing on the commission also. At the same time, Lara had to be picked up from school in an hour's time. Maybe if they went for a quick ten minute spin...

"Yes certainly, Sir," Beres answered. "If you'll just give me a minute." He quickly arranged for the Lotus to be wheeled out of the showroom and on to the busy street. In another few minutes, he was sitting at the wheel of the car, with Declan beside him ecstatic.

Berkeley Square was as ever spinning with a constant flow of traffic from every direction. But Beres knew the back streets. He pointed the car in the direction of the least congested route to the Westway. That was the nearest motorway and long enough to test the Lotus' engine to the max.

Beres cleared the traffic in no time, handling the Lotus like a seasoned rally driver. It was rare to see a young black man at the wheel of a car more expensive than most people's houses and no matter what luxury car he drove, Beres never failed to garner the admiration — reluctant or otherwise — of bypassers. While nearly all the black people who saw him would give him a respectful nod, whites would merely stare with dropped jaws and mouths wide opened, their brains unable to make head or tail of the messages their eyes had just sent — the ultimate fear of a black penis.

Declan didn't notice the reaction from passers-by. He had a slightly moronic look on his face as he studied every detail of the sportscar's controls. Beres had a knack of being able to judge his customers. It was a psychological thing. The Africans tended to go for a Mercedes Benz while the Americans tended to go for Jaguar. The Aston Martins and the Bentleys were usually preferred by the English, who were also always keen to stress their limited budget, though wealthy. Beres also had the knack of sussing the reasons why a rich man would come into his showroom looking for a flash car. Sometimes it was an ego thing; they needed a dick extension. He always advised those sort of guys to go for the big Bentleys. They never failed to impress. For those who wanted to pull women he would suggest the fast sports cars, preferably a convertible. They were guaranteed to tease the most hard-to-pull woman into submission. And if the customer simply had more money than sense, he would suggest the Continental R at £168,000. He'd already sold two at five grand above the list price. It was outrageous to pay that sort of money for a car and he personally would never do it, even if he could afford to. But there were so many people out there with more money than sense.

While his friends thought he should enjoy the bachelor life newly-foisted upon him, Beres wished more than anything for the nice, safe comfort of a home he could depend on; a nuclear home with a child, one mother and one father and however much he hid his tears and heartaches, he couldn't stop dreaming those silly dreams. Everybody thought him a fool to want to rush back into marriage, but he couldn't help himself.

He looked at his watch. He had just 45 minutes in which to allow his passenger the test drive and to make it to Dulwich to pick Lara up. It was going to be tight. In fact he already knew he wasn't going to make it. The teachers weren't going to be too happy about it, but a quarter of an hour late was hardly a matter of life and death. He hated the idea of his daughter being the last child left at school, still waiting to be picked up when all the other kids had gone home, but that was the working baby father's reality. Lara was the most important person in his life, but trying to keep a full time job while making sure that she didn't miss out on anything in life was a juggling act that was hard to perform for a single man but he had managed so far, with only a few disapproving grunts from Dan Oliver. He turned left at the Paddington end of the Edgware Road into the slip road to the motorway and pulled over.

"Oh right, it's my turn is it?" Declan asked eagerly. They got out and changed positions. Though Declan climbed into the driver's seat confidently, he couldn't believe how hard it was to make the machine go. Beres assured him that a Lotus takes weeks to get used to. Declan nevertheless stalled three times. Eventually they were on the open road, notching 90 mph with relative ease.

"Of course I'll be looking at some comparable cars before I make my final decision," Declan informed his passenger as they zipped from one lane to another, overtaking everything in their path. Beres hung tight to his seat. Declan was preparing him for the inevitable disappointment of a no sale. The other salesmen at Dan Oliver's would have taken this as the cue to start maligning all the known competition to the car they were touting. Beres knew this didn't really work. What you see is what you get and if Declan Galloway-Smith didn't like what he saw that was tough. He looked at his watch again. Half an hour to go. It was more important to pick Lara up if Declan wasn't buying.

"The Lotus Esprit is not the most expensive or fastest car you'll see on the road, but it is one of the most exciting," he offered salesman-like. "Head off towards Shepherd's Bush!" he shouted anxiously as Declan moved into the fast lane as if he intended to drive all the way to Oxford non stop. They managed to cut across three lanes and into the slip road leading to the Bush. Beres was speechless as Declan held sway over the fast lane. Maybe it was an attribute of the rich or maybe it was a man thing, but it wasn't the first time Beres had seen a man transform in the driver's seat of a powerful machine. Behind the wheel of the Lotus, Declan's self-esteem seemed to soar. Like a whale amongst plankton, he felt utter contempt for any other road user.

Beres remembered the dream that had been floating into his subconscious night after night. A dream so near he could reach out and touch it. He dreamt that he was making love over and over, but he couldn't see who the woman was; her face was always hidden by a mask. After dreaming that same dream for several weeks, he managed only last night to finally lift the mask off and behind it was the face of the woman he had been making love to, only it wasn't a woman but a man. He awoke in a cold sweat, ashamed and scared and promising himself never to dream that dream again.

As they neared the Shepherd's Bush roundabout, Declan slowed to 70mph and Beres took a moment to study his client closely.

The biggest problem with being a luxury car salesmen was that there were too many losers addicted to test driving expensive cars, who just wanted the opportunity to drive a car they could only dream about owning. People who would go to any lengths to get a free drive. Beres had become an expert in sussing out the time-wasters, even as they assured him they were genuine buyers who would write out a cheque on the spot the moment they had got a chance to burn some rubber in a Porsche or Lamborghini. He usually humoured them for a minute or two in the showroom before pointing to the door politely but firmly. Dan Oliver's showroom couldn't afford to cater for the supermarket crowd and Beres really couldn't afford to humour jokers for more than ninety seconds. It was a constant battle for the salesman looking for firm sales as the time wasters were extremely resourceful. Once they had parked their ageing Ford Sierras out of sight and stepped into the showroom with its gleaming luxury cars and £100,000 price tags, they would transform into a South African wine tycoon, a rich American divorce lawyer or an English country squire sitting on a pot of inherited wealth. Spotting the time waster from the serious buyer had become a major part of Beres' job.

Declan took the Shepherd's Bush roundabout at 45mph, dodging in and out of the traffic coming from each junction.

"Look, take it easy around the roundabout!" Beres demanded sternly. "If you just double back, we'll drive back down the Westway."

Without a good woman by his side, Beres felt insecure. He was an above average man and he was available, but he just didn't have the confidence to exploit it. He had even been running down to the gym five times a week, busting sweat, determined not to be the the only person in Brixton not making love on Valentine's night.

Beres' patience was wearing thin. He didn't have time for fun and games no matter how much commission he could earn from a sale. He looked Declan up and down and couldn't help wondering about him. It was hard to know whether a customer really had money or not and Beres' own litmus test was to make a rough valuation of their clothes. He expected them to dress at least as sharply as himself.

It was then, as they turned off the roundabout to head back up the motorway that Beres' mind was made up about his customer. As Declan turned the steering wheel, his Casio watch slipped down his wrist and into full view. It was no coincidence that Beres then asked what he did for a living. No wealthy man, however prudent, would wear a plastic watch. He had an imposter at the controls of the car.

Declan muttered something about 'a private income' but Beres was unconvinced and he pulled the key out of the ignition. Declan had no choice but to pull over to the hard shoulder as the car slowed down.

"Get the hell out of my car, man!" Beres shouted. Courtesy and salesmanship were now superfluous.

"I say, " Declan declared, "we're on a motorway. What do you expect me to do? I demand that you return me to Mayfair."

"I said, get the hell out of my car!" Beres repeated, but this time the glare in his eyes warned Declan he meant business. The man stepped out of the car sulkily and Beres climbed into the drivers seat, kissing his teeth angrily. He wasn't bothered what Declan did, the man was a fraud out for a free test drive. Beres glanced at his watch. He had only fifteen minutes to get to Dulwich.

DO THE RIGHT THING

Every man wants to do the right thing, but that's easier said than done. With St Valentine's Day only two weeks away, most of my friends are under manners setting up some constructive planning, because Valentine's is the one day when excuses won't be accepted, lateness won't be forgiven and nothing but the best is expected. That means no dibbi-dibbi business, strictly limousines and dinner for two in a posh restaurant, up West, before the show. That takes some serious financial planning. And then to wrap it all up, dessert at your place all night long, and believe me, I know men who are doing their physical training for that one! Personally, I don't care too tough for Valentine's, nor for birthdays and anniversaries neither, yet I'm preparing for it, plotting it meticulously like a chess grandmaster plans his next move, because women act as if you've given them a dose of herpes if you don't have the flowers and a box of chocolates on the day. Then they start talking murder if you don't spend the night with them. Lesley's like that. "Johnny, I expect to be doted on and pampered this Valentine's," she reminded me. Pauline's like that as well. That's my problem. How to juggle things smoothly between two women on Valentine's night and still manage to satisfy them both. Though there's still another two weeks to go until the big day, I've been training for it since the summer. That's when Lesley told me she was pregnant. Pauline told me she was pregnant the day after. Pure worries and tribulation. Both babies are due on Valentine's week and Pauline and Lesley are both demanding women who won't be satisfied with no part-time Valentine's business. I'll be well under manners trying to be in two places at the same time and eating two dinners, but that's a small price to pay for domestic harmony.

Mama's always saying there must be something wrong with me because I can't stick to one woman. That's not strictly true, because I've been together with Lesley for fifteen years. It's just that I haven't been faithful all that time, I don't know a single man who has. But Mama's convinced that the devil has possessed me and goes to church every Sunday to pray for me. She's always saying, "You and Lesley should have another child, another grandchild for me to look after in my old age." I haven't got around to telling her that she's got two grandchildren by two different women coming soon.

Now, I'm not like all the other men out there. Mama always taught me to respect my woman, that's why I stand firm and take responsibility for my actions. My baby mothers can rely on me to provide for them — economically, spiritually and in every other respect and aspect. But when I really check it, the reason that I'm in this dilemma is through their insecurity. Lesley's been feeling insecure since she turned thirty. No matter how many times I assured her that there was no possibility of me leaving her for a younger woman, she needed reassurance. Now she's got the best insurance policy on the way — a brand new baby to remind me that a relationship is a fifty-fifty business, twenty-four seven, three sixty-five. And yeah, I can dig that, because she was like that from the first day I met her.

She was only sixteen, fit, and dark like ebony when she moved to Brixton from Bexleyheath with her family, yet she climbed to the top of the local look good chart in a matter of weeks. Everyone knew immediately that someone was going to snap her up and soon. I got in there quickly, with all the charm I could muster. I was nineteen, six-three, slim and good-looking. I not only had a driving licence, I also had a car, if somewhat battered and uninsured. I soon smooth-talked her into dating me.

They say there are a thousand ways to love a black woman, with my sixteen-year-old ebony princess I learned a thousand and one. She taught me to leave the blitzkrieg business behind and take things gently. I took my time, courting and romancing her slowly for a month, acting the perfect gentleman and only allowing myself to steal a goodnight kiss on her cheek after the second date. Young people today take sex for granted, with Lesley I was to learn that when a woman does it she does it well and makes sure it counts every time. I allowed myself only sneaking glances at her body while discovering that the more I learned about her, the more I yearned for her. She was a fun-loving young woman, ambitious, independent and into fitness an' dem way deh. She was sensitive and passionate and knew exactly what she wanted from a man. What she didn't want was to be second place to anyone in a relationship.

"For my friends it's a question of how good the man looks," she used to say, "but for me, it's different." She claimed she didn't care how pretty her boyfriends were as

25

long as they intended to honour her like a princess. I had found myself a young woman with character, ambition and plenty of dignity.

We spent many hours together, just walking and talking and holding hands. I took her to my favourite spot in Brixton, the walled garden in Brockwell Park. Those who haven't been there don't know what they're missing. It's the most peaceful, serene spot in South London, a place where I go to when I want to be spiritual and meditate, a million miles away from the heat of downtown Brixton. I introduced Lesley to the spot and of course she loved it. It never fails to impress the women. You know how lovers have their particular spot, well the flower garden in Brockwell Park is mine and Lesley's.

Then St Valentine's day came around. I took her to the Diamond Rooms venue in Crystal Palace. Love was in the air. Elegant FM were holding one of their popular lovers 'turnaround balls', where the ladies ask the men to dance! Satisfaction guaranteed every time!! It was a wicked night, with pure lover's music courtesy of the three boom sounds in session and an 'x' amount of top PAs. Soprano B from south London featuring Musclehead at the controls and Bingy Bunny on the microphone stand. Also from the big, rotten apple New York, Ramses Hi-Fi with Babyface... That night was to go down in musical history when the legendary deejay King Dominic rode a donkey on stage to make sure no other sound could test his people that night. That stunt nearly tore the place down and thanks to King Dom's showmanship, 'nuff men went home to get the good bedrock from their women that night, with everyone agreeing that it was the best St Valentine's night they had ever had. Copasetic.

Dressed in a criss new silk suit and with one hand caressing a bottle of Heineken and the other slipped surreptitiously around Lesley's waist, I felt older and bolder than my nineteen years. I knew it was my night, I was the king and Lesley was my queen. She had a very attractive body, beautiful and curvaceous. I was proud of her, proud to have her by my side and I felt triumphant over every other star bwoy in the place.

Her parents were on holiday in Jamaica, so I felt no way about walking her home at five in the morning and following behind her into the sumptuous living room of their Landor Road house, where I made myself comfortable. I never really used to smoke at this time so it was to my surprise when Lesley pulled out a bag of the strongest smelling herb I had ever come across from behind some paperbacks on the book

26

shelf.

"It's my father's," she said sweetly, pushing the sensi in my direction with a half-torn packet of red Rizla. "Papa says it builds up your stamina."

I shouldn't have rolled the spliff and worse still, I shouldn't have smoked it, but my heart was full of Lesley my better judgment having gone out the window. I loved the way she made me feel at ease, so at ease, as I drifted slowly on a different vibe. My body was relaxed and my head felt light, but spinning higher and higher out of control...

"Let's take a shower... together. I'll wash your body and you can wash mine."

Lesley's words lifted me without a sound off the comfortable sofa and up the stairs towards the bathroom. I hit the light switch as we undressed, plunging us into darkness as the gushing sound of the shower accompanied our breathlessness. Lesley kept the shower temperature on cold, as if our own body heat was steaming over and needed to be cooled down. It didn't bother me, on the contrary the cooling effect of the water, got me more horny if anything. I caressed her body slowly and sensually, her skin was soft and smooth, breasts small and firm. This was a sixteen-year-old girl with class.

That night, we made love like I had never made love before. We started in the shower and fell out into the hallway, down the stairs and into the living room. All the time gripped in a passionate embrace with one another. Lesley simply screamed, with pain or passion I didn't know which, but it worried me. There were times I had to cover her mouth speedily so that her screams wouldn't wake the neighbours and have them calling the police like there was some major crime going on. I thought I was more experienced, but Lesley had plenty to teach me about this love-making business. I had always thought that I knew where that certain spot was on a woman. Lesley taught me different and showed me I had been caressing the wrong place all these years. The moment she showed me where it was, it was like I was a born again lover and could make her reach new heights. Anyway, I am a man and men don't tend to have the stamina to go on as long as women. Well, I learned one more thing that night. When we had already made love three times and my manhood was in pain, begging for a rest, I suddenly felt Lesley's hand yanking it for one more go. I pleaded for mercy, but she simply ignored me, got up and went out to the kitchen for a moment. She returned with a tub of strawberry ice cream and handed it to me. I didn't understand, but that didn't stop me from diving into it without further ado. Within moments, my manhood once again started to rise without pain and I was rearing to go again.

Women increasingly demand a man with stamina, 'cause nowadays they feel no way about objecting to a lazy body. I learned that from early on. That's why I get up at 6am every morning and run a couple of blocks to pick up my Daily Mirror. Luckily I don't start work until ten, so I eat some fruit for breakfast before going to the gym and enduring a thorough workout, starting on the bike, followed by the stairmaster for half an hour. Then I do some power training on the tricep dips machine for fifteen minutes, then get the steps out and link a routine together for a further fifteen minutes. From there it's straight down to Peckham to open the bookshop with Dax hair oil dripping down my temple and muscles bulging under my shirt.

Anyway, me and Lesley remained an item for the next fifteen years. We grew up together, got conscious together and started a family together. Nothing ever came between us so strongly to wreck the relationship. She was seventeen when she got pregnant the first time. I had just come out of college without a job. Lesley still had another year at school, so there was little money coming in. Lesley was of course right; we should have waited until we were financially stable before we had a child, I didn't realise an extra mouth to feed could be so costly. But whatever, she got pregnant and there was no way I was going to allow her to consider anything but having the child.

Having to take responsibility for my daughter and family made me mature and conscious in a way nothing else had done. I stopped raving as much as I used to and knuckled down to the business of dealing with life. I wanted to do the right thing.

I've no qualms in admitting that my flesh is weak and I never intended to stay faithful to Lesley for ever and ever. No matter who you are, temptation flaunts itself in your face on an hourly basis. Especially when I got the job of running The Book Shack in Peckham. It's a little known fact that black book shops are frequented almost exclusively by black women. All types of black women — tall, short, slim, buxom, buppie, ragga, conscious and slack, but all beautiful. There's something irresistible about a woman with a book in her hand. I just can't resist them. In between the many reasoning sessions with The Book Shack's female customers, I spent many hours catching up on the reading I should have done in college. The Book Shack was stocked from corner to corner with every black book published in the diaspora. Everything from Walter Rodney's 'How Europe Underdeveloped The Third World' to Victor Headley's 'Yardie'. The fiction shelves ran like a Who's Who of black authors — Terry McMillan, Toni Morrison, Alice Walker, Donald Gorgon, Tony Sewell, Peter Kalu, Ben Okri, Ray Shell, James Baldwin, Alex Haley, Zora Neale Hurston and many more. I had always enjoyed reading and with thousands of books at my disposal, I had the opportunity to fulfil my appetite. I decided to start from the beginning with the Bible. I had always meant to read it, but never got around to it. It took me six months that first time to read it from cover to cover. Then I read it again. From that I went on to the African history books, learning about those old ancient African civilisations and how we lived before we were brought out here in Babylon. In those days African men had three or four wives, and it was no problem. The kings were expected to have even more wives. I learned a lot of things from those African history books, most importantly I learned that I was of royal blood.

In ancient West Africa, and still today, every little village had its five royal families, who took it in turns to rule. When the current king died, the title would revert to the head of the next royal family in line. In this way, almost half the population could consider themselves royal. We laugh because nearly every Nigerian or Ghanaian person that comes over here claims to be a prince or a princess. But when you think about it, it's probably true. Then I took a stop to consider all the books I had been reading. The white man came to Africa to conquer. The best way to conquer the many tribes and countries, was to take away their leaders, which is why most of those that were taken away as slaves to the Caribbean and to America were mostly the kings, queens, princes, princesses and other members of their family. That means I am a king. And if I'm a king I must live like a king. Lesley is officially my queen, but she has to understand that a king is entitled to sleep with different women every now and then. I'm no different from Henry VIII and all those guys. Besides, the Chinese, the Indian and the black man always had 'nuff wives and it was never any problem. Then Europe came, especially England and decided they wanted to reduce the amount of kids that a single black man was having with all his fifteen women. "One man one woman," they said, "that'll bring down the population." So to make us believe

29

that it should be one man for every woman, they even put it in the Bible. Meanwhile all the country's leaders are having loads of affairs whether it be with rent boys or high class prostitutes. When I really check things, I have to conclude that male monogamy is a bad white lie. Look at what all these Conservative MPs are doing, like that baby father Timothy Yeo. Those guys get away with it all the time. Just the other day a next one had to deny that he was a batty bwoy after his wife discovered him in bed with another man!

Lesley and Pauline have next to nothing in common. I'm amazed when I look at my baby mother that I could have been in the least bit interested in Pauline. She's the complete opposite. She's light-skinned, tall and aggressive. Loving Lesley is easy because she's soft, tender and beautiful. But making love to Pauline is like breaking rocks in the hot sun. It was only supposed to be a one night stand.

I met her at one of Gussie's buppie parties, filled wall to wall with ravers wearing gold 'chops' on their wrists and rings on each fist and all with their own rags to riches stories of how they became big timers and with 'nuff Porsches and Mercedes-Benz outside to prove it. Pauline declared herself the "original browning", an engineering graduate from Birmingham who had moved down to London when she got the job as a saleswoman for a top pharmaceutical company. She said she was single and didn't have time to spend looking for a man because she had to travel so much with her job. So whenever she was in London she always needed some action, a man with the right moves to get her chemistry going. The only credentials she required was that the man's wood was long and satisfied her three or four times a day, she was happy. I didn't mind that attitude. In fact it suited me to a point. I assured her that I was a champion jockey with good technique to put her in the mood. I suppose I liked the challenge of giving a woman all the affection the longest, loveliest and leanest can afford. Either way, I had nothing to lose when I spent that first night with her. Her face was a bit on the rough side, but her body looked too good to resist and she knew what to do with it. I had to pass a compliment. There was no need however, Pauline felt that compliments only wasted "good grinding time." I quickly discovered that as much as she passed herself off as the typical buppie in public, in private she loved to play dirty. I woke up early the next morning exhausted, in a strange bed with a naked woman beside me. The events of the night before came back to me slowly and I focused particularly on how good the bedrock was. It was nice, but not half as nice as when I make love with my own woman. I tried to sneak out, but Pauline woke up and was quickly revived, refreshed and ready to go at it again. I didn't get out of there until early that evening and even then she begged me to come back soon, but I had already decided I would only see this woman infrequently if at all again.

From the beginning, I've tried to do the right thing and avoided lying to Lesley. At the end of the day, I'm just a guy who loves my woman and I don't want to see her unhappy. She's asked me how many times I've been unfaithful all the years we've been together. I admitted to a handful of times. It's lucky I didn't say more, because she went into a deep depression and put me on recession for a month. Can you believe it? I had known the woman all these years and she suddenly decided to use pussy power to control me. She simply locked herself tight and refused to give me my rights at bedtime, even though I begged her and told her I was feeling so much love for her.

"If you believe in what you're feeling," she said simply, "and you want to make love to me, then be prepared to work hard for it." And of course, she had to tell her mother I had been unfaithful. Even I could have told Lesley that her mother's response would be "throw him out!" But Lesley loves me and she knows I love her too and that I'm a good father. Winnie's thirteen-years-old now and her mother would rather her child had a father than not and a good man is hard to find.

I could tell from the evil look in Lesley's eyes when I got home after spending the night and day with Pauline, that I was due for another spell of recession. I had been gone twenty-four hours without a phone call and I would have to pay the penalty.

"So where've you been?"

I simply kissed my teeth as I tried to assess what was going on in her mind. I had considered many options on the way back, but none of them seemed convincing enough. I don't like Winnie hearing us arguing, but I couldn't shift her off the sofa where she had made herself comfortable, lying full stretch with her eyes glued to the television.

"Cho', I'm a big boy, you know Lesley. I was out with my crew. It was Saturday night, I was out raving as usual, so stop acting like it's the first time ever."

I must have had guilt written all over my face, because Lesley wasn't even listening.

"It's Sunday evening, now, Johnny. We haven't heard from

you or seen you in twenty-four hours. You've been out all night and all day. We didn't know if you were dead or alive. That's disrespectful, Johnny. I've got better things to do with my time than sitting here wringing my hands and worrying about you."

"Look Lesley, I should have called. I'm sorry. But don't worry, no problem, next time I'll definitely call, don't worry about a thing."

The mood she was in, nothing I said would save me from recession. Nothing. I put an arm around her nevertheless, but she flung it away.

If Lesley hadn't put me on recession that time, I would have probably never gone round to Pauline's flat again. But I needed my oats and she could be relied on to make the trek over to Norwood worthwhile. I spent a lot of hours in bed with Pauline during that month of 'recession' and always came away ready for a good night's platonic sleep beside Lesley. I knew there could never be anything serious between Pauline and myself however, because what I had at home was steak, compared to the quarter pounder with cheese waiting for me every evening at Pauline's flat. No man can hide his thoughts from a woman. The moment I started thinking about steak, Pauline started feeling insecure.

I started spending more time at home with Lesley and Winnie, ingratiating myself as much as possible by performing little chores around the house. Even then, it took another week before Lesley was prepared to lift the 'recession'. I was relieved. I'm a man who needs sex on a regular basis and it took a lot of willpower to stay away from Pauline's while I was still on recession, but I succeeded. It was a Saturday night when Lesley decided to stop the alms house business. I had plied her with roses and chocolates all week to let her know I had a guilty conscience but was still very much in love with her. By Saturday afternoon I was blowing kisses across the room to her, hoping that this little love game would put her in the mood. After sending Winnie to bed that evening, Lesley blew a kiss back to me and I understood that recession was done. It was a long and sensuous night and we awakened the next morning our two hearts beating together as one.

I was pleased and unsurprised when Lesley informed me that one night of reckless, unrestricted, uninhibited, unprotected love was to make me a father again. The day after, Pauline called The Book Shack to tell me her "wonderful news." Deja vu.

I went around to Pauline's that evening for the first time in weeks. As usual she tried to drag me down on the floor in the hallway the moment I stepped in. I managed to fight her off. I had more important things on my mind.

"So how did you get pregnant?" I asked deadly serious.

"Oh please, Johnny. If you don't know how people get pregnant, then go back to infants school. Remember how we were after the party, how close we two got for one hot second and then you came around day after day for more? Well those hot seconds resulted in a little baby on the way."

"But you said...?"

"Have you ever heard of contraceptive failure? I hope you know that the pill doesn't always work." She had an attitude about her, almost shouting at me as if I had done her something bad. I guessed that she was probably irritated because I hadn't been by or called for weeks.

"So you're saying the pill didn't work? Sue the company then."

"Well it's much simpler than the pill not working, Johnny. I simply forgot to take it."

"You forgot...?"

"Yes. I've had a lot of things on my mind lately."

Somehow I didn't believe her. Taking the pill is like brushing your teeth. You wake up and you do it without thinking about it, but you just don't forget.

"Well, if you're pregnant, you're pregnant. I'll have to deal with it."

"Deal with it? Is that all you can say, Johnny?"

"Well what the hell do you want me to say? On the phone you tell me I'm about to become a father when I wasn't expecting it."

"I thought you might say what you think. I don't know whether you're happy about it. I want to know whether you want me to keep it, or whether you want me to have an abortion or what you want."

"Don't even talk to me about abortion! You know how I feel about those things. You shouldn't even be thinking about that when you're pregnant with my child, you know. You can poison the baby with evil thoughts before it's even born."

"Right, at least I know you want the baby. That much helps."

"I said, don't worry about a thing. I know my responsibilities."

I told her about Lesley and she said never mind; as long as I never stopped seeing her she said. As long as I kept coming

33

around to give her the good bedrock, she was happy.

That night I lay in bed with Lesley reflecting on the past few days' events. Now what a lot of people can't understand is that I am a man who will never abandon my children, no matter what. I grew up with both parents at home and I know a lot of people my age and younger, having children and having to raise them by themselves. Everywhere you look nowadays, you see 'nuff baby mothers, struggling to bring up their children on their own, struggling to survive without their baby fathers. That's why you hear people talking about black man this and black man that and how we don't take responsibility for our youts. That is not strictly true though. You have certain men out there who are prepared to stick around and give a helping hand. Men like me, who know that every child needs a father and a mother, who know that it is our responsibility to make sure our children grow up to become respectable men and women, to raise them up in the rightful ways, to move their minds and give them direction. I was sure that the right thing to do was to tell Lesley all about Pauline, but I had to be careful of what I had to say and choose the right moment, else my mouth could get me into something my wits weren't going to be able to get me out of. Tonight wasn't the right time.

"Turn off the lights and light a candle," said Lesley snuggling up beside me. "I'm feeling romantic tonight." I turned over and kissed her, trying to forget my troubles. She whispered sweet words of love in my ear. "Light a candle and come to me. I want to love you all over."

"I want to love you too." I repeated over and over again.

We made love with my mind on other things. I was thinking of my mother and how she used to say, "be careful my son, think before you make a gamble with your heart."

Six months later, I've managed to juggle things smoothly: performing my duties to each woman and keeping things sweet as both their bellies swelled. I still haven't got around to telling Lesley about Pauline. But about a month ago, Pauline started giving me the living distress about being a father to my child.

"I'm having to cook and eat for two of us and you're going to have to take responsibility for two of us. I hope you know that your duties include spending time with your child?"

I looked at how her stomach had become big and beautiful but her tongue remained sharp and aggressive as ever.

"Look what is it with you, Pauline. I didn't want any kids. I said that from the first day. Then you tell me different and

34

now you're talking like I'm your knight in shining armour who's going to scoop you up and ride off into the sunset the moment the baby's born. Get real. You knew I was never going to leave Lesley, because she is my baby mother. Now you're on the same level as her, it's still not the same thing. She's come to expect certain things as a baby mother, whereas you haven't come to expect those things. I'll still be living over there whatever happens."

Pauline stared at me with fire in her eyes. I knew she was planning something, but dared not ask what. I had made the mistake of confirming her fear of never having me to herself. Her long pregnancy, she often told me, had made her realise that she wanted us to go legit. Now I had confirmed that it could never happen, she was unhinged with rage and I saw from the look in her eyes that there would be hell to pay for all of this.

"So have you told Lesley that you've got another kid coming?" she asked defiantly.

"Don't worry about that, man. Me and her is cool. I tell her everything."

Mama used to say forget trying to find the perfect woman. "You're never going to find Miss Right, not in seventy years anyway, and that's all the time you've got. Just find a woman who will make you happy, she'd say, a woman who you're proud to hold up as your queen, every minute and every hour of the day, "a woman to love and honour and yes, even to obey." The Old Man didn't do any of that, which is why Mama has tried so hard to make sure none of her sons makes the same mistake with their women. Out of four sons I'm the only one left for her to pin her hopes on. That's the only reason I lie to her.

We told her, all of us — me and my brothers — to leave the Old Man. For twenty years we told her. But she kept saying, "I've made my bed, so I'll lie in it." The day he died, she became a new woman with a cashed £100,000 life insurance policy in her bank account. She went on that round-the-world cruise she'd always dreamt about and came back looking ten years younger. She says that now she's seen the world, all she wants to do is spend her time and her money making sure that her family stays a family. The Old Man must be rolling in his grave, because he figured that he'd be collecting the £100,000 on her, and he would be going on that cruise.

Mama will help me out with the cost of providing for two new babies, I know she will, but telling Lesley about the other kid is something I'm going to have to do all by myself.

35

BEDROOM BOUNTY HUNTER

Linvall put it down to the Harley-Davidson. There was something about his motorbike that attracted the women. Dressed from head to toe in black leathers, he felt a dozen eyes on him as he climbed off the ex-California Highway Patrol Electra Glide. It was unusual to see a black biker at all. With the leather travel pouch slung over his shoulder, he walked slowly and deliberately just like Clint, into Camerabatics, the photographic shop on the World's End side of the King's Road. He threw the pouch onto the counter and pulled out a dozen rolls of colour slides he needed developed. The shop assistants all knew him and were always keener to serve a professional who knew what he was talking about than the frequent amateurs that strolled in looking for idiot-proof cameras.

The tall white woman at the counter explaining that her film had jammed in her camera turned around, obviously impressed at the handsome young black man who had stepped in to a chorus of greetings from the boys behind the counter.

"You still riding that old monster," Ralph laughed from behind the cash register. "Blimey, I'm surprised the filth doesn't do you for that. It's a bloody nuisance to society. When are you going to get yourself a nice running Cortina like everybody else."

"You should try reading George Orwell's *Animal Farm*, mate," Linvall replied affecting a cockney accent to blend in with the surroundings, "two wheels good, four wheels bad."

Linvall ordered a couple of new lenses, a dozen boxes of light sensitive paper and a hundred rolls of film. He pulled off his helmet to reveal a short mane of flattened funki dreds. He ran his fingers through the hair and shook them into place. He was handsome in a stylised sense.

"Excuse me, are you a photographer by any chance?" the tall white lady beside him asked. Beres turned around and noticed her for the first time. She was in her mid-forties and despite a few unflattering lines, still held the beauty of her youth and an alluring smile that could be called sexy.

"Well I have been known by that title," he grinned, "I don't know if the people in here would call me one."

36

Linvall shared the cliquey joke with Ralph, who doubted whether 'photographer' was the right title for him.

"My name's Lucy Fry," she said, "I'm head of Light Entertainment at Channel 3 TV..."

"Yeah, I know who you are," Linvall said recognising her now. It was his job to know who the big names were on the celebrity circle and Lucy Fry was no ordinary media bureaucrat, but led the kind of life that had turned her into a celebrity also. She had been caught many times by the paparazzi and had her photographs spread all over the tabloids, literally with her panties down.

"Well you might be just the person I've been looking for," she continued. "I've got a new show planned, a very hip, fresh, young show, and I'd like you to come in to audition for a presenter's job."

Linvall's head swelled slightly as she handed him her card. He looked at it, his mind a blur. He had heard it happen to friends of his, but now when he was being offered a shot at fame and glory, he didn't know what to say.

"Call me up later this afternoon and we'll arrange for you to come in. Do you have a card?" She smiled sweetly. Linvall played it cool and pulled a business card out of the breast pocket of his leathers and handed it to her. He promised to call. Laden with orders, he flung the saddle bags over his shoulder and walked coolly out of the shop. He kicked the Harley into life with a deafening roar and raced off. He had played it just like Clint would have.

Down at Linvall's studio in a converted church on Stockwell Road, Candi Clarke was performing rather than posing. She was the up and coming South London model people were talking about as the new Naomi Campbell. Linvall expected her to go all the way to the top. He had discovered her, he had created her and for that matter it was he who had marketed her as the Face of Black Britain.

"Candi, you're not relaxed. You're moving around too much. Just play it natural. You're supposed to be modelling a line of beachwear."

It had been the same for the last two hours, he hadn't got one decent shot. It was unlike her. She was only sixteen, but had learned fast and could now be considered a professional. You usually didn't have to tell her anything, because she knew how to make the camera fall in love with her. But her mind was elsewhere and Linvall began to wonder if he was wasting his time. Then he saw something in the viewfinder that made him think again, something that looked good.

37

Maybe he was taking the wrong approach. Maybe he should be working with all this extra energy and not try to tame it down, but use it to his advantage. Models that couldn't keep still usually meant bad photographs, but this was different, this was Candi Clarke and if anybody could make the pictures come out brilliantly, she could. He stuck a Shabba Ranks cassette into the tape machine. He knew that Candi couldn't resist *Wicked In Bed*. He looked her semi-naked body up and down casually through his lens. She had the perfect body for modelling, perfect eyes, mouth and hair. And she also had the perfect attitude; she didn't give a damn. He began with fairly tame poses, with Candi sitting on a rocking chair wearing only a wet t-shirt, her eyes peering out at the camera from underneath the wide-brim of a straw hat, and covering her pubic area with both hands, her long legs crossed, while the sounds of Maxi Priest and Shabba blasted from the machine and she did it without complaining. It was four in the afternoon and they were making amazing pictures and after all, that's what she lived for — to make pictures that would be remembered for years to come. That was true immortality in the modelling world.

"I've got something to tell you," Candi said nervously as Linvall switched off the lighting so they could both cool down for a short break. "I won't be doing any more photographs with you after today."

Linvall's heart sank. He had feared something like this. "Why not?" he asked.

"This agency in New York wants me to fly over there and work exclusively for them. They've got me an apartment in Manhattan and they're paying me more money than I could afford to say 'no' to," Candi answered, unable to look her mentor in the eye.

"Well do what you want to do. I think you're making a mistake. We had plans here. The money's been tight, but we're moments away from it." He wanted to use much stronger language, to tell her straight, that she was dissing the programme, but it would serve no purpose.

"It's no use trying to talk to me about it, Linvall, I've talked to my family, I've talked to an accountant and I've talked to a lawyer and they all say I'm crazy if I don't take this offer up."

Linvall was angry. "You think you've made it all on your own. You're forgetting the two years I spent with you, two years of unpaid time taking more and more photos of you, building up your portfolio and taking it around. And this is how you treat me."

"I knew you would take it like this," Candi said sadly. "Can't you just accept that this is business. That's all it is, business."

Linvall's ulcer burned at that; he knew she was right but he didn't want to hear it from her. All he could think about was that his golden child had slipped away from him. On the eve of fame and glory, God had refused him this chance to prove that wealth would not change him.

He sent Candi home early. Linvall's heart really wasn't into taking beautiful photos of her now. He sat down by himself, just staring ahead trying to think things through. Billie Holiday had replaced Shabba and her echo resounded throughout the studio. Linvall examined the facts. In the last six months he had personally earned £20,000 acting as Candi's agent and photographer. People had warned him that it was a conflict of interest, but he was actually doing the job of agent as well and felt he deserved it. Anyway, Candi had also earned £20,000 and he thought it fair. It wasn't a great deal of money in the industry but she was really just starting out and he had expected their earnings would quadruple in the next year, there had even been calls for Candi to catwalk in Paris and Milan. But that wasn't to be, not with him anyway. Candi was off to New York and he would never be able to afford to hire her. He would probably have to sell the Harley to cover the credit card debts he had accrued thinking that he was now a high roller. Those were the facts. Linvall didn't want to start touting for freelance work around the magazines again. Candi had been his insurance against that. Maybe something would turn up. He was a good looking black man with potential and youth, something always turned up.

He must have fallen asleep because the late afternoon winter darkness had fallen. His mobile phone was ringing.

"Hello, is that Linvall Henry?" the English schoolmistress' voice asked. "This is Lucy Fry from Channel 3. I was expecting a call from you this afternoon."

Linvall apologised and said he had been busy.

"Are you still interested in coming for an audition? We're pushed for time on this project and I'd like to see if you're suitable as soon as possible."

"Well I'm free right now," Linvall said, only half-seriously.

"That will be fine," Lucy quickly agreed. "You know where the studios are don't you, overlooking the Hammersmith flyover?"

Within half an hour Linvall had arrived in her plush office

with its panoramic views of London at the top of the TV studios.

"I can't offer you a strong drink because I don't keep any. But I've got some herbal tea," Lucy Fry said hurriedly.

"Herb tea is fine," he said jokingly, as he flung himself down on a comfortable armchair and his saddle bag on the ground, "that is the latest craze isn't it?"

The humour was lost on Lucy who busied herself at the little kitchenette discreetly tucked away in a recess.

"Now the sort of presenter we're looking for," the producer began as she returned with the tea in a bone china cup, the tea bag still floating in it, "is somebody who's in touch with what's happening on the street level."

Their hands brushed against each other's as she handed Linvall the cup. He noticed she had incredibly soft hands for a woman who couldn't have been younger than forty-five. She sat down on an even more comfortable oversize armchair opposite him. "Someone who can check what's going down on the Frontline in Brixton at the same time as what's happening on the rave scene." She admired his beautifully designed funki dreds briefly

"So let me get this straight," Linvall interrupted, "if I'm the presenter, I make it my job to know every change in fashion, style and music. Well that's no problem, I know the latest chat, the latest dances and anything else of importance that's occurring street-wise. I'm a conscious man first, foremost and last."

"So what do you do with your time otherwise, when you're not taking photographs of beautiful women..."

"I'm always working hard in the studio or in the dark room developing photographs and all that sort of thing. You know how it is, a photographer's life is never done."

"You don't have any girlfriends?"

Linvall wasn't sure whether the question was part of the interview or just a general inquiry. "Well, no, not at the moment?"

"How come?"

"What?"

"How come a young, handsome, successful man like yourself doesn't have any girlfriends? You're not gay are you?"

"Give me a break... I mean, no."

"Well why haven't you got a girlfriend then?"

"Well, you know how it is, up and down; if you're always busy like me, it's hard making a relationship work."

Lucy studied him hard, smiling.

"I bet you've broken the heart of every woman you've met and if I know black men well enough, I'm sure you've sown your seed every which way you've looked."

Linvall was genuinely taken aback. This was definitely not a normal audition. He didn't know whether she was praising him or insulting him or what she was getting at, but he had a sneaky suspicion he was going to find out.

"No, you've got the wrong guy for that. I'm not like that."

"Please," Lucy said with exaggerated disbelief.

"No, really. I couldn't have built up my career as a photographer if I had women all over the place."

"And no children at all anywhere?"

Linvall was now anxious to get to the bottom of the questioning before he revealed too much about himself. For a moment it had seemed like Lucy was making a pass at him, but he wasn't so sure anymore. He was accustomed to women falling for him. Many of the women he knew as friends had offered up their bodies at one time or another. All kinds of women, from the modern black woman with ambition, but no man to match her, to the bored wives of men who they had married before realising their husbands were really not going anywhere. Most of the women he got off with were just inquisitive, he knew that. He could almost see them thinking, 'well if he's that bright and he's that charming, maybe he'll be interesting in bed'. It was almost too easy for him. All you needed it seemed, was a trendy haircut, a pair of designer jeans a modicum of intelligence and potential. But he had to be extremely careful. There were too many women out there who wanted to chain him to a wedding ring, a house in the suburbs and three kids on the floor with another one to come making four.

Linvall wasn't expecting Lucy's next move. Without a word, she walked to her office door and locked it from the inside. She then walked across the office to her ample desk and pressed a button on the telephone to tell her secretary to take messages and hitched herself up on the desk taking off her high heeled shoes without backstrap, keeping her eyes fixed on the handsome young black man staring incredulously in front of her. She was the first woman Linvall had seen who polished her toenails. They were red and sexy to drive men wild. He maintained a calm, if nervous, smile trying to watch the proceedings dispassionately. But Lucy Fry's speed and daring was beginning to overwhelm him. She pointed a finger at him to come toward her. Linvall approached the desk with caution, her eyes enticing him further. She could have been his mother and for a moment Linvall thought about his Oedipus Complex. Close up he decided to take the initiative and tried to kiss her, but she turned her head away and said she didn't like kissing, only sex. In a moment she had pulled his head down to her breasts and smothered him. It didn't take long before they were locked in a rhythmic embrace on the solid oak desk, Lucy Fry's legs pointed to the ceiling with Linvall breathless between them. She was a peculiar sort of woman wanting no kisses but pure unadulterated sexual power, heat and no easing of thrust. It took an hour of muffled squeals from her before she came, biting Linvall's arm hard as she did so to stifle an explosive scream. The panoramic views of the fully lit city below increased Linvall's sense of the fantastical situation he had found himself in. He felt more like Clint than ever. He recalled a scene in *Dirty Harry* and pulled himself out of Lucy Fry and smacked her on her behind. She was grinning and he took this as an indication of his skill. Linvall believed he was a good lover and he knew that what a woman like Lucy Fry needed was a hard dick. He eventually climbed off the table. It had been great making love on the boss' desk, in an office after hours. It gave him the thrill of power at his fingertips. He pulled on his leathers and with his saddle bag slung over his shoulder took his leave.

"I want that job," he told Lucy seriously. "So, give me a call about it." He unlocked the door and let himself out, leaving her still moaning on the desk.

Outside, the corridor was quiet, most of the daytime staff had gone home. A young black cleaner with a red, green and gold tam on his head gave Linvall a knowing smile and a wink as he left Lucy's office, as if they both shared a secret.

It was now evening as he left the TV3 building. Linvall climbed on his motorbike; he was sure he wouldn't have to sell the Harley after all. As far as he was concerned he was about to embark on his new career as a television presenter.

GOD BLESS THE CHILD

Libra — Now is the time to work hard at those New Year resolutions you promised a month ago. Friends will tempt you away, but stick to that new regime you've worked out for yourself.

Beres smiled as he drove the Lotus through the gates of the Harriet Tubman Preparatory School, out into the busy traffic. He was thinking about how quickly Lara had grown up. Somehow she acted more mature than her age, like when last summer he caught her practicing her kissing technique on an orange so that when her first kiss came she'd know what to do.

"I don't mind you being late, Daddy. I wasn't bored because I had my books with me and I knew that if I started my homework now, I wouldn't have so much to do later on."

Beres turned to his daughter, ever the practical woman of seven years of age. He loved her. And he knew she loved him, that was why she never complained of standing around after school. She always made life easy for her father.

"Is this your new car, daddy?"

"I wish it was, darling. But you know Daddy doesn't have the money to buy a really expensive car like this."

Beres looked at his watch. He had to drive straight back up to Mayfair otherwise Dan Oliver would report the car stolen to the police. He had been gone over two hours.

"So what do you say to a Monday treat?"

"Oh yes, Daddy... Yes, yes yes. What treat? No don't tell me, let me guess... Can we go swimming? That would be nice."

"Let's go swimming on Saturday, yeah? I was thinking that I should treat you by taking you out for dinner?"

"Oh yes, Daddy. That was my second choice... let's go to McDonalds."

"I'll take you somewhere better than McDonald's," he promised, "you can have hamburgers, but at this place they're better hamburgers than at McDonald's."

Lara leaned her head back against the car seat, a big expectant smile on her face. She loved her daddy's treats.

Beres parked the Lotus outside Hollywood Dreams in Covent Garden, which American film stars Dick Martin, Ricky

43

Blackman and Bill Bates had recently opened jointly. He and his daughter climbed out of the Lotus followed by the indiscreet eyes of tourists who thought that he must be a black American film star with his daughter. Beres wasn't a film star, but he was a regular customer at the restaurant. Frank the doorman winked at him as he waved them through.

"So you've brought the missus this evening," he joked.

Beres simply smiled. Inside, the restaurant was packed to the brim.

"Kathy!" Beres called to one of the waitresses trying to cope with the constant stream of orders.

"Oh hiya Beres... How are you doing, dear? Table for two?"

"Yeah, that's right. But look, I've got a favour to ask. This is my daughter, Lara. I've got to pop back to work for a few minutes. Could you keep an eye on her and help her out with her order."

It was fine by Kathy. Beres was a good customer who always left a big tip. She smiled at Lara, who smiled back. "Come on, love," she said, "I'll find you a nice table and we'll get you something really nice to eat before your dad gets back."

Within seconds, Beres was back in the Lotus and roaring off towards Berkeley Square.

At 28 and earning huge commissions selling fax machines, Beres had been the most eligible bachelor in town with a promising future ahead. The more successful he became, the greater the number of potential wives who made themselves available. But Beres knew exactly what he wanted. He had drawn up a shopping list of the type of woman he was looking for — kind, fun-loving and a university graduate so their children would have at least one parental role model in education. Sonia fitted the bill perfectly and from the very first time he blessed his eyes on her, his heart took over while his head took a much needed rest.

Beres met his wife while on a holiday in Tenerife with Johnny and Gus. Sonia had completed her finals earlier that summer and was taking a well-earned rest with her best friend, Grace. She played things cool during that holiday and also when Beres plied her with calls, flowers and little gifts on their return to London. She was living on the North side at the time, but that didn't deter him from pursuing her with the vigour of the confident salesman that he was, yet she just

44

didn't seem interested and Grace did her best to ensure that she didn't lose a best friend or gain a best friend's husband. Sonia finally conceded after a month and he took her out for the most expensive slap-up meal she had ever eaten at a high class French restaurant in Knightsbridge, followed by an evening at the theatre. He was the perfect buppie, surely he had a lot to offer a woman intelligent enough to win his heart as Sonia had done? Most men would have got the message when it took another four weeks to get her out on a second date, but Beres wasn't giving up that easy. When he was with her he felt a fire raging deep in his soul which told him that he was in love, he had no choice but to pursue her. Nothing could have daunted Beres' spirits in those early days. He was bewitched by Sonia, hypnotised, and the more she wanted to cut him off the more he was convinced she was the solid rock that was missing in his life. He had found the love of a lifetime, he just had to convince her of it.

Sonia was born beautiful and spent much of her time in front of a mirror to make herself even more attractive. She had become so used to hearing compliments about her looks that she had grown to expect it. So Beres' efforts were nothing special to her, only his persistence. She wasn't ready to give up being a beautiful woman to become a good wife to somebody as everybody expected her to. She had other plans in life, she just didn't have the means to achieve them.

It took all his skills as a seasoned salesman, but Beres finally succeeded in winning her hand. Sonia made it clear from the word go that she expected the good life and that she didn't want a commonplace marriage and even though Beres had proposed after only the second date, she insisted on a twelve month engagement to get to know each other. In those next months Beres learned that Sonia wasn't interested in having kids and growing old and fat as a mother. She wanted to stay slim, young and attractive as long as possible and wasn't interested in stretch marks before she was thirty-five at the very least. "It's not *your* hips which have got to expand," she would counter whenever Beres tried to convince her otherwise, "it's not *your* tummy which is going to swell, *you're* not going to go through any kind of pain."

To all their friends, Beres and Sonia had a real good thing going. They were the exemplary buppie couple, with a successful marriage, a big house in the suburbs, and his BMW and her Mercedes parked ostentatiously in the driveway for all the neighbours to see. He, the kind of man that women like to read about — handsome, well dressed, well toned muscles, hard working and ambitious. And most importantly loyal and faithful to his wife. She, a woman that could turn any man's head, attractive, elegant and intelligent and who modelled herself and her husband on the pictures of the perfect buppie couples she had seen displayed on the pages of *Ebony* magazine. Though visually they made a pretty pair, dressed from top to toe in the latest Donovan Love creations, their relationship had its problems like any other. They weren't compatible, but like chalk and cheese. He was the serious, conscientious type, while she was erratic, carefree and perhaps naive about the responsibilities of married life. And she seemed to lack that sense of real passion towards him, but flirted infamously at parties. But Beres saw his wife only through rose-tinted spectacles and his close friends were helpless to do anything but humour him. For them, the only thing left to wonder was whether the marriage would last or whether Sonia would be tempted elsewhere. They could see she was restless and threatened to flee the nest eventually.

In other ways Sonia seemed an ideal partner. She was able to give Beres good advice in his business life as well as his personal life. It was her idea that he set up in business for himself. Beres saw the benefits immediately. He'd be able to spend more time at home with his wife, and what could be sweeter than that? It was also her idea that he started wearing bright ties and re-style his hair in a low-cut, fashionable fifties style.

The baby had been an accident. One of those awful moments when the condom burst just as Beres was about to climax and because he was moving so frantically he couldn't feel the rubber pop. But no matter how much he swore that he didn't know he had a puncture, he always got the feeling that Sonia didn't believe him. Especially as she still brought the subject up several years later.

He had said from the word go that Sonia and the child would be supported to the fullness. That's why he brought the wedding forward, even though she didn't feel they needed to. As far as Beres was concerned, the only way to avoid his children being called names by anybody was to go legitimate. He arranged the church wedding with all the trimmings in record time, though not fast enough for little Lara who was born two months prematurely, the day before they were due to walk up the aisle.

Beres' hopes that the birth of the baby might transform Sonia into a homely woman with traditional 'mother values' weren't to be realised. The first few weeks were okay once

46

Sonia had gotten over her post-natal depression and was full of dreams about her life with her new daughter Lara. She spent most of her time with the baby and didn't seem to mind. She was always cuddling the child and carried her around the house all day no matter what. Everything was going alright until Sonia became despondent when her breasts began to dry and shrivel up. It was down to the gym for a month of intensive workouts, with her new best friend — Delores, a woman she had met in the labour ward — and back to her original shape. All outward signs of childbirth disappeared, the stretch marks, the wide hips and so on and she was once again slipping into her expensive designer clothes with ease. Still, Beres' hopes of another child were premature. Sonia insisted that she didn't want the breast milk back, nor the tight gourd of a stomach she had when the child was inside her. Instead, once Lara started attending prep school at the age of three, the focus of Sonia's life lay increasingly outside the family home as she spent her weekends raving with Delores. She still liked to look beautiful and indeed, she seemed to have grown more beautiful with time, experience and childbirth. As long as he got to play his Sunday morning game of football with the team, Beres willingly looked after his daughter while his wife raved. Sonia was more the socialite anyway and needed the good life that their new-found wealth afforded them more than her husband. Since the birth of his daughter, Beres preferred to spend the evening at home than go out to the numerous events they were always invited to as members of a new black elite. Whatever else they did, they would always spend Sunday afternoons together. Sonia would cook a wicked pot of rice and peas and chicken and Beres would pop open a bottle of champagne and some juice for his daughter. His parents had brought him up to believe that the family who eat together stays together.

Nobody wants to know you when you're down and out, but Beres soon discovered that a fistful of dollars gained you instant entry into the buppie elite. He then ran a successful electronics shop on Tottenham Court Road, selling faxes, computer hardware and mobile phones. Most of their business was export to the rich territories Beres had developed while selling faxes internationally. It was those export sales that helped him ride the recession, though on a knife edge.

What you're worth on paper was was all that counted in the world of the buppie and certainly when you took in to account all the stock they had on credit and the mortgaged property they owned, Beres and Sonia were millionaires.

Suddenly everyone liked them and invites to the most glamourous social occasions started arriving with the morning post. Sonia insisted that they attend as many as possible, "It's important for the business that we go out and meet people socially," she would say. Beres was indifferent. He enjoyed being on the panel of judges for the annual Miss Black UK competition, but he wasn't into the formal stuff at places like the Jamaican High Commission, nor was he ever comfortable as a member of the UK black high society. So while Delores accompanied Sonia to the events, Beres would stay in and read his daughter a bedtime story until she fell asleep in his arms.

To Sonia's disappointment, money didn't change her husband's life as it had hers. While she wanted to experience the thousand and one things that new found wealth offered, Beres was different, some people would say he was a bit of a bore. They hardly went out together to the cinema, or to parties, or even the pub. Beres was happy being able to provide well for his family, proud to send his daughter to a private school and giving her the best start in life he could afford. Money could do no more for him, in fact he found it rather distasteful talking about it. For him, happiness meant something more than exotic holidays and expensive cars. It meant more than the latest designer clothes. Happiness for him was being with his wife and daughter, and no matter how much Sonia tried to get him to listen to opera and read poetry, he was happier with a Marvin Gaye album and considered an X Press novel a "good read".

Though he worked hard in the early years of the business, Beres admitted that maximum respect was due to his woman for her advice and contributions to the company. He had no interest whatsoever in the paperwork of the business, so Sonia enrolled in an evening class for book-keeping. She was a voracious student and soon began to do the company's books from home

To her husband, this woman was one of a kind and made him happy in every respect and aspect. He considered himself lucky to be the man in her life and when he came home from work she usually had a hot tub running for him to relax in.

Their dreams had come true. They lived in a huge detached house on Streatham Common, set in an acre of land, sent their daughter to the Harriet Tubman Preparatory School and indulged in a life that others only dreamed about.

Beres and Sonia's relationship had seemed so perfect, as marriages do before the initial passion has waned, it was a real shock to their friends when she left him. But who feels it knows it, and Beres felt it bad when he returned home with Lara one Sunday afternoon from a dinosaur exhibition at the Natural History Museum, to find his wife gone, her car gone and two envelopes sitting on the kitchen table. Beres tore open the one addressed to him and read:

Dear Beres,

There's no point in kidding each other, things haven't been going sweet between us and they're not getting any better. Maybe we need to put some distance between us, some breathing room, I mean we need time to think about it all and I need space to think. I just need some time to clear my head and straighten things out. I'm sorry it had to be this way, but you would only try and stop me. Take care of my baby; I'm sure you'll bring her up well and it will give you no reason to come after me. I'll call when I've got my life together.

Sonia.

Beres was paralysed, rooted to the ground, devastated, unable to move. He simply stood with the letter in his hand staring at it, as his life shattered in a million pieces and his eyes started to water. He hoped that his wife had merely acted on impulse and that she would be back home by the next morning, but there was a penetrating coldness about the letter which suggested otherwise. After what seemed like several hours of meditation, Lara entered the kitchen from the living room where she had been watching cartoons on the video.

"Daddy, I'm bored now, I don't want to watch the video anymore. Where's Mummy?"

At first Beres didn't know how he should play it, but he decided against bluffing his daughter. He handed her the envelope addressed to her. Lara read the typed out letter slowly. Beres stared at her hard as her face grew downcast. She finished reading the letter and ran upstairs hurriedly. Her father waited a few minutes before going up to his daughter's bedroom where she lay sobbing quietly on the bed. Beres picked up the letter which lay beside her and read it:

Darling Lara,

Mamma loves you very much, but I have to go away for a while. Be good and I will write as soon as I can.

Mamma.

49

Thinking back on it now, Beres couldn't understand why Sonia had walked out when things were looking so good for them. She had everything a woman could ask for, the very best of the very best and money was no object. She had a beautiful, healthy daughter and a husband who respected his woman and believed in marriage as a partnership between two equals. It didn't make sense. She had never complained of being unhappy, there had been no tell-tale signs, not that he had seen anyway. So he assumed she had run off with another man.

Beres didn't go in to work that week but simply went through the motions at home and left the running of his electronics shop to the staff because he half-expected Sonia to come home, if only to see her daughter or to collect the expensive clothes she had left behind in her wardrobe and he wanted to be there when she came. For days he walked around like in a dream, unable to fathom the full extent of what had happened. He'd wake up in the middle of the night, soaked in a pool of his own sweat and anxious about his daughter after suffering the recurring nightmare where his daughter was being snatched away from him. Women go on about their men abandoning them with kids, but what about the baby fathers? Nobody speaks up for them. You come home expecting your wife to be there taking care of things, you don't expect to come home and find a note waiting. He had become a desperate man and resorted to desperate means to find his wife, like driving to her mother's in his pajamas, sitting outside, keeping surveillance, certain that Sonia would turn up; but she didn't and he had begun to believe that the old woman really didn't know her daughter's whereabouts. He also kept surveillance outside Lara's school, and outside Delores' house, but there again he drew a blank. The straw he clutched at for his sanity, became shorter and shorter in the hours he spent sitting outside his wife's favourite restaurants, hoping. He also sat outside the church where Lara had been christened — even though Sonia wasn't a regular churchgoer -- but there was always a minute chance... and as he sat there his mind turned to memories of his childhood, a stable childhood in which his mother had managed to keep the family together, through thick and thin. And when he thought about it, his parents went through a tougher time, as one of the first wave of black immigrant workers who came to clean up after the war. And his mother was always there to take care of every little thing, as his father was always proud to state, he had never once set foot in the kitchen throughout his married life. His parents had managed to bring him up and send him to a private school throughout the lean years and were still happily married after 38 years, while he with all the advantages that his life now afforded him, only managed seven. There was something wrong with the arithmetic.

As one week turned to two and still no sign of Sonia, Beres' feelings turned to bitterness. He thought of all the women he had turned down because he loved his wife and children more than anything in the world. And when Johnny Dollar and the rest of the gang used to tease him that "with all your money, you should be pulling in 'x' amount of pussy," he would always laugh and answer that he wasn't a stud and that no woman could make him feel as good as Sonia. There had even been times when his love for Sonia had waned, sure, but he remained faithful. It's hard for a man to continually turn a blind eye when beautiful, horny women are constantly throwing themselves in his face and then to come home to a wife who's got a headache. She didn't say it in so many words, but Beres knew that his wife had begun to find sex boring and he had made several attempts at variation. When he suggested that they should make love on the kitchen table, Sonia looked at him as if he was a lunatic. It was like he couldn't please her, whatever he did. Their sex life wasn't what it used to be, but Beres nevertheless felt lucky to have a lovely home, a fine wife and a wonderful daughter.

By the third week, it was clear that Sonia wasn't coming back. Beres let Lara have the first two greeting cards her mother sent, but then he started hiding them out of spite. Whatever she thought of him, how could a woman abandon her daughter? How could she miss out on Lara's upbringing like this? Missing out on her daughter's education. She didn't know whether Lara was doing well or badly at school. Missing out on all the family photographs and home videos which would record Lara's life for posterity. Every woman, every mother should want to be part of that. It went against all logic to think otherwise. Now it was down to him to tell his daughter about things like her period when it came and that was definitely the mother's job, because she knew much more about it.

After that first month alone Beres resolved that he could no longer rely on Sonia to be part of their daughter's upbringing, but he wouldn't give social services an opportunity to take Lara away. They would jump at the earliest chance to prove that a black man was incapable of bringing up his daughter. Well, he wouldn't give them that break. He didn't need anybody's help to turn his daughter into a wholesome member of society. He bought a copy of The Complete Baby Father's Guide and went about learning everything in detail. He soon became an expert on children.

Six weeks after Sonia had walked out, Beres had still not returned to run the shop, but he took Lara off on holiday instead. They drove down to Cornwall, where they rented a holiday flat in St Ives. From there they made their way down daily to Hayle Sands, where Lara spent the days with her new-found local friends running freely on the white sand beach. On their second day there, Beres decided it was time to speak plainly to his daughter. After dinner at an elegant restaurant in town, they returned to the holiday home to watch television.

"You know your mama's not coming back, don't you?"

Lara didn't answer, her face remained glued to the TV screen on which Tom the cat was once again getting a hammering from his rodent adversary. Like her mother, Molara Cleopatra was a beautiful baby who grew lovelier every day. And intelligent too. She started to talk early, walk early and before long started asking mature questions, "When was there ever peace in the world, Daddy?" she once asked. Those who believed in that sort of thing always attributed Lara's precociousness to the fact that she was born on a full moon, the year of the big storm when half of Britain was flattened by high winds. She herself was a lot calmer than her birth legacy. She wanted to be a violinist when she grew up or a ballet dancer or possibly a show jumper.

"I know you heard what I said, Lara, but I'll say it again..."

"Yes Daddy, I know she's not coming back," Lara interrupted dolefully.

"Well, how do you feel about that?"

Lara turned to face her father. "Why did she leave you, Daddy?"

"I wish I knew, honey. I've thought about it but I really don't know. Do you?"

"I know she used to cry a lot, when it was just me and her at home. She used to sit in the kitchen and cry and when I asked her why, she said it was because she wasn't happy."

"Really? I didn't know that; nobody told me. Why didn't she tell me? Why didn't you tell me?!" Lara recoiled, unused to her father raising his voice at her. Beres saw her eyes water and immediately regretted his words. "Look I'm sorry, honey," he said reaching over to embrace his daughter. "I didn't mean to shout. It's my fault, I should have known if

52

your mummy was unhappy. She didn't say anything else?"

"No, no she never," Lara sobbed. "I just want my mummy back... When's my mummy coming back?"

"I said I don't think she's coming back. Grown ups have fights and sometimes when they have fights they don't want to see each other anymore, even when they're married. Or else they stop liking each other as much as they liked each other when they first met. Me and your mother have been married for seven years and we've known each other for eight years. That's a long time you know honey. Maybe she just got tired of being with me after so many years. I'm sure she'll explain everything when she's ready."

Six weeks quickly turned to two months. Lara was back at school, but Beres had still not set foot back in his shop, he just couldn't face it. He had lost his lust for work and only half cared if the company survived or not. As far as he was concerned, the business could run without him. He had employed enough people to take care of things and the staff could now start earning their salary. He promoted Denise, the secretary, to manager, while Desmond and Maxi had learned their trade from the master and could run the salesfloor in his absence. If only things could run that smoothly, he'd be laughing. He had however, forgotten about the 'secret ingredient' of his success. With Sonia absent, nobody took care of the book-keeping and it slowly fell apart until one day a creditor slapped a winding-up order on him and within fourteen days, the shop was closed down, the stock auctioned off and the disgruntled staff made redundant. Beres was bankrupt. Christmas with Lara would indeed have been cold as well as lonely if he hadn't got himself the job at Dan Oliver's in record time. His commissions there had saved their home and Lara's education.

Beres fell asleep on the sofa in front of the television. He had only just managed to get Lara to sleep; she had been complaining about a tummy upset all evening. Now the ringing phone woke him up. If he had known his life would be turned upside down by the call, he wouldn't have answered it.

"Hello. Beres? Hello..."

He recognised the voice immediately. A rush of adrenaline flooded his head and his heart throbbed with palpatations.

"Hello. Beres, is that you? It's Sonia." His wife's voice echoed hauntingly in Beres' ears like a *duppie* from the past. To get a call out of the blue after six months...!

FOR A FISTFUL OF DOLLARS

Linvall lived in a large New York-style loft apartment converted from a disused church on Stockwell Road. It was huge. There was so much room and the ceilings so high that you could have got four one-bedroomed flats in the huge space which doubled as a studio, and wherever one looked the signs of the tenant's career were evident. There were camera lights and back drops and framed, enlarged photographs. At one end of the reception hall size space, Linvall had installed a residential portacabin which he had turned into a dark room. His bedroom was also a portacabin at the other end of the loft. And in between was the vast area he used as his studio-cum-living room-cum-breakfast room. There was also a tiny built-in shower room with a toilet, and a stove, sink and fridge, over by the windows demarcated the kitchen. It was definitely the home of an artist, not everyone's cup of tea, but part of the bohemian style to which Linvall believed his life belonged.

He was flicking through the pages of some women's magazines, admiring the clothes and the photographs when the phone rang. It was Lucy Fry.

"I thought you'd be out partying," she said. "It's Saturday night. You're young and supposed to be out enjoying the best days of your life."

"Why did you call if you thought I was out?"

"On the off-chance. I had a dinner date with Oprah Winfrey, would you believe it, to discuss a TV special we're producing with her, but she didn't make her flight from New York and I couldn't think of anybody I'd rather be having dinner with, instead, than you."

"So you're taking me out to dinner?" Linvall asked sleepily.

"Yes, if you can make it, I'd really like to see you this evening."

"It all depends," he said teasingly. "What's on the menu?"

"Oh, something you just won't be able to resist," she purred down the line.

He thought about it with a big grin on his face. "And what's for afters?"

54

"More of the same... irresistible."

It was an offer he couldn't resist. She gave him her address in Hampstead Heath on the North side. "I can be around in half an hour," he said looking at his watch. She said that was fine. "Just hold tight and keep that dish stewing nice and hot for me."

Linvall found her large Victorian house on Heathurst Road easily. "You're most welcome," Lucy Fry said, receiving his bottle of white wine in one hand and embracing him tightly with the other.

Linvall entered, his eyes gazing around the magnificent property before him. He couldn't believe the opulence in which she lived. Lucy Fry lived in the entire three-storey building by herself. The property seemed even larger than it was, because she had converted each floor to hold just one room. On the ground floor was a massive kitchen-breakfast room. From there a wrought-iron spiral staircase in the centre of the kitchen went up into the middle floor which was a combined sitting room and study. The spiral staircase then continued another flight up to a lavish bedroom with en suite bathroom with a shower and a skylight. The entire interior of the house was styled in an 'ethnic' theme, tastefully decorated with fine acquisitions from the Orient and Africa. It was a magnificent testament to what loving care, taste and a lot of money could do for a house.

"So you like my place?" Lucy said proudly, as she pulled the cork from the bottle of wine and poured. They sat down on the rug in front of the sitting room fireplace and sipped.

"Like it, I love it!" Linvall replied enthusiastically. "This place is extra safe. I'm sure you don't have any problems coming up with ideas for television programmes when you live in a place like this?"

It hadn't occurred to Linvall that Lucy Fry could have this much money. He now noticed how pretty her clothes were and how expensive her jewellry looked. He took another sip of wine and laid his head back on the comfortable rug, he was on a level vibe, copasetic. Lucy went off to "get something stronger." She returned with a packet of king-size Rizlas a half empty packet of Silk Cut and a lump of black hash in a small transparent plastic bag. She sat down on the rug beside Linvall, cross-legged, humming to the sounds of Al Green which emitted softly from some well-hidden speakers and began to roll the fattest spliff he had ever seen. She lit it and the room quickly filled with the evil-smelling aroma of strong hash. She puffed away meditatively and had smoked half the spliff before she passed it over to Linvall. He declined.

"I don't take those things anymore," he said with a hint of disgust in his voice. "I left all that behind years ago."

Lucy looked at him puzzled, but shrugged her shoulders and continued smoking until there was nothing left but a roach.

"A good spliff always puts me in the mood for sex," she explained, turning to Linvall and yanking his crutch roughly. He wanted to grind her anyway, there was no doubt about it. The setting had put him even more in the mood and he could see how much she needed a sweet lover man. He didn't have time to dwell on it however, Lucy had begun to feel hot and had a dead serious look on her face. She unbuttoned his jeans hurriedly and pulled them off, nearly tearing up his briefs. It was time for a work out. Lucy only needed one movement of her hand to strip herself — she had no bra or panties on — after which she laid herself out on the rug, with her two legs skinned out, one pointed east and the other west. Before he knew it, Linvall was on top of her, biting Lucy's large and sagging breasts. Unlike the sex at the TV studios, here there were no inhibitions and Lucy Fry screamed like crazy, begging Linvall to "bite harder!" She suddenly struck out, swiping Linvall on the head hard before shoving his head between her breasts again, shouting, "I said bite harder, keep biting, don't stop!"

Linvall found her an exhausting partner, although she still wasn't into kissing. She explained that she wasn't into any ticklish business. She was only interested in a big heavy dick to make her jump, dance, wail and sing and she demanded nothing less than the full boom bye bye between her legs.

Lucy had already enjoyed three orgasms and was now begging Linvall to come. He held out as long as he could, teasing, before he released the floodgates. She lay on the rug for a long while after, staring at the ceiling motionless, as if paralysed. Linvall returned from the bathroom upstairs where he had gone to wash himself. He saw the enigmatic smile of contentment on Lucy's face and knew that she had a funki dred on her mind. He was now hungry, that was what she had invited him around for in the first place.

"Well we can either cook something here or we can get a take away. There's an excellent Chinese restaurant down the road which does take aways for special customers like myself."

"Boy, I'm too hungry to wait for any cooking," Linvall confessed. "I thought you had cooked something already.

Let's just take the Chinese."

They walked down the road together, Lucy holding tight to his arm. She may have been old enough to be Linvall's mother, but she didn't care what passers-by thought. This young black man was giving her what she needed.

It took about ten minutes to get their orders. The waiter had seated them at a table by the entrance to wait and Lucy huddled up close to Linvall every time customers entered the restaurant bringing with them a cold, sharp draft from outside. Linvall felt conspicuous with the older white woman cuddled up beside him, but he had decided to let this one ride and see where it took him. He shivered, it was a cold night with the wind blowing and a flash of lightning signalled an approaching storm. They returned home with the food quickly. He was starving.

"I hope you're not one of these 'single black men' with a woman and child lurking somewhere in his past," Lucy chatted as they ate. "I don't like men who lie to me. Remember, you need me to open doors for you." Linvall assured her again that he was a bachelor boy and free to do whatever he wanted. He was getting the distinct impression that she had decided to have a more permanent affair with him. "Because I wouldn't like to have a scene with a man with kids somewhere. As soon as I hear a guy's got a child, I feel that they've let some other woman down somewhere, and if he did that to her he'll do it to me. When you think he disrespected her, you don't want to be the next one he disrespects. Even if he gives me a valid reason it's still at the back of my mind and I feel the kid's always going be more important than me.

"It's not always the man's fault. You get women who trap men into fatherhood as well."

"Whether he got trapped or is just spreading his sperm irresponsibly, I'd only be interested if he cut all ties with the mother. By that, I mean if their sexual relationship was completely over. It helps if both partners hate each other, I'd be more inclined to get involved with the man then."

Linvall was well aware of the reluctance by certain women to date a man with a child. It brought added responsibilities, financially and timewise. But the real fear for most women, he knew, was the dreaded ex, the baby mother or ex-wife. Women know better than anyone else what other women are like and the tricks, the deviousness, the lengths that the ex will go to get things her way if she still wants the man. Even those women who would have been prepared to put up with

57

the inconvenience of ready-made motherhood to a child who wasn't naturally theirs were reluctant to tolerate any rumpus with the ex.

The meal finished, Lucy was feeling horny again. Linvall didn't leave the house for the next three days. Each morning he would wake up and insist he had work to do and each morning she would feed him a high protein breakfast and convince him to stay "just a little longer." She called in sick on Monday morning and would have done the same on Tuesday if Linvall hadn't dragged himself away, reminding her she needed to sort out his presenter's job.

UNDER PRESSURE

You get all sorts of people coming in to buy diamonds nowadays, not just people with a lot of money, but everybody from the ordinary hard-working raggamuffin types to the big-shot celebrities, and even old ladies realising their worth and investing in them. Everybody's got money or at least if they can afford a car, they can afford a diamond. And you get enough respect when you wear a diamond. Except for at Gatwick Airport where every black newly-arrived is put in a special 'nigger line' however they're dressed.

The first bleary-eyed Jamaican passengers eventually came through the customs hall into the arrivals lounge more than three hours after the plane landed. They looked rough and confused like their predecessors who came to these shores by their hundreds and thousands by the boatload, to take a big time job and settle. My parents were amongst them back in the fifties. But no matter how long they lived in England, not a day went by without them dreaming of returning to settle in the home they loved. You hear plenty of people who live over here talk about how they're so English they even like to eat cabbage and potato chips, but after thirty years Papa's belly still preferred a good plate of rice and peas anytime and he was glad to have made the decision to return home. I'm glad they've gone back. The pressure on me to get married and start a family is a lot less when they're thousands of miles away, although there's still the mail service, the phone and the fax. More importantly, their relationship seems to have improved since they returned. It's like they're in love all over again. There's nothing better than seeing a couple still in love after forty years of marriage. That's what the magic of the bright sunshine of the Caribbean, the bright blue seas and the hilltops kissing the skies can do for you.

I finally saw them. Papa, unmistakable in his spotless white panama hat, the same one he wore when I last saw him on the day they left for Jamaica.

"Mama! Mama! Oh Mamma it's so good to see you!" I cried, giving her a big hug. Mamma cried also, I knew she would.

"So Augustus, how you keeping?" Papa said patting me on my back stiffly.

"Fine, Sir. No problem. Everything is just fine, you know."
"I took charge of the luggage trolley and headed towards the car park.

"And how's Evelyn?" Mama asked looking around as if to ask why my sister wasn't there to meet her.

"She's doing alright. You know she's a big-shot solicitor now with her own practice, so she's busy all the time. She'll be down at the flat later on this evening."

The rain beat down heavily as we drove in to London.

"So why did it take three hours to clear customs?"

"Same old reason," Papa said peering at old familiar landmarks through the windscreen. "These people haven't learned anything in all these years. England is still the same racist country."

Papa was more interested in talking about the business though.

"Well, we've made an increase of fifty percent in sales year on year. At the moment I'm preparing to fill all the St Valentine's Day orders. I expect to sell about £100,000 of jewellry between now and February fourteen," I informed him. "Christmas sales were also better than expected because of the Diamond Savers Club we started. We've got all sorts of people who thought they couldn't afford to buy a diamond paying between a fiver and twenty pounds a week into our savings scheme. Also, weddings are on the increase, which is always a good thing for us. You see, despite the recession, the new black middle classes — buppies — are still out there in large numbers. Unlike their white counterparts — the yuppies who died out when the economic boom was over — buppies are increasing in number and everyone wants to be a part of this new upwardly mobile young black middle class."

Father nodded approvingly at every thing I said. It was his company but he had put it in my trust and he was happy to see that despite everything it was doing well.

My parents came to these shores in the late fifties, leaving their home in Jamaica in search of a better life thousands of miles away. They were unskilled labourers who took little with them but their eagerness to work. Like so many others they only intended to stay a few years then go back home, but they ended up in England for more than half of their lives. Then two years ago, they joined the 200 Jamaicans returning home to settle each month from Britain, Canada and the United States.

The promise of a tropical paradise had never seemed quite enough to lure them back home until the Old Man's heart attack, when after a lifetime of hard work and cold winters they retired. They left as unskilled labourers but returned to Jamaica in glory as the new middle class from England. They bought a rambling colonial-style, three-bedroomed house in an acre of land in one of the most affluent areas on the North Coast, close to where English authors Noel Coward and Ian Fleming had lain their hats to indulge in a lust for young black boys. It really was a magnificent house. I've been over to visit twice, and each time lent a hand landscaping the pretty garden with its English roses, orchids and privet hedge and with palm trees and an assortment of fruit trees blanketing the back.

"Life is sweet in Jamaica," my father declared pompously, "and we're sure we did the right thing."

I remembered the shock they got when they first returned. They had last visited the island of their birth when they left at the ages of nineteen. After the drabness of London, sunshine and acres of sandy beaches were powerfully seductive. But nothing could have prepared them for the violence, corruption and poverty of the island. "I have no illusions about life in the Caribbean," Papa had insisted before they first went off. And now when he returned he was first to declare, "I'll be the first to say that it can be frustrating trying to get anything done in Jamaica. The system is breaking down, the roads are full of potholes"

"But it is still better to be in your own country than in a foreign country," Mama added. "I'm surprised we waited so long to return. Why stay somewhere where you're not wanted when Jamaica's begging you to come home?"

My parents were fortunate enough to have money coming in on a regular basis in UK sterling so they never suffered the effects of a sixty per cent inflation rate in Jamaican dollars. But no amount of money could protect them from the consequences of the massive unemployment situation.

"At times I feel like coming straight back to London," Papa said. "Because of all the problems. I wouldn't advise anyone to go to Jamaica to settle without a lot of money behind them. Everywhere you turn there is corruption, and the politicians are the worst of all. You can't move without paying out money somewhere?"

Jamaica was like a foreign territory to them when they first got back. Many of their friends and family had either died or themselves emigrated to the US or Canada. And my parents were perceived as tourists in the country they called their own.

"The moral standing of the country is at an all time low," Papa continued. "People have little respect for each other and crime is so rife that you have to live in a house with iron bars around it. Everyone assumes that because we lived overseas we have something to steal."

"Yet, for all this I don't regret our decision to return home," Mamma insisted. "Not one bit. People back home laugh and say we were crazy to come back, but that is where our hearts are. We always planned to spend our last years there, I just wish the government would do more to improve conditions."

It didn't take her long to get around to what was really on her mind. "So how about you?" she asked enigmatically.

"What, me? Oh I'm alright, you know how it is Mama. I'm staying healthy, I'm eating well, I'm doing my exercises." I could have mentioned that I was still playing football on Sunday mornings, but I knew they didn't want to hear that. Sunday was a sabbath for them. They thought I should be in church, not playing football on the holy day. I swung the car right off Chelsea Embankment at Battersea Bridge. At the sight of the abandoned power station, Papa took some delight in remarking that at least Jamaica would have done something about such an eyesore by now.

"But is there any special young lady in your life yet, Gussie? That's what I'm asking," Mama continued.

I knew it was coming, so my reply was prepared.

"I've had some bad luck lately, mama. You know how it is. I've met a couple of nice girls and I hoped each time that something would work out, that maybe this was the right woman. But... I've just been unlucky. It's never quite worked out."

"That's exactly what I wanted to talk to you about," Papa interjected loftily. "I've been worrying about it so much my head hurts, I haven't slept properly for a week. You mus' marry. You cyan't keep putting it off. You've got a stomach ulcer at such a young age because your life is not settled. Life isn't easy, you know. You think you'll be young for ever, but let me tell you that's not the case. And when you get older, you'll realise why you need to go into a marriage partnership with a good wife. I can't hand over the business to you until you show maturity, experience and responsibilities as a married man. I want to see you in a stable relationship first; with a wife, home, children and a solid foundation. If you're not careful too late will be your cry; too old for the nice young girls, and the only women left will be the ones nobody else wants."

62

Papa would have continued like that for the rest of the day. He enjoyed nothing better than lecturing to his children about family values and other virtues. The journey from the airport had taken almost two hours and when we got to the flat overlooking Clapham Common, we were all in need of the refreshments I prepared. Even though I lived in the large and tastily-furnished three bedroomed flat, it belonged to my parents. They sold the family house when they left for Jamaica and installed me in the flat to make sure they always had "somewhere to come back to in London." And of course from the moment they stepped in through the door they treated the place rightly as if they owned it — and so did I. There were two messages on the answer machine. One from Evelyn checking that Mamma and Papa had arrived safely and one from Caroline asking whether I wanted to go out that evening. I called her office. Caroline was still in court. I spoke to Evelyn briefly then passed her on to Mamma and Papa.

I like and admire my parents and want to be like them. When we were a strictly Sunday service church family, I dragged myself out of bed every morning after a rough Saturday night, to accompany the family to church to oblige their belief that the family which prays together stays together. Five years ago, the Old Man became a 'fundamentalist' after a heart attack forced him to realise he was getting old. He was the only one surprised when it finally came. He'd spent thirty-five years of his life sweating for his family, first as a carpenter then selling jewellry from a market stall, before going into the diamonds business full time. I respect him for trying to provide the best for his family, but I'd rather not be the cause of his early death. Mama had long come to terms with marrying a workaholic, but she nevertheless let out a big sigh when his heart attack came as if it had taken a lot of worry off her mind. Afraid that he might die in England, the Old Man immediately made plans to emigrate back home, as Mama had wanted for so long. They soon discovered that the house they had paid £10,000 for fifteen years ago was now worth £200,000 and bought their colonial style house just outside Oracabessa on the North coast with their savings and with the spare cash, the Old Man bought a flat with magnificent views of Clapham Common and went into the diamond business. Most definitely.

Caroline returned my call. Despite her insistence to maintain her chastity on our first date, something in her voice told me she wanted me. After my wasted efforts on that first night at the hotel, I thought she might have changed her mind about our St Valentine's Day date, but on the contrary she was even more eager.

"I really enjoyed myself on our one night together. Everything's cool with me, I hope everything was alright for you and I'm really looking forward to our Valentine's date. Meanwhile, I wanted to see if you would like to go out to the theatre. There's a wicked play performing at the Shaw Theatre called 'The Late Great Black Man' and I've managed to get some tickets, the only problem is that they're for tonight."

"That's no problem," I said confidently. I wanted to see her again and maybe, just maybe, there was a possibility...

People were already queueing outside the theatre when I arrived. After a couple of minutes, Caroline turned a corner into view, dressed in a dazzling black two-piece, with glittered edges, and her hair done up in a high beehive. She looked stunning, as several of the men present remarked. I felt secretly proud and took her arm to lead the way in.

After the show, we took a cab to Covent Garden, where we had a late supper at Brahms & Liszt. Caroline was composed, despite the resounding hush that greeted her entry. She's either used to it or indifferent to it and I haven't met a woman yet who's indifferent to the power of her beauty.

"So what did you think of the show?" she asked.

"It was okay, a bit intellectual for me. I prefer a good sex comedy with Oliver Samuels myself. But it was alright."

"Oh you like Oliver as well?" she remarked impressed. "It's usually the women that go for him, that's interesting."

"Well, you know, I like to support the cause you know."

"Oh I agree," Caroline added. "I think it's fantastic to see all these black theatre companies appear out of nowhere and producing plays which the black community wants to see for a change. And they've managed to survive without a penny from the Arts Council when other theatre companies have gone bust. Did you see 'Black Heroes In The Hall Of Fame'?"

"Of course I did. That's my favourite show..."

We had been getting on famously and it seemed like we had only exchanged a few words of chit chat when she pulled out her disappearing act again.

"I'm going to have to leave, Gus. I've got a big day in court tomorrow and I've got lots of work to prepare. I have to brief the barrister and all that."

"Damn. I was hoping I might go back to yours," I said despondently.

"Don't rush it, Gus," Caroline said unimpressed. "I had a really great evening. And I'm looking forward to going out with you again. I'm sure there'll be lots of opportunities to go home to your place or to mine, but let's each go to our own homes tonight. Okay?" She smiled, a sweet teasing smile. I was teased and couldn't resist.

"Look Caroline, I don't know how to say this, but I think I've got some strong feelings for you... I don't know what to do about them. I need to see you, I need to see you tonight. And I need to make love to you."

"My, is this some kind of proposition? I should be flattered. Well, I can't deny my strong feelings for you also..."

"How strong...?"

"Well, from the first time I saw you, I've wanted to make love to you..."

I gulped, thinking 'yes!', I had struck it lucky after all. A waiter informed us that the bar was about to close. We were the last ones in and all the staff were waiting on us, but there was still time to hone in for the kill.

"You don't really want to go to an empty home do you? Wouldn't you like me to come around and make things a bit more comfortable? You do live on your own don't you?"

"Yes. There's just me and my Siamese cat Josephine."

"Well, just imagine, there'll be me, you and Josephine, just the three of us, snuggling up close. Close your eyes. Can you imagine it?"

"Are the lights turned down low?" Caroline asked, her eyes shut tight.

"They're not, but I'll turn them down low if that will help."

"Yes, turn them down low, or even better, light a candle and curl yourself up with me and play some Barry White music in the background. Yes, curl your feet up on the sofa."

"Okay, my feet are curled up on the sofa and my tongue is slowly, softly caressing your ear," I whispered close to her ear breathing hot air gently over her.

"Oh yes, I can see what you mean," Caroline purred breathlessly, "it feels good already..." Then suddenly she pushed me away. "Stop that though. You're making me feel sexy and I don't know if I want to feel sexy tonight."

She opened her eyes and shied away from the smiles of the waiters who had now taken interest in our little love games.

"Seriously, Gus," she said determined, "I have to get back. So if you don't mind getting me a cab."

Caroline offered to share a cab, but I wasn't in the mood. I didn't want to make a habit of being prick-teased by her and when she waved me goodbye with the words, "see you on Valentine's Day," I thought, 'not if I can get out of it'.

65

DON'T TAKE IT PERSONAL

Beres replaced the receiver. He couldn't understand why his wife had called after all this time, but he had agreed to have her around for dinner the next day. The woman was out of order and he cussed her at first. How did she expect him to react? He wanted to find out whatever it was she had on her mind. He hoped she wasn't playing around. He was just about coming to terms with the realisation that she was gone for good, just about getting over her. He had been through too much pain to allow her to put him through it all again. Deep inside though, he knew he was still weak for her. When a person gets under your skin you can never get over them unless you have a proper clean break. His heart still yearned for her.

Lara woke up.

"Daddy, my tummy's still hurting me."

Beres was now becoming worried. Lara had complained about the tummy upset ever since thy got home. He had thought it was just indigestion and given her a glass of liver salts to drink before going to bed. It was now midnight and she hadn't got better.

"What was the last thing she had to eat?" the emergency doctor asked, disgruntled at being called out at this time of night.

"What did you eat at the restaurant, darling?" Beres asked his daughter who was reeling in pain. She told him she had ordered a hamburger, followed by a milkshake.

"A hamburger?" the doctor repeated incredulously. "You give your daughter hamburger to eat? Well, that's the problem, I don't need to go any further. You give your daughter hamburgers to eat and you're asking for trouble. If you're going to give her meat to eat, next time buy the fresh meat, not the one that's been sitting in a freezer for years."

The doctor gave her a mixture that would help clear her system of the last vestiges of the hamburger. "She should be alright once she manages to go to the toilet," the doctor explained as he packed his bags and made his way hurriedly out of the house.

The doctor was right and the mixture did the trick. But

Lara had very little sleep that night and there was no point in sending her off to school. Beres decided to stay at home with her. He hadn't slept much the night before either. Each time he tried to sleep, the dream of his now unmasked lover was waiting for him there in the pillows and in the sheets, waiting for him to come to bed and dream it all over again. Staying awake had given him a lot of time to think. He thought about how he had Sonia's love in the palm of his hands and how he lost it. Maybe if he had spent more time with her, going out together, maybe she'd still be there. He thought back, covering the same ground he had covered a thousand times in the last six months. He remembered their arguments verbatim; like the time Sonia had got upset when he laid down the hardline regarding their daughter. It had started with a television programme on mixed marriages.

"What would you say if Lara brought home a white guy when she's older?" Sonia asked totally unprompted.

"Not in my home!" Beres answered brusquely without giving it too much of a thought.

"What about if she came home with an Asian man?" Sonia persisted.

"I said not in my house," Beres repeated somewhat irritated. "No way is my baby marrying anybody but a true black man."

"I think she should be able to marry who she wants," Sonia retorted. "She's an individual, Beres. I don't want you messing up my daughter's head with prejudice. That's not the right way to bring up a child. I don't want her all messed up later in life."

"What is all this about? I'm not telling her to be prejudiced. She can marry an ugly man, a rich man, or a poor man, I don't mind. But I personally don't want my daughter bringing home a white man. She's going to have enough problems in life without getting involved in mixed relationships."

"Oh come on Beres, that's a load of rubbish. You've been in mixed relationships — and you survived. And I've been in mixed relationships, they didn't do me any harm..."

Beres became agitated. Sonia knew full well that he didn't like talking about his past relationships and liked less hearing about hers. But she pursued the issue.

"If I hadn't met you, I could have ended up marrying a white guy..."

"Look, do I need to hear this?!" Beres burst out. "Let's just drop the subject, okay? But let me tell you now, if you think I'm going to stand around when my daughter brings home a white man, you've got another thing coming. That issue is non-negotiable."

What had started out as a peaceful evening at home in front of the television had degenerated into an argument about a hypothetical situation that was in any event several years off. Sonia continued murmuring something about "my child should be able to grow up and live her life without all our prejudices. You need to listen to yourself and hear yourself speak sometimes!" There had been several similar arguments in the last year of their marriage. But Beres refused to allow them to spoil a good relationship. He was always first to apologise, kiss and make up.

They got into an argument another time when the builders were in, building a refectory at the back of the house. Beres had to endure hearing the workmen making comments about how "fit" his wife was. From that moment on, Beres didn't like them. On a particularly hot day, a couple of the builders asked for a drink. Beres got them a glass of water each. They looked at each other and said, "Ain't you got nothing stronger, boss?" There was no way he was going to allow them a squeeze after the way they had been chatting. He told them there were no beers in the house. At that moment, Sonia came out of the kitchen saying, "Of course we've got some" and produced a six-pack from the fridge. Beres was determined not to be outdone however and swiped the beers back from the builders outstretched hands with the words, "I said there were no beers in the house."

Sonia never liked it when his friends came round either; especially Johnny Dollar, because when he came around all they ever did was talk football, play cards and watch TV and she certainly wasn't happy when Beres told her that Johnny was expecting two kids by two different women.

For Beres, Sonia's friends caused as much disruption in their domestic affairs. Particularly Delores who had just split up with her husband and had taken up the habit of arriving at their house at 9am every morning. As the boss of his own shop, Beres didn't think it necessary to go to work before midday. He worked hard and deserved his morning lie-ins with his wife. He used to look forward to a morning of making love, pillow fighting and other love games when he returned home from driving Lara to school, but Delores' early morning visits had made that impossible. Beres, who normally didn't like to leave his yard before midday, was suddenly leaving at nine in the morning to avoid his wife's best friend.

Thinking about it now, Beres had to admit that they had

unnecessary small fights. Maybe he should have done the chores a lot more. But it was hard to think that Sonia would walk out of their home for something like that.

The doorbell rang at 8pm sharp. It was just like Sonia to be punctual. Beres opened the door and his estranged wife stepped in, exquisitely dressed in an expensive fur coat that fitted her to perfection. Beauty is in the eye of the beholder, but Sonia carried it around with her. She had a striking sense of style, clothes-wise and otherwise, and an instinct to flaunt it; topped with a defiant air that lacked refinement. When you walk beautiful and think beautiful, people will always perceive you as beautiful. Beres thought he had never seen his wife look more beautiful. Her skin looked fresh, her eyes alive and the two lines across her forehead had disappeared. She had spent half their marriage trying to get rid of those two lines with creams and massages. She was so beautiful that he couldn't resist pulling her towards him and trying to give her a gentle, passionate kiss. The emptiness in her lips left him cold as she gently pushed him back. The two stared at each other in silence.

"I'm sorry..." Beres began.

"What?"

"I shouldn't have done that."

"Did you want to do it?"

"Of course I wanted to do it."

"Then that's no problem. I didn't want to do it, that's the only problem."

It was stalemate. The subject changed by mutual consent.

"Where's my baby?" Sonia asked casually.

"She's upstairs asleep. She was ill last night and didn't get much sleep."

"Ill?"

"Nothing to worry about, just a stomach upset. She ate a hamburger."

"You're giving my baby hamburgers to eat? Well, I think I came along in the nick of time."

Whatever had gone through his mind the hundred times he had thought about what he would do when Sonia came back was now long forgotten. He no longer wanted to shout at her or ignore her or throw her out. He wanted to be reasonable and work something out.

They passed the time away with polite, stiff pleasantries. Sonia asked about how Lara was doing in school. Finally dinner was served. Not being a natural cook, Beres had

69

applied all his culinary skills to the meal and what he had come up with was callaloo and chips.

"So, have you got another man?" Beres asked her eventually, as they sat down to eat.

"No, why do you think that?"

"Well, I've been racking my brain trying to think of why you left and I haven't been able to come up with an answer."

"It was nothing to do with you Beres, it was me. I changed and wanted other things out of life."

"But you had everything? I know women who would give up their right arms to have half of what you had. You wrecked our home Sonia, and there's no excuse for that. You had a beautiful home, a beautiful daughter and we were happy, or at least I thought we were happy. You deceived me. I couldn't bring myself to tell people that my wife had walked out on me!"

Lara entered the dining room at that moment in her pajamas, holding her teddy bear and struggling to wipe sleep from her eyes. She yawned before realising who the woman eating dinner with her father was.

"Mummy! Mummy!" she cried with joy as she ran to Sonia with open arms. Mother and daughter embraced each other warmly. "Mummy, Mummy. I'm so glad you're home, Mummy. I've missed you so much. Christmas was so lonely without you, Mummy. Please say you'll stay."

Tears came to Sonia's eyes. She had longed to see her daughter agin, longed to hold her, to kiss her, longed to talk to her. "Well let's wait and see what happens shall we?" she said hugging Lara tighter.

"Lara darling, you'd better go back to bed. You know you've got school tomorrow and you've got to get better."

"But I'm not sleepy anymore Daddy."

"Well go up anyway, me and your mummy are having a heart-to-heart and we need to be alone."

"What's a heart-to-heart, Mummy?" Lara asked turning to her mother.

"Well... it's when two people have to talk seriously and truthfully about how they feel."

"Oh alright, I'll got to bed. But don't go Mummy. Please stay the night."

"I'll see darling," Sonia choked wiping a tear from her eye as her daughter kissed her goodnight and went off to bed.

"It's no easy thing for a mother to fall from grace," Sonia said, looking for sympathy.

"You didn't fall, you took off," Beres interrupted

unsympathetically. Sonia burst into tears, but Beres wasn't impressed. "And it always ends up in the damned weeping," he said heartlessly. He had the upper hand now and he wasn't giving it up. Sonia had seen how much her daughter missed her; she'd be the one begging to stay.

Sonia stiffened as if she had been expecting this kind of onslaught for a long time. She was ready to face the music.

"Look Beres, I wasn't happy at home and I needed to get away. I didn't want to tell you because you'd try and change my mind as you've done so many times."

"When have I ever changed your mind?"

"How many times did I tell you that I wanted to go off travelling on my own. All I wanted was a few months to myself, doing the things I wanted to do and going to places I wanted to go to. I wanted to go pony-trekking across the Khyber Pass or canoeing up the Amazon, not going on a package holiday, but you always convinced me otherwise."

"Yeah, but I didn't know that had anything to do with you being unhappy in the relationship and wanting to leave. As far as I'm concerned you can go hang-gliding from the top of Everest if it means that much to you."

"Look, I'm not young enough to spend this much energy arguing over something that doesn't have any meaning now. Let's talk about why I came here.

"You want to come back home, don't you? Well that's cool, but this time around we're going to have certain rules you're going to abide by."

Sonia's surprised expression suggested that Beres had caught the wrong drift.

"Look Beres, I'm not moving back. I'm not the same girl you used to know, stop and think it over. The reason I'm here is that I realise I am a mother with responsibilities. That's why I've come to get my daughter. I don't want any arguments about it Beres. I want to take Lara with me and for her to start a new life with me."

Beres felt despondent rather than militant. The best years he had known were the years he had had with Sonia and at that moment he would have given anything to have her once again. Anything but his daughter. Lara was not negotiable.

The doorbell rang at that moment. Beres threw a long, cold stare before answering. He recognised the face at his door immediately. It was somewhat older and plumper than he had last seen it, but it was definitely Grace, Sonia's old friend, whom he had first met all those years ago on the Canary Islands.

71

"Are you alright, darling?" she said rushing over to Sonia and embracing her.

Sonia saw the puzzled look on her husband's face.

"Grace was waiting for me outside in the car," she explained.

"Yes," Grace added belligerently, "in case you decided to get stupid and violent. I warn you, I'll go straight to the police."

Beres still looked puzzled. He turned to his wife.

"What's going on?"

"Er, Grace is my girlfriend," Sonia answered shyly, "I mean my *actual* girlfriend."

When a black man falls from grace he has nowhere to run. When Beres twigged, there was only one thing on his mind.

"You'll never see Lara again," he promised as he shoved the two women out of his house. "You will never see Lara again, you hear me?!"

NO DISRESPECT

The doctor looked at me puzzled. His brain couldn't make sense of what his eyes were telling me. Yes, he had seen me earlier that day. Lesley had been called in for last minute check ups on the same day as Pauline and only a matter of hours separated their appointments. Even though I had changed my clothes and shaved off my stubble, the doctor had no doubt that it was me. He gave me a bemused look which confirmed it. I returned a deadly look which warned him not to say anything as I hadn't got around to telling Lesley that I was expecting another baby by a different woman.

"So have you experienced any problems with the pregnancy?" the doctor asked matter-of-factly, as he listened through the stethoscope to the sounds coming from Lesley's belly. "No? Good. And the morning sickness has stopped finally? Good And I hope the father is doing his share of the chores." He glanced at me pitifully, before addressing Lesley again. "You need a lot of rest. Put your feet up, because the baby's due very shortly and at this stage you need to take it easy."

"You heard that!" Lesley rejoiced turning to me with a victorious smile. "The doctor says I'm to put my feet up and that you should wait on me hand and foot."

I smiled nervously and the doctor smiled ironically.

Phew! It was a close shave. I couldn't believe it when I learned that their appointments were so close together and both women had insisted that I do the right thing and accompany them to the clinic. I haven't had the opportunity to tell Lesley about my other baby mother. I feel guilty about deceiving her, but right now it's better to be economical with the truth. I should have done it months ago, but now she's heavily pregnant and needs my support. I can't risk giving her news that could distress her at the moment. I'm going to have to break it to her gently after she's given birth.

I've had many months now to chew over the situation. If Lesley and I could have afforded it we would have probably had more kids, but as it was Winnie remained an only child. Now I am getting two kids for the price of one and I can't really say I'm too happy about that, but as all children are God's children, you have to love them. That's what I said to

Lesley when I was trying to prepare her for what's to come.

"You know seh all children are Jah Jah's children, don't you? That Winnie and the baby you've got inside of you are not your children alone, they're Jah's children. You do know that don't you?" I said mysteriously as a hint. Lesley turned and looked at me suspiciously, searching my eyes for a clue. She knew it was a trick question and didn't want to be caught out.

"Yes..." she nodded nervously, unsure of her answer.

"Good, I replied, "because Jah's expecting more than one child this year."

I was close to telling her, but I just couldn't. The look in her eye told me the time wasn't right.

"Well, if you ask me, Jah's had enough children for a while," Lesley offered ominously. It really wasn't the right time to mention the other baby, so I stood silently, a nervous king with king-size problems.

'What a man thinketh of himself so shall he be,' Christ said. So if your character is kingly, you become a king. Being a sagittarius makes it worse for me, because sagittarians are ruled by Jupiter and Jupiter's a king also. With this reaffirmation I try to carry myself like a king at all times with an air of royalty about me.

A king, at least any king worth his salt, hears the cry of his people. The king's duty is to serve his people, as opposed to the people serving him. So if my baby mother's crying about a particular problem, I'll hear it. I'll be passionate if needs be and try to fulfil her needs. If anyone of my family or friends are crying ,I hear their cry and try to help. In the land of the blind, the man with one eye is king. Right now the cry of our people is to build an army of righteous youths to help educate mankind, raise our consciousness and take us to the next stage of our evolution. Every black man is supposed to be building an army, to help people think positive in terms of long term investments and family structure and other things. It's a mission too big for one woman and sometimes a man has to recruit soldiers. I guess you could say I'm one of these people who would like to change the world.

There was a time in our civilisation when there were ten men to every woman. A time when nine men would say, 'Johnny, we and you have to share Lesley'. And whether I liked it or not I would have had to deal with it. That was in the old days. Today things have changed and if the lyrics of the record are correct, 'man shortage ah gwan'! Now if that's the case, I don't know any woman who would like to be the odd one out if the law says one man one woman. If they were the ones left out without a man and without a child, they would cuss us every day for being faithful. Imagine the situation if women were in the majority — whatever the statistics are — yet men were remaining faithful and monogamous. You'd have all sorts of problems. There was a man driving his car in New York. He stopped at a traffic light and suddenly a gang of girls surrounded his car and with a gun pointed at his temple, forced him to lick every one of them. Can you imagine what kind of society we'd be living in with all these frustrated women? One thing I know for sure, women don't like being around other frustrated women, because they're the first ones to comment on a particularly agitated friend that "what she needs is a good grind — look at her she can't get no man..." I've known guys who got six, seven years in jail for some misdemeanour because they had to face a female judge who hadn't had a grind for a year. Those guys are always first to speak out against capital punishment, I'm telling you. When I show women that scenario they usually agree that it's true and say, "we can't be so selfish, we must learn to share."

I've had women cuss me when I've refused to give them a grind. Once when Winnie was two-years-old and Lesley took her to Jamaica to meet her grandparents, I spent a whole night with a woman without grinding her. I was only interested in kissing and cuddling. With my woman away I just needed someone to hold, that's all. I tried to explain that, but this woman was hungry for a man and she couldn't take it no more. She didn't give up trying the whole night long and cussed me the next morning. "Why yuh don't give me a grind?" she moaned."Enh? Why yuh nevah read your bible? You nevah hear Jah say 'go forth and multiply'? Yuh think Moses could afford to have just one woman with the statistics like it is? Yuh mad! Each one of Moses' sons had to have more than one woman. That's why Solomon was the wisest man, because there's so much idiot like you about the place him haffe have a thousand woman, enh. Cho'! Yuh come to England come act like white man, to rahtid! Talk about one man, one woman... You fool, it's Africa we come from you know... And you should know better as a righteous man..."

It's of particular interest to Mama why a man has two women when he's getting enough sex at home. For me personally, that Lesley and Pauline's characters are so contrasting adds spice to my life. Pauline is fiery. She'll throw things at you in an argument and I can't resist trying to tame

75

that little lion. I tease her remorselessly. While Lesley is really placid. Most of the time she's just happy to be my woman and take care of her family. She treats me like a king in my home and usually has my dinner waiting for me. I like the best of both worlds.

"Well, you can't have the best of both worlds!" Pauline screamed at me. She had finally taken my advice to stop raving and had even taken up buying baby food and knitting little booties to put herself in a motherly mood, but she seemed to have become more irritable as a consequence. I was trying to work out a compromise that we could all live with. It was easy, I would divide my loyalties between the two homes. I would spend four days at Lesley's and three day's at Pauline's. It still remained for me to discuss things with Lesley, but from the Pauline's reaction it wasn't going to be an option.

"Why Johnny? Why do you want to get rid of me?" Her watery eyes searched mine for an answer.

"I don't want to get rid of you, you don't understand."

"You promised me, promised me that you would look after me and the baby. You told me, 'no don't get rid of it', and now you want to abandon me. Why, Johnny, why?"

"Who said anything about abandoning? Woman; just calm down and try to reason it through."

"I'm going to kill you!" she screamed.

I don't know where the knife came from, all I saw was the blur of Pauline's hand as it came towards me. I sidestepped the thrust and grabbed her by the wrist. I could have hit her when I saw the breadknife in her clenched grip. I managed to shake it loose and hold her down. When I thought she was calm enough, I decided to return the knife to the kitchen, out of the way. I hadn't taken but a few steps when Pauline rushed for the bathroom. I moved quickly after her and only just caught her in time as she tried to empty the contents of a bottle of sleeping tablets into her mouth.

"I want to kill myself!" she screamed again, "leave me, I want to kill myself!"

I had begun to get irritated and wished I had never met the woman, but the situation was a delicate one and had to be played with caution.

"Look, I'm sorry, Pauline. Forget everything I said. Of course I'll be with you full-time when the baby's born. Come on now," I said cheerily. "Let's forget it. You know I'm going to take care of you and the baby twenty-four sevens, three-sixty-five. I would have said anything to avoid any more of the alms house business.

"Just tell me the truth, Johnny," she said sobbing slowly. "If you don't want me just get out of my life. I'm thirty-years-old Beres, I'm getting old. I'm scared of being stuck by myself with a child."

"Of course I want you, Pauline. I want you and I want the yout'. You can rely on me. No problem." I managed to convince her that everything was cool and she calmed down. "So you've managed to get it off your chest this morning," I said with a smile as I embraced her close, "and a long time you did want to get it off your chest, right?"

"I've been trying to get it off my chest all the time," she said sniffing in staccato. By the hungry look in her eyes she had been biting her nails and itching and willing me to come through that door before we got into the argument. Now the argument was done, she remembered her appetite. Pregnant women seem to have bigger appetites. Pauline requested the serious kind of loving, genuine kind of loving, with hugging and kissing, not to mention caressing. Pregnant or not, when a woman gives you that certain look, poor jimmy just can't help growing.

"I know you're hot, Pauline. I know you when you get hot. You get that look you've got in your eyes."

"Yes I am feeling hot, she said invitingly as she took off her blouse to cool herself down, followed by her skirt and then her panties. I was feeling hot also and threw off my jacket as Pauline fell semi-naked on the bed with her legs spread out and her pregnant belly pointing to the ceiling. From the look in her eyes I could see she didn't want no ticklish business, she was looking for a big heavy dick. My body, tense, steamy and sweaty lay with hers, but my mind, clear sharp and honest was on the other side of town.

I looked at my watch and groaned. I was supposed to have been home hours ago. I had to get up, but I knew it wasn't going to be easy.

"You're not getting up already are you?"

"I have to, Pauline. I have got other things to do as well you know. I can't simply drop everything." I climbed into my jeans and continued dressing.

"What shall we call our baby?" Pauline said suddenly changing the subject.

"Whatever," I said impatiently, "as long as it's a Bible name, I'm cool."

"Oh try and take a bit more interest, Johnny. It is important."

77

"Well you choose a name and I'll choose a name. A loved child has many names..."

"Nigerians like to give their children loads of names. My friend Funmi's Nigerian and she has about ten names. Apparently, the Yorubas allow every single uncle and aunt present at the christening to each give the child a name. They take their names more seriously than we do, because they feel a name really means something. It tells people who you are, what you are and where you're coming from. Funmi's brother's name means 'God be praised', because their father was dying of food poisoning at the time his son was born."

I continued dressing without saying anything. I was in too much of a hurry to allow myself to be drawn into a discussion about baby names. Pauline continued...

"Mark, that's a good name. It's a name you just kind of use, people don't question it and it's a Bible name. I wish my parents had called my brother Mark and not Angus... Father was so psychic and sure that it would be a girl and born on his birthday. The baby was born on his birthday but turned out to be a boy, so they weren't prepared with a boy's name, so he didn't care and mother chose the name out of a magazine in a hurry."

I was dressed and ready to go. Pauline seemed only then to realise that I really was going.

"So what are you going to do now, screw me and leave me?".

"None of your business," I said firmly. It was not negotiable, I had to go.

"I'm making everything my business. Where are you going?"

I simply looked at her and kissed my teeth, slamming her front door behind me. She had just got some first rate loving, she was hardly going to top herself straight after. I understand women. They don't want to be 'hit and run' victims in a relationship, but I had already decided, months ago, that I was going to stay with Lesley after the kids were born and try to work things out. She was my long-time woman, the woman I wanted to continue being with.

RECESSION AH LICK

Beres was glad to get out of the house. Linvall wasn't enthusiastic. Gussie needed to take his mind off things, and Johnny wanted to go out for a drink with the posse afterwards.

Brixton Massive FC were not the most disciplined soccer team in the London League, usually only half their players turned up for the 'compulsory' Thursday evening training sessions, but with the forthcoming final match against the Harlesden Ruffnecks, the team manager Fat Willie had organised a team night out together. It was the only way he could guarantee that the whole team showed up on time. Beres had obliged by getting a deal on a U.S.-style stretch limousine for the night and everybody had arrived dressed to the nines in their party clothes. Somehow, the whole team had to squeeze into the limo, with Beres behind the wheel.

"So these are the wheels," Johnny shouted above the mayhem as he climbed in. "So gimme the keys, nuh." he said admiring the limo.

"What for?"

"So I can tek it for a test run. Gimme the keys man." Johnny bumrushed his brethren, tickling him and searching him all over.

"No, seriously, this is no joke," Beres pushed him aside. "If it was my car, I would let you drive it, you know that."

Miraculously they all managed to squeeze into the car but not without a good deal of pushing and shoving.

"This is the big one," Fat Willie barked. "You think you're bad, well in a week's time, you're up against the cream of the cream, the finest, most brutal team in the league. They've won the cup four times in a row; the only team to have done that. And do you know how they've won? Because they've wanted to win and they've trampled over everything in their way for that bit of glory at the end of the rainbow, just to lift up that cup and hear the cheers from their supporters. They want to carry the cup back to Harlesden once more, and they've got a secret weapon..." Fat Willy produced a photograph from inside his jacket. He passed the pic around. "That's Animal De Souza... the roughest, toughest centre half in the league. This guy bites your legs. He instills fear in the hearts of the bravest footballers. Harlesden have won every game he's played in this season while their opposing teams have lost half their players on stretchers. If there's any talent between you, I don't want to see it on Sunday. Forget talent and just go for the goals, because the cup final is strictly war — South London versus West London. Winner takes all."

The Brixton massive players muttered their disapproval of Animal and added that he had the ugliest face they'd ever seen.

"I know this guy, you know," Everton Small pipped from the front seat of the limo where he was squeezed tight between Beres and another player. "'Cause I used to go to school up Harlesden way. I'm telling you, he is ruff."

"Can you give us a character profile?"

"Well, all I remember is that there were two things that got him angry: when someone said his dick was too small, that started enough fights at school, and I remember another time when we were fifteen or sixteen, about six of us ah play cards..." Everton couldn't stop himself from laughing as he recalled the memory, "playing blackjack and someone said to him, 'your girlfriend's saying you eat under sheet'... Animal went crazy, 'Wha'dya mean me eat under sheet, me is a Jamaican, me nuh eat under sheet...!' Four of us had to hold him down to stop him committing murder that night. And then his woman comes in and says, 'what you mean you don't eat under sheet? You must stop tell lie?!"

The entire limousine erupted with laughter.

"You see wha' me ah seh," Johnny appealed to his fellow passengers, "every man must put his woman under manners."

They laughed some more.

"The most important thing to remember, and I know some of you are going to try your hardest to forget, is that each of you needs all the stamina he can muster up on the night. That is why after tonight, I'm imposing a total sex ban on the team."

The dissentious uproar from each and every member of the team threatened to turn the proceedings into an insurrection.

"You must be joking!" Carly Jones shouted, "you think my woman will agree to that?"

Johnny tried to be reasonable.

"Come on Willy, you can't ask for a total sex ban. It doesn't bother me personally, because to tell you the truth me deh 'pon 'recession', but I know that some of these youths ain't going to be able to take it. Not a whole week. Okay, have a sex ban the night before, I can understand that because it's an important match, but you're asking for too much with a week..."

"You all think this is a joke don't you?" Fat Willy sounded frustrated, "This is no joke you know. In a week, you go into battle and the only way you're going to survive is if you save all your energy and take out all your pent-up emotions on the Ruffnecks next Sunday. It's my final word, after tonight I'll be checking upon you all and anyone who breaks the rules doesn't play in the final."

There were still some unhappy murmurings, but everyone knew that Fat Willy meant business.

Beres eased the brakes and pulled in to the kerb outside Gregory Peck's nightspot in Soho. This was to be the first watering hole of the night, where a man could pick up a woman with style. The passengers climbed out, one by one. To the punters queueing outside, who supposed the passengers emerging from the limousine to be an American pop group, it wasn't surprising that the bouncers waved them straight into the venue ahead of the line.

Beres gunned the motor and drove to find a car park with three adjacent parking spaces. Even if the tight narrow streets of Soho made it difficult to drive a yank mobile of this size, it was still an ego trip driving a car that threatened to eat up the road. The sleek charcoal-grey limousine belonged to a hire company to which Beres had sent many of his clients and in return they usually allowed him to borrow a car for the night. The stretch limo was the most ambitious loan Beres had made there so far, complete with chrome wheels, power steering, power brakes, a powerful motor, air conditioning, automatic heat, short wave radio, colour television and a telephone, four carburetors and two straight exhausts.

Inside Gregory Peck's the crowd were in ebullient mood. The disc jockey was armed with 45s and some dubplates by his hip and, it seemed, could do no wrong dropping one dance tune after the other to the cheers and whoops of the crowd. This was where bored wives and girlfriends went missing on a Saturday night; trying to find some of the sparkle that had gone out of their relationships and whenever a good rhythm dropped, they climbed on the dancefloor strutting their stuff boldly, in slow motion, to dances with exotic names like the bogle, the gingy fly, the nanny, the butterfly and the santa barbara. It was like a party rather than a club and the Brixton massive FC team were at the centre of the dancefloor, turning it into their own little party. Johnny had a beer waiting for Beres when he arrived.

"With all the driving you've got to do tonight, you need at least one strong drink, man," he assured his friend patting him on the back. "Then go forth and multiply. Have you never read that in the Bible?"

Some of the team had already pulled women, good time girls who were into raving and adult fun and sat around their table giggling and asking for expensive drinks. Johnny had a woman on each arm, one an attractive, 5ft 4, curvy divorcee whose name was Carol and said she was bringing up her eight-year-old son positively and independently and the other, Denise, a 31-year-old personnel officer, who said she was looking for an uncomplicated working man. They were both victims of the latest fashion for wigs and claimed they would never go to dances without one. In fact, they never left home without one.

"I saw a man with a weave on down in Camden Market last week," Carol said smiling ironically, "it looked kinda good from the front but when he turned around and I saw the join, I was in stitches."

Johnny didn't think it was a laughing matter at all.

Some men were born to nice up dance, Beres and Gussie preferred to stand by the bar and sip their drinks as they watched the action in a cool profile.

"So what do you think of Willy's sex ban?" Beres asked.

"To tell you the truth it won't have much effect on me, I'm on recession right now anyway," Gussie admitted. He told Beres the story of his unsuccessful attempts at bedding Caroline. Beres had little sympathy for him.

"You're getting old, Gussie, you're not supposed to be running around trying to screw different women at your age. It's getting embarrassing now and you're not even scoring. Just find yourself a woman, a permanent thing, get married. It will do you some good."

"Yeah, yeah, yeah, same old story," Gussie answered impatiently. "How about you, B? Is the sex ban going to trouble you?"

"Personally I don't mind it, because I wasn't getting any anyway, so another few days won't make a difference."

Recession has a domino effect. When a man is under recession he won't be getting any cooked food either and the woman tends to forget her place. Instead of behaving like a woman in the bedroom and kitchen they'll go out with their friends. It gets so bad that you start wondering if they're grinding anyone else. Some men get paranoid and try to get their women to account for every minute it took them to get

82

home from work. Recession makes other men independent and they suddenly learn how to iron clothes and how to use the microwave. A man can't endure recession. It doesn't sit right until it's over. It's a constant burden. You can't focus on anything without becoming bitter, and it drives some men from being a one-woman man to being a ten-woman man when they realise that it makes as much sense to have spare women as it does to have a spare tyre in your car — if one doesn't work, then you try the other. Beres had never allowed the effects of recession to get to him. Gussie was different, recession had driven him to drinking double shots of rum rather than his usual glass of champagne.

"The Ruffnecks have got a sex ban as well, you know," Fat Willy chirped from behind them. He had his arm around a suitably ample woman. "They've had a sex ban for a month now and they all stick to it religiously. That's why they win the cup every year. It makes sense."

Only half of the team re-entered the limo for the next leg of the evening. The other half had opted to go off with the women they had met in Gregory Peck's. If this was going to be the last night of sex for a week, they didn't intend to waste any time. The limo was still cramped however, because some of the others had brought women in with them. Beres steered the car expertly through the narrow Soho streets as his passengers continued their party in the back seats by popping open a bottle of champagne. The car purred its way through the sex capital of London where a billion pounds a year changes hands for a little sex; where a woman who was prepared to spread her legs a little could get a raise and walk away after a couple of years with a nice little bundle and now the dark crevices of the Soho streets were filled with nervous black women, whose heavily painted faces barely concealed the bruises of their souls. Something happened to the men of Brixton massive FC as every few yards a black woman walked off the kerb to flaunt her stuff for the potential customers inside the limo. It hurt each of them deep in their souls. They were embarrassed, angry and silent.

Later, as the limo purred towards a blues dance that Fat Willy knew about in Hackney, Johnny vented his anger about the increasing number of black women selling their bodies in Soho.

"I blame all this slackness on the media and the artists who are chatting pure nonsense on records. Just the other day I came home and heard my twelve-year-old daughter start singing a song about, "Me 'ood in ah your hole and matey can't take it out..." When I finished slapping her on the bottom she turned around and said she's going to get a gun to point at me. If you don't believe me, ask Lesley. I'm telling you, things are getting dread out there. Some man nowadays have nothing to do but cuss-cuss woman. Why not talk to them nicely, sweetly, you can get anything you want eventually, but when you cuss a woman, it's like cussing your own mother and you see the results of that on the streets."

The women in the car all disagreed with Johnny's argument and blamed men for all of the planet's evils. One even said she thought it was a good thing that women could be independent by becoming prostitutes. Johnny was on form however and wasn't going to let them get away with shifting the blame.

"Women are the problem on this earth," he said confidently. "Men know what they're doing, women haven't got a clue."

The men in the limo were warming up to Johnny's argumentative style. They knew he was only playing devil's advocate to set off a good old-fashioned war of the sexes.

"Alright," Johnny continued, "this is a question to all the women, I want you to answer it. You might say I'm feisty, but answer it anyway. Why is it when a woman's going anywhere it takes her three hours to do her hair even when the man's cussing for her to hurry up and then she complains, 'Just cool me dear, you want me to leave the house in my bra and panties? Me nuh have nothing to wear.' Yet the wardrobe's full of dresses."

The men agreed solemnly that it was perfectly true. The women simply kissed their teeth and looked out of the car windows nonchalantly. But Johnny wasn't finished.

"Why is it when women go raving they always go to the toilet in twos and threes?" The Brixton Massive players all cracked up with laughter. That was a scenario they each knew all too well. The women said they had had enough and would get out at the next party.

"Raving ain't what it used to be," Gussie lamented. It was seven o'clock in the morning and after attending three more parties, there were only a handful of people left in the car: Johnny, Gussie, Beres, Linvall and Fat Willy who had already dozed off in the front seats next to Beres. There was little traffic on the street as the limo cruised its way alongside Clapham Common to drop Willy off in Balham. "Back in the old days, I used to listen to Sir Coxsone, Fatman Hi Powah and Shaka sound systems. That's when raving was raving. The blues dance used to be cool in those days. Girls used to look their best, guys used to be well dressed, smoke a bud maybe, but no cocaine. Will it ever be the same again?"

"Those days are long gone man. What you talking about, things move on, music moves on and the youths move on with their style and culture. Remember in the old days, rasta was predominant. In those days when you took a stroll down Brixton High Street, you thought every youth had turned to rasta. Rasta isn't answering the questions of the youths nowadays. These youths aren't saying the same as us, that they come from Africa and they want to go back home. These youths are saying they're Black British Jamaicans or Black British Nigerians, or whatever, and they're dealing with the things that are important to them out here."

Gussie sniffed. He was talking raving, not getting into a political debate.

"I say bring back the old days anytime, because I can't take the nowadays raving. That's why I stopped. Bring back the old vibes again. A little blues dance on the corner, where you paid a pound on the door and entered and everybody was well behaved. Nowadays it's a roughneck thing. Even the girls rave in track suits and trainers. Remember the deejays like Big Youth and Trinity, Prince Far I, I-Roy, Dillinger and all those guys?"

"How you mean, man? Of course. Names like that can't fade away. Like the great Tapper Zukie."

"And of course U-Roy, the great U-Roy, the father of the deejay school"

"Dreadlocks educator of the school," Johnny added. "You see in those days, when you and your woman weren't getting on so well, you went raving and just... cool, you know. Nowadays, there's really nowhere to go for our generation, that's why we can't afford to get into arguments with our women, we get t'row out with nowhere to go." Johnny turned to address Beres in the driver's seat. "I see you're staying out of this one, Beres. Don't worry man, I'm still going to send your application to Blind Date."

"Not me," Beres assured him.

"You sure? Because me know yuh lonely right now. Yeah man, me know you lonely."

"Yeah but it's no problem," Beres insisted.

"What do you mean 'no problem'?"

"I'm sorted already."

"Oh, you sort out? So only last week you said you weren't sorted out and now you're alright? Boy, you're fast, Beres."

HARD AND STIFF

Everybody knows that rich white girls are easy to get. Linvall didn't think himself different from a lot of other guys who had gotten their break and taken it. Lucy Fry was his passport to a career in television. He saw her every night over the next few days. He was her companion at all the big-time receptions and parties she attended, raising more than a few eyebrows amongst the suits and ties of the entertainment industry; dinosaurs from the days when the only young, black men at such events were cleaners or waiters. Linvall knew that these big knobs didn't respect him, but he ignored it. Lucy Fry wasn't his ideal choice of a date, but she looked fit for her age, a good deal better than some of the women there half her age.

She invited him to a dinner party she was having at Heathurst Road. A sea of expectant faces were gathered around the dining table awaiting him when he arrived. There was Jean, a parliamentary private secretary, Ralph, a merchant banker and Lauren who was a British Airways air hostess. They talked and had their ways and had their games, drinking alcohol, talking about the state of the world and stupid things.

"So what do you do?" asked Ralph over coffee.

"I'm a photographer."

"Really? Oh how very interesting." Except it wasn't, not to Ralph and he quickly changed the conversation to money and power.

Linvall only just managed to escape him out into the garden for a breath of fresh air. The garden was massive, a combination of three separate gardens where the tenents of the adjoining houses agreed to knock down their fences so that they could all share one huge communal garden. It was fabulous, well kept and immaculate. Through the patio doors Linvall watched Lucy and her guests chatting and laughing and knew that he wasn't interested in being part of their world.

Even though Linvall was reluctant on his side to take Lucy out to a ragga show, as she wanted, she insisted that the exchange of culture between them should be a two-way traffic. So he invited her down to his loft and cooked her a

86

chicken and curry. He knew what he wanted from this relationship and he was going to hang around long enough to get it. Even though it was still too early to put anything down on paper about the presenter's job, she assured him that as far as she was concerned he already had the job and the buck stopped with her. He had her eating out of his hand and had even got her to lay off him on all the third degree stuff about honesty and baby mothers.

But she was a very demanding woman. She hated to be home alone at weekends and wasn't interested in a sex boycott because of a football match. She liked coming home to a man with a dick between his legs big enough to fill the empty feelings between hers. She wanted him to perform long and often. The physical regime was taking its toll on Linvall. He was already in serious training for the Championship match but found himself having to add another couple of miles to his circuit every morning just to keep pace with Lucy's demands.

Lucy Fry proved to be the kind of kinky, independent, professional woman who took pleasure in intimidating men and never explained her actions to anyone. Sex, good food and shelter were the only things that mattered to her and they grinded for hours and hours, until it hurt. Sometimes Linvall longed for a black woman instead and had to concentrate hard to keep his eyes on the prize, while Lucy revealed that her recurring fantasy was to fuck a dozen men she didn't really know, just for fun. Otherwise she suffered fools lightly, "There's a sucker born every minute, try not to be one of them," she warned Linvall. She was born with the power of privilege and expected the servitude of men, yet she needed Linvall to continually assure her that she had soul. And she would be instantly relieved and refreshed. But he had an attitude that bothered her and she couldn't understand why he didn't warm to any of her high-flying friends. "Why are you so angry?" she would ask. "These moods must come from your childhood." She still tried to convince him of the joys of foreign films, French coffee, Sartre and cigarettes. "Try to be impartial and positive and open to new ideas, Linvall," she said as she presented him with a copy of Sartre's *Existentialism Is A Humanism.* But he wasn't interested in the lessons taught by crude white men. More than anything, Lucy wanted Linvall to show her how to hang tough and loose like a black woman. He told her to just be cool, very sharp and all together, that her chest was made to wear a bra and to cut down on the filthy language when they were grinding.

Taking fashion photographs had been Linvall's dream since he was at secondary school. When others spent their money on girls and comics, Linvall's weekly allowance went on film and developing paper. And whilst everybody else was learning about William the Conqueror, Linvall was flicking through the pages of women's fashion magazines and saying, "Yeah, one day that's going to be me." He dreamt of being surrounded by beautiful women from all over the world, as he pressed a camera shutter. But he hadn't taken many photographs in the last few days, his passions having been consumed by the thought of a television presenter's job. And a decision had to come soon because he had bills upon bills waiting for him at home — fuel bills, light bills and parking tickets — and the stock market wasn't flowing, neither was the interest rate, the talk was of the pound running slow and there was no photographic work to be had since Candi left him.

Lucy said she loved him but Linvall didn't believe a word. She was the kind of woman who needed a man to cling to. He had learned that when a woman says, 'I love you', it really only means you're being a good boy at the moment and everything is cool. But any which way he tried to live his own life, it would be like 'love don't live here anymore'. Lucy felt she had him wrapped around her finger, but Linvall thought he knew different. Only time would tell.

88

WHO SAY BIG MAN NUH CRY?

Beres had got his hands on a couple of tickets for a show at The Chrysler Ballroom in Carnaby Street, featuring the male strip group, 'Relax' — the black Chippendales — and invited me along.

"Come along, Johnny," he urged down the phone line, "it could be a giggle. I've got a baby-sitter for Lara."

I agreed that we could both do with a night out away from our troubles.

"If nothing else, I hear those shows are full of sex starved women. We'll probably be the only men there!" I said enthusiastically.

"I've just heard so much about these guys," Beres said. "Every woman I meet is going on about them like they're really horny. I just want to see what all the fuss is about."

I made a point of not frequenting the tiny, glass-walled, basement, Chrysler Ballroom in the old days on account of their door policy. It was ostensibly a black club catering in the main for a buppie, soul music clientele. Yet they had a policy of not admitting dreadlocks. As far as I knew, Maxi Priest, Lenny Kravitz and I think the dread in Loose Ends were the only locksmen to ever set foot in the place in the old days. Now Patrick, my personal bredrin, couldn't get in the place. He got vexed and organised a boycott of the place by all the dreadlocked celebrities. He told pop group Wadada, singer Mighty Massive, actor Everton Jones and many others about the boycott and they all said 'yeah', they would come down and demonstrate outside the club, but when push came to shove, the only ones that showed up were me and militant reggae producer Einstein. But that was years ago. Since the recession the Chrysler — like every other club in town — has realised that dreadlocks' money is as good as any other and not only do they welcome dreadlocks now, but they positively encourage them. On certain nights, the person with 'the longest dreadlocks' wins a bottle of champagne.

The place was packed when we got in, but somehow we managed to squeeze ourselves and our drinks between a group of tanked-up secretary types, with men on their minds, waiting expectantly to see some fine examples of black manhood.

As we sat down, I noticed one particular buxom woman give me the eye.

"You noticed that woman was giving you the once over didn't you?" Beres informed me.

"Yeah, yeah, yeah. Big deal," I replied; the woman wasn't my type. "You can't trust a woman with a big behind and a shy smile."

"You were saying earlier, this woman Pauline is distressing you."

"Distress? You don't know the half of it, man. She's the living duppie. I tell you I regret ever meeting that woman. She'll wreck my domestic life given half the chance. It's a fatal attraction, that's what it is, a raas claat fatal attraction."

"I bet you love it really though. Come on admit it, Johnny. You're running two women at the same time. Most men I know would give their eye teeth to be in that position."

"You wanna swap positions with me? Or you know any man who'll take the woman off me and he's welcome to her. Anyway, all she can do is screw."

"Remember, Johnny, the golden rule: a man must maintain a period of celibacy to maintain his dignity."

I looked at Beres hard. Despite his recent troubles he seemed content. He said he had doted on Sonia long enough and was now ready to settle down with a new woman. It no longer mattered with whom he settled as long as she was different.

"It's alright for you to talk about celibacy, Beres. You're used to it. It's like if you don't smoke cigarettes you won't understand why people find it so hard to give up, but me personally, me nuh inna the Tarzan business. And all the cold shower business, me nuh inna it. Black man nuh easy, y'know."

"So what are you going to do about your 'dilemma'."

"I don't know exactly," I shrugged. "There are two women and two babies in between. Which do you choose? My biggest fear is to end up like these fathers who put themselves up for their kids to admire yet never spend time with them."

"One of the women has to lose, you know that don't you, Johnny? And you're going to have to pay for that loss."

"Necessarily?"

"It's the rules of life. You can't have a baby without paying for it. Ask me, I should know. Maintenance is a dirty word that's going to come back and haunt you. A couple of guys I know up in Tottenham are getting clobbered by this new maintenance law."

He was right, he was the world's expert on paying the price for fatherhood, but he wasn't cheering me up. He had stayed celibate for such a long time pining for Sonia that it must have taken all his strength to stop himself dragging her into bed.

"So how are you coping with Lara?"

"Oh she's no problem. She's growing up to be a right little lady. How's Winnie?"

"Going through that problem age, you know, no respect for her elders, disrespect in every aspect. Sometimes I think it's no use talking to the youth of today. It's like hitting your head against a brick wall, because they just go out there and do the same wrong things... Winnie's only eleven and already all she is interested in is the batty riders. It's no good. I've told her that as long as she keeps away from the crack and bad bwoys and goes to school to learn some knowledge, she won't have no problems from me."

"I think you've got to do more than that. Children must be awakened spiritually, mentally and morally."

"I couldn't agree with you more. But this is the age of television, when parents are losing the battle for their children. I don't know who Winnie listens to most, me or Shabba Ranks. You'll face the same problem when Lara gets older, believe me."

"The only reason television is winning that war is because the concept of 'family' is dying out. I want Lara to grow up seeing a mother and father about the place and seeing that they share spiritual values and read their history and their culture and maintain a sense of dignity. It's important for kids to know who their fathers are when they meet them on the street."

"I want my children to grow up prepared to leave babylon," I said.

"I want my child to know about black philosophy," Beres added. "To understand the type of issues Farrakhan is always talking about: why blacks must spend more with each other — because there'll be more to spend on the race."

"Raas claat!" I exclaimed impressed. "You're a raas claat closet Garveyite! It's nice to know that you care about your kid's future too. I wish more men out there cared."

We were now on our fourth doubles of rum, a bit too merry to have noticed the increasing buzz of excitement around the club, until the voice of a compere came crackling through the loudspeakers at an unbearable volume.

"Girls, ladies, women and the one or two men who dared

91

to come tonight... good evening. We hope there are no jealous husbands in the audience, because tonight they won't be able to control their women. Because ladies, the show you are about to witness has been described as 'Orgasmic' by The Voice, 'Penetrating' by The Gleaner and 'Well hard and well stiff', by Express magazine. Ladies are you ready? Ladies are you ready? Then please welcome, all the way from Hollywood, Jamaica, five men who make Michelangelo's David look like Pee Wee Herman... Put your hands together for Relax Incorporated."

The five he-men strutted on stage to the sound of Tone Loc's 'Wild Thing' dressed in the stetson hats and cowboy boots of the Wild West and little else. The women were screaming like crazy. Everywhere you looked there was mass hysteria as the Relax boys paraded their bulky torsos up and down, out of step to the music, and dropping bits of clothing as they worked their way through the track. They went off stage and returned to a rapturous welcome dressed in Click suits and toting fake pistols yardie-style. This time the song was Shaggy's 'Oh Carolina'. They still couldn't dance to the rhythm, but the women didn't seem to mind as each time one of the dancers inserted the barrel of the gun into his mouth and sucked slowly, the crowd erupted. It continued like this for forty minutes, without respite. It was hard to see what was happening on stage, beyond the sea of female heads encircling it. The glimpses we caught left us in hysterics. The biggest and blackest of the five men had the smallest penis, while the shortest one had the biggest dong I had ever seen. I couldn't help cracking up each time he tried to do the running man, because it looked like there was a good chance the dong might hit him in the face!

We sat down at our table once the spectacle had removed itself unceremoniously from an unexpected stage invasion. Only two of the women who had previously shared our table returned. The buxom woman who had her eyes on me and her friend, a pretty little thing, but way too skinny. They informed us that their friends had gone home.

"Can we get you ladies some drinks?" Beres offered always the gentleman.

"Oh yes please," said the maaga one whose name was Suzette. "We're both drinking babycham."

"Babycham?" Beres echoed with a disgusted look on his face. "Why not real champagne? I'm sure you ladies prefer the real stuff."

"Oh well, yes, that's even better, thanks."

Her friend, the buxom one who's name was Patsy, said something about Beres sounding "posh" and asked me what I did for a living.

There are only two types of men in the world: breast men and arse men — after all those are the parts of a woman's body that most men favour. An arse man is a crafty little sucker. His woman can't trust him, she's always got to look over her shoulder to see what he's up to. He'll say that he's faithful when he's grinding all over town. But that's the way he is, when he says 'up', he means 'down', when he says 'big' he means 'small'. Then you have the breast man. He's got nothing to hide. He's big and he's bold and doesn't mind showing you that he loves two of everything. I'm a breast man, myself. I just wasn't interested in Patsy.

"So what are two charming ladies like you doing in a place like this?" I asked to get the chit-chat going.

"Oh we're just out for the fun, like everybody else," Suzette said. "It's strange to see men in here. I bet you two have only come here to check out all the women there'd be."

"Personally, I find it degrading," Beres said. "To see men parading like that on stage, as a man I find it degrading."

"Oh that's interesting," Patsy said. "I've never heard a man say that other men have degraded their entire gender. It's usually women who say they find Page 3 degrading."

"Well it's degrading for me and I can't for the life of me see what women get out of it."

"I think women go to these shows, because they want to see some nice looking black men up there on stage, because few of them have a man that looks that good at home. There's a shortage of black men anyway and a good man is even harder to find, so you can't hang about. I'm tired of sleeping alone; if the Lord worked a miracle for me to find a man that looks like they do, I would go for him. Even if you know you're not going to get the guy, you can admire his muscles and dream about them. And then I think you get some women who come here, because it's the one chance they get to dominate and exercise total control over a man. We pay our fifteen pounds to come in and that means we own them. We own those guys up there on stage. We can do anything to them. We can scream and they'll take their clothes off. And then when it's all over we go home without having to deal with all the aggravation of having the man around on a permanent basis.".

Even though we didn't fancy the women, they turned out to be really nice and we enjoyed some wicked reasoning with them for the next hour. There was an embarrassing silence as we announced our departure to the women. Nothing had been said, but there was a sense of "your place or ours?" in the air.

"Please don't take it personal,"I reassured them, "maybe we could all get together some other time, but we've got to go right now."

I relaxed, leaning my head back into the deep pile of the minicab's rear seat as the driver raced down to Brixton. Beres beside me was also unsober and well knackered. There was nothing to do but chill and listen to the sounds of Mr Grooves on Classic Reggae FM blasting through the car speakers. Mr Grooves was one of the better radio selectors catering in a 'ragga free zone' for those of my generation who remember the old style roots revival music. I was being dropped off first, and we had almost reached my yard when a dedication came over the air as clear as daylight.

"Yeah this one's going out to Johnny Dollar, moving and grooving somewhere out there in the Brixton region of town... and it's coming from your woman, Pauline, in the Streatham side of things, and she says 'I love you and you're going to get the good bedrock when you drop by tonight'."

I almost choked. Beres heard it also and couldn't stop himself laughing.

"Boy, she's going to be bawling for you tonight when she finds out that you're not coming that way. Or you want the driver to drive you there instead? It's not too late you know."

"You're crazy man," I said, peeved at the public display of Pauline's affections. I didn't approve of the way she was flexing. It was risky business. If Lesley heard that dedication and put two and two together, I don't know how she'd take it. I climbed out of the cab. I definitely had to put Lesley fully in the picture at the first good opportunity.

I heard the first scream as I searched for the right key to our front door in the moonlight. I knew straight away what it was. It was happening, there was no time to lose. I was in the flat within seconds. Winnie rushed over to me in her night dress, panic stricken.

"Daddy, Daddy, the baby's started coming!" she cried.

"Have you called an ambulance?"

"Yes, I've done that. They're on the way."

"Well done..."

I rushed in the direction of the screams which seemed to be getting louder. In the bedroom, Lesley was lying on the bed screaming with labour pains, her legs spinning in the air like a ferris wheel.

94

"Don't worry, don't worry, darling. I'm here now. What do you want me to do?"

"Nothing... it's alright..." Lesley panted between gulps. "Just make sure the ambulance gets here soon."

She continued screaming in short loud bursts and in between she breathed deep and steadily, doing exactly as the midwife had told her to. I was in a state of panic, but fortunately the ambulance came within minutes and the baby held on until we got to hospital.

I was with her all the way, holding her hands. Child birth is still the greatest experience a man can witness. No matter how many times you've seen it, you feel closest to God when you're in that delivery room giving comfort to your woman as she pushes and she pushes until there is an earthquake in her womb. Finally the head was within reach and the midwife brought the child into the world a week prematurely. It was a boy. I fell down on my knees and broke down in tears. It was the same when Winnie was born. It was an emotional and spiritual time for me and I said a prayer, thanking God. My baby was alright, with all of his toes and all of his fingers, his tiny willy and glassy eyes and little elbows that bent every which way. He was the exact likeness of Lesley in his face, so pretty and his tiny, stubby hands were like minuscule versions of hers, but he was a Lindo and every now and then he smiled to prove it. I was elated, once again I had witnessed the most perfect of God's creation come into being.

There was a queue of pregnant women waiting to take Lesley's bed the moment she vacated it, so they sent her home the next day, which was a good thing. I had so many plans for my son, the sooner he came home the better. Lesley was almost like new, except for the big belly which remained for another two weeks. I asked her what it had felt like giving birth to our son, Jacob.

"Winnie felt different. With Jacob, it felt like a steamroller had stalled inside me."

Lesley loved her new son. She didn't let him out of her sight for a moment and she fussed over him like I had never seen her fuss before. Winnie also loved her new brother and didn't begrudge him anything for relegating her to second place in our affections. Far from it, Jacob gave her a chance to prove that she was more mature than we had given her credit for being.

We spent most of those few days of bliss holding our baby and passing him between us. Friends and family dropped by, but we didn't go out anywhere. I had got somebody else in to run the bookshop and the Saturday school. I was taking a couple of weeks of leave to get to know my new son. I couldn't get enough. Lesley sang to the new baby about love, while holding her breast in her hand as she always did when she fed him.

Childbirth seemed to have made Lesley even more attractive. Seeing my beautiful baby in the arms of her loving, beautiful mother, did something spiritual to me. Every morning I would wake up and get down on my knees and say 'Thank you God'. I thanked the father for putting me back on the right path and showing me that unless I changed my ways, I would never be worthy of all the grace he had bestowed upon me. Every night before I went to bed I would say another prayer. I even began to say grace before eating.

I helped a lot with the baby at the beginning, because Lesley was distressed with a lot of cakes to bake. After years of working as a secretary for a city bank, she had set up a nice little profitable business, baking designer cakes from home. She started off baking as a favour for a friend who was to be the bride at a big society wedding. That five-tier Empire State Building design went down a storm and the orders started pouring in. Word of mouth is the best advertising there is. When people saw how well Lesley could turn a simple cake into a work of art, someone else would say "I must get her to bake a cake for my little boy on his birthday. He would love a cake that's shaped like a football." The word spread like wild fire. She had only been doing it a year, but she was now considering moving to proper premises and taking on staff. I became domesticated and suddenly took an interest in painting and decorating, washing up dishes and laying carpets and linos. I found myself enjoying it. Though I had always maintained that I wouldn't change nappies, I even started doing that, because I knew the work needed to be done. And whereas I had always avoided leaving the phone numbers of where I was going to be of an evening, I now took it up by habit. The big problem before was that I never phoned home so I took up phoning from wherever I was. I now appreciated that a little bit of concern is important.

Yes, I willingly did the chores. It made me feel less guilty. I had still not told Lesley about baby mother number two. It was a delicate situation so soon after childbirth. I had to wait until the time was right. The baby was already drinking stress milk and what I had to say to her would have stressed her even more. I knew what I had to do; I had to get rid of Pauline, but my problem is that I'm not a cold-hearted person who can say 'goodbye' and walk off and it's done. I'm too loving for that. Besides, whatever my feelings towards her, I still had a yout' on the way by her and that was something that had to be sorted out, sooner rather than later.

In between my family duties, I spent a lot of time reading books, looking for a way out hidden between the pages of Toni Morrison and Zora Neale Hurston. I couldn't find anything, not for men anyway. While women had their voices to fight for their rights, nobody was speaking up for the humble black man. Woman problem — a king size problem that needs a king to solve it.

WOMAN RUN T'INGS

Scorpio — meetings and interviews go well and decisions are finalised. A lump sum of money could be coming your way, but you may be paying out lots as well. Parties are in the air and you don't know whether you're dreading the weekend or looking forward to it but it could turn out to be more fun than you reckoned.

Beres inhaled and exhaled with the effortless ease of a fullbred athlete as he ran the events of the last week through his mind again, his legs carrying him another circuit around the park. 'Life is a bitch,' he told himself again. He glanced at his watch. A bead of lukewarm sweat splattered itself across the face of the Swatch and dribbled down to its strap as Beres' face broke into a half-smile, he was ten seconds down on his time. But the little pleasure that this offered him was quickly replaced by nervous indigestion, a reminder that he didn't know what his next move would be. He hadn't gone to work since Sonia came round. He was too concerned as to what she might do. He kept Lara away from school also, but he knew that he couldn't do that indefinitely. And then this morning, he had got a legal letter informing him that Sonia was applying for custody of their daughter. One thing for sure, Lara wasn't going back to her mother. His wife had proved herself unfit to be a mother. Woman was made to comfort a man. The first thing to do was call Evelyn.

"Pottinger Simmons Solicitors," the businesslike voice on the other end of the line answered.

"Yeah, is Evelyn Pottinger about please?"

"Uhm... I'm afraid Miss Pottinger isn't available at the moment. can I ask who's calling?"

"Yeah, tell her it's Beres."

"Hold on one second please..."

Beres knew that Gussie's sister would know what to do. They had known each other since childhood, in fact they had even dated once. But that was in their early years. They had both married since and were now just good friends.

"Beres, long time no hear..." Evelyn's voice chirped from down the line.

"Well, I'm always here, you know."

"Yes I know, it's my fault also... I've been really busy

lately... Look, were you calling for anything in particular or can this wait until later, I'm on my way to court."

"No, I can talk to you later, but just answer one thing quickly... Sonia's taking me to court for custody, do I have any chance of winning?"

"Oh damn. I'm really sorry to hear that. What a cheek that woman's got! After all this time. It's been, what... six months?"

"That's no problem Evelyn, just tell me, have I got a chance of winning?"

"That's the terrible thing about it. Except in unusual cases, the court is always going to give custody to the mother."

"Even if she abandoned her child...? Even if she walked out without saying a word and disappears for six months? How can the court do that?"

"That's how it goes I'm afraid. It will be difficult to prove that she abandoned her child."

"After six months!" Beres didn't intend to shout at Evelyn but that's how it ended up.

"It doesn't matter. People are allowed to go away and leave the child in the charge of the other parent. You've got no proof that she abandoned Lara."

"Supposing Lara doesn't want to live with the mother who left her to fend for herself? Supposing she'd rather live with the father who's been taking care of her ever since? Doesn't the court take that into consideration?"

"Yes they do, if the child is of an age which the court considers old enough to make that decision. If Lara was ten or eleven-years-old, that would be taken into consideration, but seven... I'm afraid that's a borderline case."

"Well there's no way Sonia's going to get one penny out of me."

I'm afraid there's not much you can do about that either. If she wins custody she will automatically be entitled to a slice of your income. It's the same the other way around. If you had won custody, she would have been obliged to pay for the maintenance of the child."

"But you've just said the man is never awarded custody. That means the woman's able to hold the man to ransom with this Child Support Agency thing. So you're telling me Sonia can have her cake and eat it. I have to pay her for depriving me of my daughter?"

The line went silent for a moment, with neither willing to take up the baton. Evelyn finally spoke.

"Look, if you want to talk to me later about it that's fine.

But let me transfer you to my partner. She doesn't have to be in court until later this afternoon and she's nodding over the desk here that she'll take your call. Is that alright, Beres?. Her name's Caroline, Caroline Simmons. Look I'll call you later, once I'm out of court."

Beres' mind was filled with a thousand different thoughts, that ranged from anger to bitterness. The putrid taste in his mouth soured his vibes even more and he wondered whether he would be able to control his temper if he ran into his ex-wife. He was Lara's father and always would be. He refused to allow Sonia to take that away from him.

"Hello, Beres, this is Caroline Simmons, Evelyn tells me your wife's just thrown the gauntlet down in a custody case, is that so? Well, the first thing I can suggest is that you don't try to contact her and then that you get yourself a good solicitor as soon as possible... Hello... are you still there Beres?"

"Sorry, my mind was thousands of miles away. Caroline, isn't it? What were you saying again?"

"I was advising you to get a good lawyer."

"Well, you're a lawyer aren't you? Could you represent me?"

"Er... actually, it's a bit difficult... you see, I have a policy of never taking the man's side in custody cases. I only ever represent women."

Beres was irritated with the answer. His initial pain had been caused by a woman and here was another woman rubbing it in.

"You're not allowed to do that are you? I though lawyers had to take on any cases that came to them?"

"That's not strictly true..."

"So let me ask you one question: why do you refuse to represent men? Don't we have a right to legal representation as much as women?"

"Yes of course, but that's not the point. I just have a policy, because personally I think it's more important that women, rather than men, win custody of their children and the courts generally agree with that."

"Look don't worry about it okay, I'll speak to Evelyn later. But personally I think your policy stinks. "

He slammed the phone down. He had no time for such foolishness.

SWEET AND DANDY

How come women can't get it into their heads that when a
man says no, he means no? I've been saying no for years, but
it's like my words fall on deaf ears. 'No' is the first thing I say
when I meet a woman. I say no to love, no to permanent
relationships and no, definitely no, to babies. Now I don't
mean no disrespect to any woman, but that's how I personally
stay. Until Miss Right comes along, I don't want any woman
clinging to me tight, playing on my conscience. As much as I
want to be one of the lads, a ladykiller puffing up my chest
out on street and carrying on like I'm big and broad, deep
down inside I've always known that one day I'll find the
woman I want to spend the rest of my life with, the woman I
want to build up a home and start a family with. She'll be a
virgin maybe, but not necessarily, but she'll be a woman I can
hold in high esteem, someone I can place on a pedestal and
worship, not some one-night stand. The whole point with a
one-night stand is that you're not supposed to see the woman
no more. Marriage is a thing which I personally take very
seriously and having children also. I read my Bible regularly
and it tells you that those kind of things ain't no joke.
Marriage is not just a ceremony, it's for a lifetime and
children aren't just for Christmas. And the same with the
family, without a strong family behind you, how are you
going to be able to face life squarely and still succeed? I'd be
nothing today without the support of my family.

So all these things go through my head each time I meet a
new woman. That's why I'm still a bachelor and proud of it.
I've had my chances, many chances to be a baby father, but I
don't need the ego trip of having children to make me feel like
a man. Why be a baby father? Why not hold tight until the
right woman comes around and make it legal?

Now Caroline's coming on like I'm a potential baby father.
She called me up on Friday morning to remind me about our
Valentine's date on Sunday, "I know you're a busy man and
you might forget," she said. And then she dropped the
bombshell on me. Would I mind if she brought her six-year-
old son, because it's so hard getting a baby sitter on
Valentine's night? I couldn't believe it. The first I hear about
any kids is two days before, when she invites him to join us

for dinner. I suggested we cancel the date, but she insisted, "Vernon won't be any trouble at all," she promised, "we won't even notice he's there." I had bad vibes about everything. I wasn't that keen on seeing Caroline on Valentine's anyway, after our last two dates had reaped nothing to write home about, even though she had a way of adding a sultry promise in the tone of her voice, I suspected it wouldn't bear fruit. But I'm stuck with her because Evelyn will take it as a personal diss otherwise and like the 'Ten Commandments of Love' warns, 'Hell hath no fury like that of a vexed sister in league with a scorned lover'. Most definitely.

The main reason why I don't want to see Caroline on Valentine's is because I met a woman who's beauty and charm alone made my head spin and before I knew it I was asking her out on Valentine's Day. Now, I'm not the kind of guy who easily falls head over heels for a woman, but when I say this girl was 'fit'... Believe me. I double-booked myself in the knowledge that Valentine's is the day when even the hardest heart is inclined to soften. If I could get her to give me a squeeze, I'm sure it would improve the qualities of both our lives and there's no better day to convince a woman of your credentials than on Valentine's. She came into the shop just a couple of days ago. I was attending to another customer, so I didn't see her. Then I heard all this giggling and I spun around. She had her back to me, dressed in a matching, red two-piece that clung tight to a perfect coca-cola bottle shape. I had a sparkle in my eye, but thought nothing more of it as she was accompanied by a smartly-dressed Eddie Murphy lookalike.

"Can I be of any help?" I said to the back of her head. She turned around and flashed a smile that melted my soul.

"I certainly hope you can," she replied.

She wanted to try on different rings, to see which one matched her skin the best. The man she was with was a real Johnny-come-lately who carried a pocket-size mobile phone and insisted constantly that "money is no object." However, he had a distinct inclination towards the lower priced rings. I started with the medium priced rubies and made my way down to the sapphires. With each ring she tried on, her companion would immediately ask, "How much is that?" Finally, he was distracted by a call on his mobile phone and I got a chance to carry out my thoughts.

"Is that your boyfriend?" I asked quickly.

"No," the girl asked.

"Husband?"

"Oh no, of course not," she laughed again. "Courtney's only an 'admirer'. Why do you ask?"

Courtney must have heard what she said because he winced. I didn't want to diss him to his face..

"I'd like you to model this for me," I said thinking quickly on my feet and pulling out an expensive pearl necklace from its glass case and sliding it around her neck. It looked perfect, sitting atop her low cut neckline and seemed to glisten against her ebony skin. "Oh that is so beautiful," she said when I produced a mirror for her to see.

"Well... model it at dinner with me on St Valentine's Day and it's yours."

Unfortunately her companion had finished his call and nosed his way back in quickly.

"Yeah, that's a nice necklace," he said confidently. "So, how much is that?"

"£100."

"What! A ton for that?" he kissed his teeth. "Take it off, Chantelle. It doesn't suit you anyway."

She removed the necklace, handing it back to me with an alluring smile. I took the necklace from her and slid it back around her neck. "It's yours," I said with my most charming smile. "Compliments of the house."

She kissed me gratefully.

"That's really sweet of you. Here's my number," she said, handing me a business card. "Whenever you feel the urge to see the necklace... give me a call."

Her companion grunted something about being in a hurry and almost dragged the lovely Chantelle out of the store. I laughed to myself as I watched him exit in quick time. I could afford to think nothing of spending £100 on seeing Chantelle again, but I didn't know many other men who could. I read the card, Magnum Films, Chantelle Breakspeare, Associate Producer. From the expensively printed card and its West One address, I deduced that Chantelle Breakspeare was more than a pretty face. I called Magnum Films later that afternoon. A sweet-sounding receptionist told me Ms Breakspeare had left for the day, but she'd call back before six to check her messages. I left my number and when I got home that evening, Mama informed me that Beres had called and also "a charming young lady called Chantelle". She gave me the number and I dialled immediately.

"Yes, Chantelle..." a sleepy voice answered.

"I didn't wake you did I? This is Gussie, you know Gussie Pottinger from The Mighty Diamond shop in Hatton Garden...

the necklace, remember?"

"Oh yes of course, hi! I was taking a little nap."

"This early in the evening... you must be a day person."

"Actually, I'm taking a nap because I'm going out this evening. I'm working."

Chantelle explained that her company was shooting a crime thriller at night in Docklands. She was due on set at midnight.

"I really love the necklace, I'm still wearing it now," she said seductively.

"In bed?!"

"Yes, I've got nothing else on, just me, myself and my necklace. I'm really looking forward to earning it."

"I'm looking forward to you earning it also," I joked. "I'll pick you up at eight on Sunday night."

"I came off the phone with a buzz of adrenaline. I knew I had hit the bulls eye and was confident that I was just forty-eight hours away from rolling around in breathless passion with the woman of my dreams. I hadn't forgotten about the date with Caroline, but I was hoping I could strike two birds with one aim of my catapult. I dialled Beres' number and set the next part of my plan in motion.

"Yo, B., how's the juggling?"

"Well to tell you the truth, I'm going through the living distress. My bitch wife has appeared out of nowhere and thinks I'm just going to give up custody of my daughter because she's decided she wants to be a mother."

"Shit! I'm glad I don't have your worries. So are you going to fight it?"

"I don't know, you know, G. The only way I can fight it is by running off with my own daughter to Egypt or somewhere the courts can't touch us. 'Cause woman has all the rights here — that's what they call justice over here. I don't get to choose justice, but my bitch wife gets to decide if I can or can't be a father. Anyway, that's not what I was calling about. I was just confirming your pick-up for the match on Sunday. I'll pass by at eight in the morning."

"Just one thing before you go," I interrupted, "are you doing anything for Valentine's night?"

"Me? You're joking aren't you. A baby father's time doesn't allow for romance."

"I've got a date for you, a seriously nice woman, perfect for you, you'd love her..."

"To be truthful Gus, I could do with a little romance in my life, but I'll have to decline. There's no way I'll get a baby

104

sitter at such short notice on Valentine's night."

"Well bring Lara along," I said enthusiastically. I told him the plan; it was simple, but it needed co-ordination. We would go out on a foursome, or really a sixsome as Caroline was bringing her son and Beres would bring Lara. Beres would drive over to Chantelle's house at 8pm and pick her up. He would meet myself and Caroline at the restaurant. Unbeknown to Chantelle, Beres would act as if he were her date for the benefit of Caroline, and I would make Chantelle think that Caroline was Beres' date by keeping as much distance as I could from her.

"You're crazy," Beres said when he heard the details. "You'll never get away with that."

"I have before," I replied confidently. "You just play your part and it will be as sweet as a nut. The most important thing though is that you end up chatting up Caroline all night long and offer to drive her home, no, insist on driving her home."

"You want to watch yourself, Gussie. You're becoming just like Johnny. After all the trouble he's been through recently, I would advise you to find yourself just one woman, a woman you can be with and spend the rest of your life with, man. I'm telling you, there's no substitute in the world to a good woman, a wife. You can have all the women, the prettiest and sexiest women in the world and they'll never be able to stand up, in my view, to a good wife."

I didn't disagree with Beres. He was still generous with praise for the good traditional marriage. Even though he had been treated like shit by his woman, he was still willing to give it a go.

Later that evening as I lay in my bed, incense burning and Tony Sewell's book *Jamaica Inc*. at my side, the Old Man knocked on the door and entered.

"We really must have a chat," he said seriously, "man to man." I knew what was on his mind, it had been troubling him ever since they got back. "You know me and your mother have been talking. You may not realise but your mother is worried about you. Every night she goes to bed worried. You're thirty-four-years-old and you don't realise that the bachelor life has got to stop!" His eyes seemed to glare in the subtle lighting of my bedroom as he towered above me, pacing one step one way and one step the other. I could tell that a lecture was on the way.

"You're supposed to have raised children already, shaped their minds, given them direction."

"Papa, don't you think I want kids as well? Don't you think

I want to start a family? It ain't easy being a bachelor nowadays you know; it's not like in your days. Today, every man wants to get married, to have that security and support behind them, but it's not easy finding the right woman. I want to be sure when that time comes that it's the right woman. I've got a long list of the qualities I'm looking for in my ideal woman, and I haven't yet found anyone to match them."

"You should get rid of that list otherwise you'll never find a woman," the Old Man retorted. "You think too deeply about these things, Augustus man. You studied too much, that's your problem. Learning is good for you, but you must know about reality also. Just find yourself a woman to have one or two pickneys with, that's all, any woman. Or come to Jamaica and find a woman. Over there you have beautiful young women who would be proud to have pickney by you. Don't think about it too long, because I'm getting old. I want to hand over the jewellry business to you, Augustus, but it's a big responsibility and I can't hand that over to someone who's only ever had to look after himself. Stop looking for the most beautiful woman in the world and find a woman who stays at home to look after the kids and never complains but takes care of you, takes care of the house, the youths, a woman who sees that they get fed and get to school on time, wearing a nice criss ironed uniform she ironed herself. No problem, man. My friends who searched high and low for the most beautiful woman in the world ended up marrying women who weren't too good for them. And the good women, the women right under their noses, they didn't see until it was much too late."

We were covering ground so familiar, I could have dozed off. I understood how he felt, but I wished he'd give me a little room. Then Papa played his trump card.

"Anyway, me and your mother have decided that we'll stay in England running the company, while you take time off to find the right woman. We won't return to Jamaica until you're happily married."

THE BIG MATCH

"Hello? Who's calling Superjam 94. 2 FM on this Valentine's Sunday morning? Hello sir. You want to send a dedication, go ahead. Who would you like to say hello to?"

"I want yuh big up my wife, Sharon seen, from Warren in South Norwood, she know seh me love her 'nuff 'nuff.""

It was St Valentine's morning but the atmosphere was akin to a gladiatorial battle in a Roman amphitheatre. This wasn't a game, it was a football match. As always, whenever the championship was being fought out by teams from opposing sides of the River Thames, there was a large crowd of mainly female supporters there to 'big up' their boyfriends, husbands and neighbourhoods. It had been difficult to find a 'neutral' ground, but they had finally settled for a pitch on the Hackney Downs, East London. The long line of BMWs and Audi's that flanked the kerb along the Homerton end of the Eastway was a marker to spectators who had lost their way.

Brixton Massive FC had been playing well all season and its players could almost taste success as they ran on to the pitch to a mixture of cheers and boos, all they needed to do was win by a two-goal margin and the championship was theirs, anything less and the Ruffnecks would once again taste supreme glory. Only one thing stood between the Massive and the London League Cup, and his name was Animal. The Brixton Massive players felt the earth tremor as the 20 stone, Harlesden centre-back rolled onto the pitch to a roar of approval. The Harlesden crowd had come to see blood and expected Animal to do his duty efficiently. Linvall turned to admire the fearsome character. He was huge. His finely-chiselled features were topped with gelled hair and he wore a tight-fitting kit to accentuate a well-toned muscular torso. He obviously spent a lot of time in the gym.

Johnny, the Brixton Massive centre forward, was intimidated by his giant-size opponent, but faced him squarely with as much muster as he could.

From the kick-off, Animal began as he intended to continue. It only took thirty seconds for him to claim his first casualty, Robbie Henry, the Brixton Massive full back who was nowhere near the ball when Animal mowed him down.

Robbie was carried off on a stretcher, his leg twisted at an angle that just wasn't possible without a clean break. His team mates looked on in horror and Animal smiled as he saw the realisation in the eyes of the Brixton Massive players that he was definitely capable of murder that morning. Incredulously Animal was awarded a free-kick for the foul on *him* by Robbie! The game progressed with only the bravest Brixton Massive players wishing to hold possession for more than a second before passing it. Still, they managed to keep the ball away from the Ruffnecks and in particular Animal. The Harlesden player's eyes flared up red as the ball was passed to Linvall. Despite his bulk, Animal covered thirty yards of turf in no time at all, sending the pitch into a mild tremor with every thud of a step. Linvall saw him coming, however, and opted for the shortest route to the goal, straight down the middle. Even as he caught sight of his target with only the uncommitted goalkeeper to beat, Animal hurled himself at the striker American football style, only managing to catch the elastic on his shorts. Focused on the goal, Linvall became oblivious to the tug, and managed to take one more step for the kick as his shorts came off in Animal's hands. The ball sailed past the Raiders' paralysed keeper into the net. Cheers of jubilation were mixed with howls of laughter as Linvall raced to the touch line for an extra pair of shorts, fending off the embraces from his team mates as he did so. Animal walked over; the remains of the shorts held disgustedly in front of him.

"You might want these back," he snarled with a big grin on his face.

Linvall stared his man out calmly. "Eat them!" he suggested as he trotted onto the pitch for the kick-off.

"Next time, it's your balls!" Animal shouted after.

Animal was a man who didn't even fear God, much less fear man. He gave the referee a knowing wink as the official looked on in terror, aware that his life wasn't worth living if he booked this monster today.

Just before the half, Everton at left wing decided to dribble the ball into the penalty area. He stood a good chance of scoring, with only the keeper to beat. But Animal's flying tackle knocked him down on top of the ball, followed immediately after by the Ruffneck's centre halve's entire twenty stones of muscle. Everton didn't stand a chance, he was flattened. Animal got up quickly and continued chasing the ball, dribbling it all the way back up the other end of the field to the deserted Brixton goalmouth, as the Massive's players ran en masse to help their injured forward. As Everton was carried off on a stretcher, the referee took the ball to the touchline. Animal had scored.

Having fielded both their reserves and certain to be reduced even further, the Brixton Massive players returned for the second half with only one thing in mind: Animal had to be eliminated. It wasn't going to be easy either because the Ruffnecks player was in his element. He picked off his targets one by one without reference to the ball. More than once the Massive's players had to duck and dive out of Animal's way as he came charging down the field looking for skulls to crack. It wasn't until they got a corner against their opponents that the Brixton team first saw their chance to deal with Animal. They had drawn straws for the most risky role in the tactic and unfortunately for him, Linvall drew the shortest straw. He trotted reluctantly to the Ruffnecks' goalmouth, where Animal stood in front of the nearside post, ready to pummel any Brixton player who dared to cover the corner.

Linvall positioned himself right behind Animal and called out loud enough for everybody around the goalmouth to hear.

"Hey Animal, me hear that have short willy!"

Everybody tensed for a moment, waiting for Animal's inevitable reply. The Ruffneck turned to face his accuser, his face contorted in a mixture of pain and violence. Linvall could have done with a toilet nearby, but such was his team spirit that he dug his grave deeper.

"And I hear your woman says that you eat under sheet... Bwoy, yuh nasty!"

At the same moment Beres, over by the corner flag, sent the ball floating in the air, high and deep towards the centre of the goalmouth. The players around the goal hadn't seen it though. Their attention was drawn in anticipation of Animal's bloodcurdling response to Linvall's comments. The huge centre-half's eyes were burning in a blazing fury. As if in slow motion he lifted his entire body weight off the ground and propelled his forehead at the bridge of Linvall's nose. Linvall ducked and Animal's head went crashing into the goalpost with a sickening thud. He slumped to the ground with a surprised look in his vacant eyes that signified the end of his role in this championship. At the same moment Johnny lifted himself high above the ground and used his head to convert Beres' cross into the net. It was 2-1. The Massive needed only one more goal to secure the championship. Johnny's celebrations were short-lived, however. A scuffle had broken out amongst the spectators. When the Brixton Massive team saw Beres in the thick of the fight, they rushed over to support their teammate.

Johnny reached, to see Beres struggling in a tug-of-love, as Sonia assisted by two officers from the social services attempted to take Lara away. Beres was struggling furiously and threatening the social workers, but they simply waved a custody order in his face.

"You're welcome to challenge the order in a court of law," the male social services officer said, pulling Lara away.

"Leave my daughter alone... you hear?! Leave my daughter alone! I'm warning you! Don't get me angry!!" Beres screamed.

"Leave her alone!" Sonia shouted back. "I'm her mother. I've got the right to have her live with me."

"You should have thought of that before then, shouldn't you?" Beres hissed, "You left her, you abandoned your daughter for six months and now you think I'm going to just let you walk away with her! You're joking!"

A crowd had gathered around the scene. The social services officers were determined to take Lara with them. Beres was determined to stop them. Without warning, he sent a well-aimed upper cut crashing into the male social worker's jaw. The man dropped like a nine-pin. Someone took his pulse. At least he was alive. Confused, Lara had started crying. The female social services officer had backed off and was now walking slowly away from the scene, calling into her walkie talkie for assistance. Within minutes, two car loads of policemen were on the scene. Beres was arrested and taken away, his hands handcuffed behind his back.

Down to ten men, Brixton Massive fought courageously to increase their lead against the now Animal-less Ruffnecks. But the remaining Harlesden footballers put on a spirited defence of their title. They knew and everyone else knew, that unless Brixton won by a two goal margin, the championship would return to Harlesden for yet another year. With only five minutes of the game remaining, Fat Willy shouted from the touchline to his team captain.

"Johnny! Plan X, Plan X! Put the X Plan into operation!!"

Johnny heard his manager's orders and nodded. Fat Willy had taken him aside at the half and told him of a little known League ruling. The final championship match of the season had to have a conclusive result. If the match ended in a draw, the teams would battle it out in a penalty shoot out and the winners would be awarded a two-goal victory margin. Fat Willy feared that knowledge of the rule would relax his players into settling for a draw and taking their chances in a shoot-out. He took the precaution at half-time to confide in his captain, however.

"Whatever happens," he told Johnny, "if we can't win by a two-goal margin, then go for a draw, no matter what."

The Brixton players were bemused when they saw their captain take possession of the ball and steam down towards his own goalmouth. By the time he got within his own penalty area however, the startled Massive defenders realised that this wasn't some cunning move by their captain, but an unashamed attempt an own goal. Johnny was forced to use his best skill to dribble past his own defenders and with just his goalie left to beat, he did a nice little side-step into the corner of the goal. The score was 2-2. Stunned, the whole place fell quiet with neither players nor spectators able to understand what had happened. A few spectators fell about laughing, followed by the Ruffnecks' players who eventually claimed Johnny's goal as their own. Only the Ruffnecks' manager noticed the satisfied look on Fat Willy's face and realised what was going on. He ordered his players to put one in the back of their own net.

"Just do it!" he ordered. "Do it now and ask questions later!"

There was only two minutes to go. The Harlesden centre forward received the ball from the kick off and turned towards his own net. Johnny had managed to explain his own goal to the Massive's players, who now realised they had to stop Harlesden scoring an own goal, by any means necessary. The entire Brixton team, including the goalie steamed down the pitch, some even out-running the Harlesden centre forward. The Brixton players had no choice but to bring down the Harlesden centre forward in his own penalty area. Despite the Harlesden player's protests, the referee declared a free kick to the Ruffnecks in front of their own goal mouth. With only seconds to go, the Harlesden centre forward faced his own goal mouth and the opposition team defending it and prepared to score an own goal from the direct free kick. The kick was powerful and ricocheted off a Brixton player and into the Harlesden net. The moment after, the referee blew the whistle for full time. Brixton had won the match 3-2. The Harlesden players rejoiced with their manager. The championship was theirs.

111

DECLARATION OF RIGHTS

Imagine spending Valentine's Day in a police cell! Poor Beres. Fortunately for him, Caroline conceded that she just couldn't allow him to sit there and suffer the whole day. "I don't like helping men in custody cases," she insisted. It took a lot of pressure before she reluctantly agreed to go down to the police station. That left me with the job of keeping 'Beres' date' company in the restaurant until he was free.

Chantelle looked even more stunningly beautiful than the first time I met her. Her sequin-bordered chiffon dress turned the heads of all the men in the restaurant, including the waiters, as she entered looking radiant with the necklace around her neck and making me feel underdressed in my casual cashmere jacket, red polo neck and penny loafers. She had the most perfect skin I had ever seen and as I leaned over to kiss her on the cheek, the sensual aroma of a lush perfume held me transfixed for a moment longer than a platonic kiss would allow.

She was in top form. I sat for a moment simply admiring her, and the sounds outside of cars and people moving about going different places became like music to my ears. I was on such a high I wanted to reach out and grab those sounds of feet and voices and bodies and the sights and dreams and mix them up together with love. I suddenly had visions! I wanted to do crazy things like walk down the Champs-Elysee with a panther on a leash and I thought I had found my Josephine Baker to accompany me.

"So how many Valentine's did you get?" she asked mischievously.

"Oh a few," I replied trying not to sound too modest. "Yeah man, most definitely."

We sat down to a combined dish of ackee and saltfish, rice and peas, steamed fish and plantain and drank Irish Moss and Guinness. Chantelle told me about herself. At work she was surrounded by the rich and famous and was often name-dropping about her meetings with Michael Jackson or Whitney Houston. But she came from a humble, single mother background and now wanted to earn enough money for her mother to never work again. "I know it's sweet and sickly," she said, "but it's true. My mother sacrificed a lot for me."

She said her mother was left alone with the responsibility of bringing her up, but worked hard to send her to a good school because she knew that a little black girl would need all the help she could get in growing into womanhood in this country. Now it was up to her to do the rest. "And now I've got some money of my own, I'm able to thank her for the things she did. Don't you want to do those things for your parents also? Wouldn't you want to be able to help them out financially in their old age?"

"Sure, I want to do all those things, the only problem is that my parents are richer than I am," I laughed. "My father owns the business, you see."

Chantelle said that her mother's experiences at the hands of a man who disappeared the moment she got pregnant had toughened her. And she was determined not to let the same thing happen to her.

"But a man will stop a woman if he's given the chance. They will always look for a way to pump you full of babies and insecurities or otherwise they just want to lift up your skirt, feel on your breasts and grind up close to you at parties."

It was tough talking, but Gussie listened interestedly. Despite her words, he couldn't see her as a card-carrying feminist.

"Why can't men understand that just because you meet a man and you find him exciting it doesn't mean you want his baby. I want opera and caviar, not babies. Babies weigh you down inside and outside. I believe in chance rather than destiny."

She paused to take a long drag from her cigarette. I sat with a big, happy smile on my face. I didn't agree with what she was saying, but the passion with which she talked was seductive.

"What about you?" she asked after a beat. "What kind of women are you into?"

I thought carefully for a long moment. "I like a woman who knows how to be a woman for a man, knows what to do to keep him."

"That's a pretty damn narrow view of a woman if I ever heard one. But that's just like a man isn't it? Men know what they like, but they don't know what you like."

"So what are you looking for in a good man?"

"Understanding and respect," Chantelle replied without hesitation. A man who understands that a woman's looks aren't as important as her personality and sense of humour,

113

however gorgeous she is. I want a man, not a boy and virtually all the men I know are boys, that's why I'm happy to live alone. I'm almost thirty and still looking for a good man. Are there any out there?"

She must have put a spell on my mind and turned me around because everything she said sounded like a compliment. I puffed up my chest with boyish pride, because here at least was a good black man and I held her hand solemnly and opted to come out straight.

"I've got some strong feelings for you Chantelle, right now the way I'm feeling I'd give up everything I have to have a relationship with you on a more permanent basis. Would you like to get married?"

"Let's take it slow," Chantelle insisted, pushing me away firmly with one hand. "When we get to know each other, maybe we can talk it over."

It sounded like good advice, but good advice does no good when you're enchanted beyond your very reason. I thought I had found the love of a lifetime, slim, trim and intelligent- the woman I wanted to marry and have children with. I was free and single and well wanted a wife. I was determined to make this sweet Valentine mine.

I succeeded in bedding her a week later. We gasped and hollered both of us and ended up on the floor in her flat, tired and exhausted, she in the corner laughing with her panties twisted around her ankles and her hair standing every which way.

"There are ten ways to love a black woman," Chantelle informed me whilst we caught out breaths. That night she showed me the first seven. I can't wait to learn the next three. She of course knew exactly what to do for a man, and I was hers, for richer or poorer, in sickness and health, 'til death us do part.

DISTRESS

"You're tuned into the crucial sounds of Flex FM, slippin' an' slidin' through the airwaves on this Valentine's Day Sunday morning, on the frequency of ninety two point two, it's yours truly, the scandalous, the 'Valentino' — Sweet Sweet Bobby Baby Love. Juggling nice and easy. Remember if you want to send your Valentine's dedications, the number is 0850 54-46-54."

It was early morning on February 14, St valentine's Day. A day when lovers the world over should be enjoying a blissful day together. But life's a bitch. I was awakened by a thump to the eye... You have some men who never learn just how cunning their woman can be, men who don't appreciate just how dirty this war between the sexes can be. I've known women who are masters of guerrilla warfare. Women who have sold their souls to get their man without the man even knowing what's going on. You see men think the war's like cricket, a friendly game with gentleman's rules. Just when he thinks the rules are clear and everything's under control, his woman turns this gentleman's game into a blood sport, a messy brawl. All, they say, is fair in love and war

Once again, I was awakened by a thump to the eye, the impact of which shattered the last vestiges of a peaceful dream. Stunned, my head raised itself vertically as if by reflex and shook itself. I opened my eyes to the sound of a sharp buzzing gnawing away at my eardrums, and as I did so, the early morning sun streaming through the curtains pierced through my bloodshot eyes and filled my vision like floodlights. In the kitchen, the radio was blaring the voice of some tongue-twisting pirate deejay giving out dedications. The throbbing inside my head continued. It felt like my left cheekbone had been crushed, but it was the back of my head that was throbbing. On the bed in front of me, Lesley's angry face warned me of what more was to come. I only had a moment to consider what had happened before Lesley's tightly clenched fist hammered down on its target again with expert precision.

"What the bumbaclaat was that for!" I screamed, only just managing to grab her hand before I was dealt a third blow. This wasn't funny. A scud missile was exploding in my head and she was ready to fire another with impunity. "What the hell was that for? Enh!" I screamed again, astride her now, she was overpowered. As if on cue, the radio deejay's words cut through the tension in the room.

"Once again, this record's going out with lots of love to Johnny 'Dollar' Lindo, down there in the Brixton side of things and it's coming from your main squeeze Pauline in Edmonton up there in the North London side of things. And she has just given birth to your new baby son. She says she's sorry you couldn't be there at the hospital for the birth, but she says she loves you very much and she can't wait for you to come by the hospital later today. So get down there fast Johnny! 'Cause this is Valentine's Day and a man shouldn't keep his woman waiting today, especially when she's just given birth to your son. Cho' man, ah wha' do you? Get down there fast, man!"

It was a crafty move. I hadn't reckoned on a play like that and I didn't know what to say at first. Lesley threw another well-aimed punch. If I never ducked my nose would be in the back of my head.

"You bastard, you bastard! You bastard..." Lesley repeated.

There was still a chance of denying everything, but to tell you the truth, I was tired of all the juggling. It had to come out at some point and this was as good a time as any. "I was going to tell you... Believe me, I was going to tell you."

Lesley neither heard nor cared for my excuse, but began to cry uncontrollably.

"How could you do such a thing like that...? How could you?"

I went into a long explanation. Told her it was an accident. "What am I supposed to do?" I asked. "Whatever I do, the yout's still mine. Don't you see that? I've got to deal with it?"

Lesley was hysterical now, getting her little self uptight made her unable to control her breathing. She gasped for air, her face contorted in pain. I hoped that she was just exaggerating the effects of her discovery, but a nagging fear that this might be for real persisted. I didn't know what to do and the only thing I could think of saying was, "Do you want me to call an ambulance? Do you want me to call a doctor?" Lesley made no response to my anxiety. Happily, her breathing calmed and eventually she lay peacefully on the bed.

But that wasn't the end of it. It was the calm before the storm. I don't know what I was expecting, but it really did shock me a way to see how badly Lesley took it. Besides the most basic grunts, she didn't communicate with me at all for

116

the next 24 hours. It was Valentine's Day, the day of romance, the day of love. But while millions of couples all over the world were reconfirming their love vows, we were like strangers. Lesley went about the business of taking care of her home and children. But I could see the pain and suffering in her eyes. I felt ashamed. It was Lesley that I loved and not the other, yet I had caused her intense misery. Love had a hold on me and there wasn't anything I wouldn't say or do to make things better between us. "I love you to the maximum," I told her. "I'm sorry for upsetting you. I want nothing more than to kiss and make up." Lesley threw me a stare that could kill as my words once again fell on deaf ears.

I deliberately stayed at home over the next few days so that Lesley could take all her anger out on me. If I was around she wouldn't have to phone someone and offload everything on them, which in turn eased the phone bill. Even though I knew I risked receiving a certain amount of verbal if I hung around, home was still where my heart felt content. And I took my part in looking after Jacob at night. Anything to ease Lesley's stress and take her mind off her troubles. I plumbed a washing machine in the kitchen and a shower in the bathroom and I bought her several bunches of roses and a few boxes of chocolates but she gave me one evil look which told me where I could shove them.

It was difficult focusing on my situation, so I once again turned to books. There's one thing about reading, if you can focus on the book, it can take you out on a vibe far away from the troubles of the world. I read voraciously because I knew that if I stopped, I would start thinking about things and tribulation would be sure to follow.

I had tried phoning Pauline several times. I had to make sure that my baby was okay. I wanted to see him, to hold him, to hug him and dream plans of his future. So while Lesley slept in the bedroom with Jacob, I crept out to the phone in the hallway. There was just the answering machine. I was surprised. I thought she had already come home. I phoned the hospital, and they confirmed that Pauline had been allowed home three days before. I phoned her flat again, and again there was just the normal answer message,"I'm not at home at the moment, but if you leave a message I'll get back to you as soon as possible."

It was the same the next day also, no answer. I called The Book Shack. I had obviously never given Pauline my home number, so she usually left messages at the shop. My assistant said there hadn't been one, however. I was truly puzzled. I knew what I had to do, so I put on my coat and Kangol hat to go over there. Lesley knew immediately what I was up to. She didn't have to say a word, when her eyes were filled with so much bitterness, her face took on a cynical expression which laid bare her deepest thoughts like an open book. I hadn't been anywhere in days and from now on whenever I stepped out the door she would suspect me of going to view my other baby. She looked at me coldly. Somehow I knew it was a mistake but I just couldn't go out the door without saying something so I said, "I'm just going out for a walk" and knew even as I spoke that she didn't believe me.

I entered Pauline's flat with the latchkey she had given me and found it to be empty. It was strange, it didn't look as if anybody had been there for several days. Now I was worried slightly, even though I knew there had to be a reasonable explanation.

Lesley's pain didn't go away as I had hoped. In fact it seemed to get worse. The more she internalised it, the more the look in her eyes turned from fire, to pure hatred and finally to murder. When you see your woman feeling that bad it affects you deeply, I don't care how hard a man is. And it changed me. Outwardly, I was still the same, but inside of me I had changed. I wanted to work things out with Lesley by any means necessary. I made a commitment to myself that I would never, ever play away from home again and I told Lesley so. She simply kissed her teeth and turned her head away in disgust.

"Why yuh nevah decide that before?" she spat venomously.

That's how it had been the whole time. I would try and make peace and got pure slackness in reply. I became a kitchen regular because Lesley had resorted to serving one single dumpling on my plate at dinner time.

"Look Lesley, me sorry!" I tried again frustrated. "I love you, I don't love nobody else. Some man love one, some love two, I love you and you alone. But I did you wrong. If I could dream my life over I wouldn't do it. But just give me a chance, please, let me explain and I'm sure you'll understand...

But shame and pride was killing her and holding a conversation with me was bound to cause more pain. I looked into her face. What a fool I had been, the last thing I wanted was to lose her.

Lesley looked at me with the tears of years of pain in her eyes. "What have I done to you, Johnny? I must have done something wrong for you to treat me like this?".

"There's nothing I can remember right now," I admitted. I

was searching hard for an explanation that would save our relationship. "But there is one thing... And if it wasn't for that, none of this would have happened... probably. It's when you use sex to spite me. Like when I'm on top of you and you suddenly ask, 'Are the dishes washed up?' and I know that if I ever say no, cold vibes and recession business ah start. It's dangerous playing on the weakness of a man. When you treat him like that, how you expect him to satisfy his needs, enh? That's what really drove me to look elsewhere you know Lesley, I was tired of the recession business."

"So, you don't remember that you have responsibility? You sacrifice your relationship with your baby son and your pretty little daughter just to be wrapped up with another woman? Two babies by two different women, Johnny... I can't understand how you could be so feisty! I thought I knew you, Johnny. I thought I knew you well and I thought you were a good man. Johnny, how long does it take to get to know the person you are spending the rest of your life with really well?"

The question was armed with a nuclear warhead, anyway I answered it I'd lose. My silence condemned me. Lesley was my long time woman, yet I had to admit she didn't know me. When she cried that I had taken her youth, I cringed because I knew it to be true.

"When I was sixteen, so many guys wanted to be with me, Johnny. Even now today, men are always coming up to me and asking me for a date. You don't believe me? Well it's true. And they beg me all kinds of things, Johnny, and you know when a man flatters you like that it can give you a boost that will last the whole day. Especially when you're not getting no sweetness like that at home. But I've never, I've never once gone with any of them, Johnny. Because I made my decision and I chose you, and I've stayed faithful to you for fourteen years, Johnny. Fourteen years!"

Then Lesley decided to start hitting me where it hurt, by using the children as hostages. The slightest little tiff, argument or disagreement and the first thing she comes up with is, "Right the kids ain't going up to see your mother anymore. It's your mother's fault anyway, why you can't keep to one woman. She probably knew you had both of us and didn't say nothing. Your family have never liked me anyway." She cried throughout and cussed bad, bad word "

Winnie stood bold as day by her mother's side, and showing contempt for the upbringing which had taught her respect for her father, said Lesley had a point. I just said,

"Cho', I don't want to take this any further."

The arguments and upsets soon began to trouble me bad. Lesley's convinced herself that I hadn't done anything for her during her pregnancy.

"I do everything for your friends when they come around and this is my repayment," she cried. "After all I've done for you, I've given you the best years of my life and look what you've done to me... You've betrayed me and I can never ever trust you again... You've messed up my head good and proper this time..."

I could do nothing but stand and see her go through the pain. It troubled me in my heart and I had doubts as to whether we would ever again be close like we used to be, talking things through together and planning the future together.

Jacob was also troubled and cried all night every night and as a result Lesley wasn't getting much sleep either. And as if that wasn't bad enough, Lesley had told her mother about my other child and now she was calling her daughter on an hourly basis to add salt to injury with her malicious comments. It was the worst week of my life. I couldn't forgive myself for having caused Lesley so much pain. I didn't deserve her, I really didn't deserve her. I considered dedicating the rest of my life to her happiness, whatever it took, because I now appreciated the years of her life she'd given me. It's a shame that it took a whole lot of tribulation like this to make me see wha' ah really gwan. I used to accuse other people of having tunnel vision, now I realise I'm the one with the problem. It took something like this for me to see I only need one woman in my life and that's Lesley. I had hurt the one I loved enough.

Lesley forced me to move into the spare bedroom. I lost my appetite completely and a stone in weight that first week. Soup was the only thing I managed to hold down and even then very little. I had become an insomniac. I would lie on the camp bed tired, but unable to sleep, while remembering all those records on which the singer sings "I can't sleep because my baby's gone." I used to think 'sloppy shit', without really focusing on them. But now I know what they're dealing with because the reality has licked me also. I thought about Beres and how he coped when his wife left him. Women offered themselves up to comfort him, but he had his wife on his brain and couldn't sleep with any of them. We all used to tell him to snap out of it and get himself a new queen. I couldn't understand when he said "after losing my wife there's no

120

other woman in the world for me.". I can see the picture clearly now though. It came to mind the other day. I still hadn't spoken to Pauline, however, and I couldn't really play my next card until I spoke to her.

Lesley wasn't wasting time waiting for me to play my card; she had already started causing friction and disharmony between me and my daughter. She would deny it and it's probably too subtle for me to put my finger on any one thing, but Winnie now looks at me in a very different light. There is no trace in her eyes that until recently I was her hero. She had witnessed her mother's hurting and crying everyday and clearly saw me as the villain, so took her mother's side in everything. If her mother now told her that cows were blue she would believe it. Unless I speak to her, more time she doesn't even say anything, but just sits in front of the TV watching Black Satellite TV waiting for the Shabba videos to come on. I put it down to the girl's youth. When she gets older she'll see wha' ah gwan. She thinks she knows everything and worse still, I gave her the confidence to think for herself. But she's a long way from being a woman. Our daughter-father relationship came to a head one night when I was trying to get into the bathroom.

"Get out of the bath," I ordered through the locked door, "and get ready for bed, because you have school in the morning."

She opened the door with a mischievous look in her eyes as steam poured out of the bathroom.

"Mama says I've got another dry-head bro.her somewhere out there," she announced standing in the doorway with her arms folded, clocking my entry. I gave her a look which warned her that I wasn't in the mood for games. She just stood there proud and loud and continued.

"Mama says if a woman called Pauline calls up I can cuss her the most amount of bad word and not get beaten for it."

I couldn't believe my ears. How could the girl be so bold and feisty to my face with the full support of her mother?

"Watcha man," I said, "you're a big girl now, nearly twelve-years-old, you're not no pickney. If I hear you cuss any bad word, you're going to feel it and not your mother. So don't even think of cussing anyone."

Winnie gave me a 'sticks and stones may break my bones, but threats will never hurt me' look and then went to bed.

Early the next morning, Lesley played her trump card.

"I might go away with the kids and if I do you'll never see them again," she announced casually.

NIGHT NURSE

Sagittarius — the time has come to put yourself first and not allow others to burden you or take up your time The last week has been a stepping stone to the rest of your life... a new friend could open a closed door... be positive.

With his daughter now with her mother, Beres ended up taking Caroline back to his place after she succeeded in getting him released on police bail. He was grateful to the woman who had initially refused to take on a male client in a custody case to come to his rescue and wanted to talk to her about his chances of having Lara home. He also wanted to talk about his feelings or simply talk to someone about anything. The only thing he didn't want to talk about was his estranged wife's sexual preferences. He hadn't mentioned that to anybody and still hoped it would stay a dark secret.

"I'm not paying a penny," he assured her as he fixed some drinks in the kitchen. "They can chase me up for child support, but I'm not paying. Sonia made her choice. First she abandoned her kid and then she returns after six months and gets custody. If they think I'm going to contribute towards that they've got another thing coming."

"You cannot get out of it I'm afraid Beres."

"When it comes to children, who's right should be first, the father's, the mother's or the child's?"

Caroline didn't hesitate to reply "the child *and* the mother's."

"Well, I don't agree with that. I think the child's rights come first. And Lara was happy here with her father. The one parent who stayed at his post and looked after her. But men have no choice to choose or not to choose fatherhood. It's down to the woman whether she wants to foist it on him or deprive him of it."

Beres had had time while sitting in the police cell to consider the plight of the baby father and he was aggrieved that while a pregnant woman could decide for any reason that she did not want to go through with it, she had options; she could go and get an abortion right from the moment of conception, whereas the man had no say in whether to become a father or not.

"If men had the same rights as women, there would not be so many kids. There would not be so many one parent families."

Caroline asked him to expand on his conclusion but was unimpressed with the answer. Beres handed Caroline a Bacardi and coke and pulled the ring on a Tennents for himself. He explained further that he didn't consider himself an irresponsible father. After nearly eight years of marriage, he had only had one child.

"Yet the law assumes immediately that Sonia is to be trusted with raising Lara before me. That doesn't make sense after her behaviour. She's already shown that she doesn't want her daughter. She abandoned her for six months, for crying out loud! If she gets custody the law is telling women out there that if they feel like getting pregnant, the law will make him take care of it, and that's not right."

Ordinarily Caroline wouldn't have had time for this. But Beres was different, she was intrigued by him. He was the first man she had met who was bringing up his child on his own. She had often doubted there was such a thing as a genuine baby father. Beres had been a shining example of that, if only for six months.

"I think you should pay your parental contribution to your wife before being asked," she said. Whatever happens you do have some responsibilities towards that child. I'm sure she'll be taken care of regardless, but that's not the same as you being involved in the child's life, and I support mothers who go out and stand up for their rights and hunt the absent fathers down for child support. That's simply going out and getting what's right for the child."

Deep in his heart, Beres knew Caroline was right. He had expected her to be anti-men, but now that he had discovered she wasn't he began to notice her properly for the first time and liked what he saw. He continued rambling throughout the evening. He couldn't understand why his hands were sweating and his inner voice was telling him to cool it, not to talk so much. But he couldn't stop those palms from sweating and the more he sweated, the more he talked. It was nearly midnight when Caroline insisted that she had to leave. She was okay to drive and she had to get home. Before going to bed, Beres watched *The Victor Headley Mysteries* on video, drinking more and more cans of Tennents and thinking about Caroline. He couldn't get her off his mind.

The next day, he called her at work and talked her into dinner that evening. Caroline chose the restaurant, Ackees, a

123

nice little Jamaican restaurant of the upwardly mobile types on Chalk Farm Road in Camden. As always, Beres dressed like a millionaire, wearing an elegantly cut, black two-piece, which he reserved for special occasions. His earlier modesty had vanished for now he had come to talk business and had no intentions of wasting time. He knew what he was after, he had thought about it for three nights now and that was all the time he needed to come to the conclusion that Caroline was the kind of person who could give him what he wanted, long term. But he wanted to do things right, the way old time people used to do. He looked at his watch as he had done three times in the last hour and polished off the remainder of his jerk chicken.

His intentions were strictly honourable but he needed somebody to fill the gap that Sonia had left in his heart. "I'm at your command," he said pulling off his shirt as they entered the living room in his house that evening, a mischievous look on his face. His manhood was hard and stiff; he had endured so long with repressed emotions building up inside him. Now he was ready and willing, and felt sure he had found the woman he was looking for, a woman who would support him through thick and thin."

"Why do men always expect sex when they start to take you out?" Caroline asked playfully. One thing led to another and within minutes they were rocking gently, Caroline on top, on the rug in front of the telly. Beres thanked her as he lay exhausted minutes later. It had been so long he hadn't been able to control himself. He lay still for a few minutes with Caroline still tense on top of him and wandered if he would ever again allow himself to trust a woman so completely as he had done his wife. The thought hadn't crossed his mind that she could have left him for another woman. Johnny had once mentioned that there was a possibility of that, but Beres had discounted it immediately. He knew his woman better than that, he thought. He should have listened to his friends a lot more. Johnny, Gussie and Linvall were always encouraging him to check other women and saw to it that he was rarely alone after Sonia walked out. They even set up girlfriends for him, although he usually declined, too embarrassed to tell them that his heart was still yearning for Sonia. But now he was slowly coming to terms with building a new life for himself. And now there was no way he'd allow Sonia to destroy it no matter what. He would get his daughter back.

Tonight with Caroline was refreshing though. Beres felt brand new. This rebirth would remain a special night in his life. She looked really good and made him feel really fine.

Caroline began to rock again ever so gently. Beres was once again hard and stiff inside her.

"Let's forget all our everyday problems and just make love," she said soothingly, running her hands though his hair.

This time it was better. They were at it for half an hour, rolling out into the hallway and somehow ending up in the upstairs bathroom still locked in a tight embrace. Caroline couldn't have wanted a better lover. He was hungry and it seemed like he had never made love before.

"I bet I know what it feels like about this time," she said teasingly.

"Girl, it's hard to explain what I'm feeling inside."

"Then don't say anything, just hold me tight," Caroline said her head running away with romantic thoughts.

125

DISS THE BLACK MAN TIME

Linvall sat down on the kerbside, his shoulders stooped in a dejected manner and his face pointing to the ground. In the last twenty four hours his life had been turned upside down by a series of events beyond his control. His woes started the day before, early on St Valentine's Day morning. He was preparing to leave the loft apartment to pick up a lift to Hackney Downs for the Brixton Massive Championship match. The pink envelope that had been pushed under the door of the main entrance gave no indication of the day to follow. It was addressed to him in a neat handwriting. He opened it slowly and pulled out the card, turning straight to the inside for the inscription: 'We two could be one. From your lover woman.' He smiled. It could only have been from Lucy. He got on to the team bus amidst the sniggers of his fellow team-mates. They were all holding copies of that morning's News of the World, which had a double page photo spread on 'TV Boss And Her Dreadlocked Toy Boy'. He was shocked to see a series of pictures of himself and Lucy cuddling and exchanging sweet nothings. The photographs had been taken through the window of a Chinese Restaurant in Hamsptead Heath. The story described him as a 'photographer', with quotes, and gave a comment from an insider at the TV station that "Ms Fry's preference for dark destroyers is well known." Linvall was shocked and embarrassed. He hadn't reckoned on his 'friends' in the press to be interested in this. He climbed off the bus and called Lucy from a call box, speaking to her briefly.

"Don't worry Linvall," she tried to reassure him, "I've been through this kind of thing before. My advice is that we both keep a low profile in the next few days and I'll call you when I think the coast is clear."

It was easy for Lucy to say; Linvall still had to face the teasing of his team-mates and everybody at the match. It seemed like the whole of London had bought a copy of the paper that Sunday morning. Linvall would have done well to cut his losses there, however, problems seem to know your weaknesses when you're down and pile up on you unsuspectingly.

It had been such a long time since he had seen Marcia, a

long time since they had talked with each other or held each other tight. It had been a very long time since they last made sweet love. Linvall stayed at home that afternoon looking forward to Marcia coming round. She had called a few days earlier and said she needed to come by and talk seriously about Lacquan. Marcia was Linvall's baby mother and Lacquan his ten-year-old son. However, Lacquan had never known the tall, motorcycling photographer with the funki dreds as his father. Marcia realised that Linvall was not prepared to enter into a joint partnership of parenthood even when she was pregnant. He was prepared to play his part financially and to drop by every other week to see his son, but he didn't have the time to do more than that, when he had his photographic career to build up. On hearing this Marcia immediately released Linvall from any of his fatherly duties and the pair split up acrimoniously before the child was born. She then took on the combined roles of mother, father, sister and friend to baby Lacquan. As the child grew older, Linvall's pleas to see him increased. Marcia didn't agree until after the boy was three and then only after Linvall had sworn to regard the boy as his nephew. She didn't mind Linvall seeing his son, she just didn't think he was a good enough role model for her son. Thus Lacquan grew up knowing his father as uncle. Inexplicably Linvall accepted the arrangement. Marcia had always expected somebody better than a struggling photographer as a father to her offspring. Not for nothing had she worked her way up from being a telephone saleswoman in the classified section of one of the major national broadsheets. She was now overall advertising sales director of the same company. Linvall couldn't match her for status or salary even if he tried. She didn't need anything from him to bring up her kid and whenever he sent a parental contribution, she would send his cheque back in a cab. Lately he had taken to just buying the boy clothes and gifts which she found it harder to deprive him of. Linvall tried to be a good father even though he had never been given the chance. In his view, the problem with the legal system in this country was that it never took into consideration the special needs of a male child to be with his father in custody battles.

Linvall often thought about Lacquan, planning all the things they would do together after that inevitable day when the boy found out who his father was. He wished that he had been more involved with the child's upbringing but he had to get on with his life and seeing his son whenever Marcia would allow. It was probably no more than once every three months that she would show up taking the kid to see Uncle Linvall and he would see how the kid was looking more and more like him. Lacquan was going to be tall like his father and he certainly had the same dimpled smile. But the more Lacquan grew up to look like his father, the more his mother did everything in her power to make sure he didn't turn out like his father, or his uncle Linvall for that matter. She wanted him to be a doctor or a lawyer and in the absence of a suitable father, the Huxtables were a credible surrogate. Lacquan never once asked about his father; Marcia said he didn't seem interested. She had told him only once when he was very young that his father lived in America and he had never mentioned it again.

Linvall loved his son and he didn't really want to hide the fact from women he dated, though he sometimes did and had done with Lucy. It was too easy not to mention his son to his girlfriends because living with his mother in another part of town, Lacquan was invisible.

However, now the boy was becoming too much for Marcia alone and she had called to arrange a meeting with Linvall to discuss what she was going to do. Since throwing her latest boyfriend out after some domestic problems, there was no man around the house to help raise Lacquan and she was becoming frustrated, though far from beaten. Nevertheless, she couldn't resist asking Linvall on the phone whether he was alone or seeing someone.

At three in the afternoon, Linvall opened the main exit to his building to a fuming Marcia. She had a copy of the News of the World scrunched up in her fist and shoved it in his face.

"What do you call this, Linvall?! Have you no shame? I call you on the phone and tell you that your son needs a role model and guidance and three days later you've got your face plastered all over the national papers with some dog that's old enough to be your mother!"

"You sound like you're about to go off on me and I don't want to take that from you. It's a bollocks story, right? She's a friend of mine — that's all it is, a friend of mine who I went out to dinner with and because she happens to be a TV chief they've made up a story."

Marcia wasn't convinced. The story was a fitting description of Linvall if she had known him a day and *what bad ah morning can't turn good ah evening*, she knew. Still, she hadn't come to censor Linvall's behaviour, even if she could. Officially, he had nothing to do with her or Lacquan and by rights his behaviour was outside her jurisdiction. She filled

128

Linvall in on his son's progress. Lacquan was doing badly in school. She had been called up to see the headmistress twice and the second time had been warned that if Lacquan got into any more fights he would be removed from the school. For some reason he was just not interested in his studies and he who used to come top in the class in maths and English was suddenly lagging behind everybody else. Linvall breathed a sigh of dismay, but there was more to come. Lacquan now ran with a local street gang after school and they had recently taken up going up to the West End on their own and stealing toys from Hamley's. She had been cautioned by the police twice and feared that Lacquan might be recommended for a spell under council care if she was not really careful. Linvall was astonished. He had no idea that his son had tumbled to such depths. While he pondered on what steps to take, Marcia spelled out her well thought out plan.

"I want him to stay with you for a while. I'll tell him that he's going to go and live with Uncle Linvall in his big flat. He'll love that, I'm sure. He always loves coming up here. I think it will benefit him to have a man around again."

Though Linvall had dreamt so many times that the day would come when Marcia would ask this of him, he was unprepared today. He couldn't say no, she would never forgive him for having declined to take full responsibility for his son a second time, yet he couldn't have Lacquan around, not now, not when his future was so unpredictable; not after telling Lucy Fry that there were no children in the darkened closets of his past. He muttered something about needing to arrange a few things in the loft in preparation and that he would let Marcia know the state of play in a few days.

It took a while for Linvall to get Marcia smiling, but he finally succeeded and got her relaxing on the oversize cushions that littered the floor of the loft. They say absence makes the heart grow fonder. Seeing his baby mother lying back on his floor reminded Linvall of the old days when they had loved each other. He couldn't resist kissing her. She returned the kiss passionately. He led her to the sofa in the centre of the room and laid her out like a feast and smothered her with kisses. First her lips, then her cheeks, neck, shoulder, arms, hands, fingertips, her belly button, her upper thigh, her thigh beneath, the slit in her dress, her knee, ankle; each kiss slow and deliberate. His eyes focused on hers, she relaxed and enjoyed it all. He kissed her legs again and began to massage her foot.

"Ever had a foot massage before?" he asked her. She shook

her head, enjoying it. "How does it feel?"

"Like heaven, Linvall, don't stop," Marcia answered breathlessly.

He released the front button of her blouse, allowing his funki dreds to fall through and caress her upright nipples. He stroked her back gently with one hand, tracing some mysterious outline that stretched from the base of her spin to her neck.

"You're turning my world crazy" Marcia gasped.

"Well, you should have married me," Linvall groaned as he entered her. "That would have been good." He had been thinking about her a lot lately, missing her. He felt silly about it, but as always he cried when they had finished, he couldn't help it. He didn't know why, but he always cried with Marcia. She was doing something right if she could still brings tears to his eyes, Linvall thought.

All that was the night before, Valentine's Day. He awoke the next morning with a hard-on as Marcia caressed his cock gently, expertly and determinedly between her fingers.

"Are you still in love with me like the way we used to be or did it all fade away?" she asked as he opened his eyes. Any man in his situation would have been forgiven for falsely pledging love, but in the cold light of day Linvall bravely went for honesty. He wasn't going to start seeing her again. All hell broke loose with Marcia, claiming that he had deceived her and slept with her under false pretences. And now she was refusing to leave the loft until she was good and ready, just for the sheer bloody hell of it. She was in a combative mood and Linvall knew that meant she would stop at nothing to get her own way. He was down at the kerbside waiting for her to calm down and leave and looking dejected when Gussie pulled over in his new BMW.

"Linvall man, what's up?!" Gussie called out from behind the wheel. He suspected that it had something to do with the previous day's picture spread in the papers.

"That bitch! That frigging bitch!"

"Who? What? Who bitch?"

"Marcia!"

"Marcia as in your ex-missus Marcia?"

"Yeah, the bitch. She won't leave my apartment."

Gussie sighed. It wasn't the first time Linvall's ex had pulled a stunt like that. Why did the man never learn?

"I knew I shouldn't have sexed the bitch."

"You never learn do you, man?" Gussie had little sympathy for his friend's predicament. "It's the same thing every time, and you always say you shouldn't have."

Linvall kissed his teeth sulkily.

"I know you're right, man. And I'm always aware at the time, but when she comes round... I don't know what it is, man, I've always got to trouble it." And he had to admit to himself that he'd had fond thoughts at the time.

"Your flesh is weak, you know, Linvall. Your flesh is too raas claat weak."

"It's not my flesh, it's the pussy. I'm telling you. But she's so messed up in her head." He rose to his feet angrily. "I don't care how sweet that t'ing is, the bitch is leaving my flat."

"So what are you going to do?" Gussie asked disinterestedly.

"I've called the cops. It hurt me to do it, but I had no choice."

Gussie filled Linvall in on the development of Beres' domestic problems. Caroline had managed to get him out of the police cell on bail, and he would have to appear in court at a later date on a charge of assault, but Caroline thought he could plead temporary insanity.

"As for Lara, Sonia has her now and Beres has to apply for visiting rights to see his own daughter."

The police arrived eventually. One male and one female.

"Mr Henry?" the policeman asked with an air of cynicism and experience that matched his years.

Linvall nodded miserably, stood up and led the way across the road to his loft. The policeman could see that he was in no mood for conversation, so he turned to Gussie.

"So he's a reggie singer then, is he?" the officer asked jovially, admiring Linvall's crown of funki dreds. "Of course, my daughter's always playing that stuff," the officer continued unprompted. "Who's that bloke she's always playin'....? Shabba... That's it Shabba! And that other fellow, Boo-Joo Bam-Tam... It's all the same if you ask me. I can't tell the difference. Call me old-fashioned, but you can't beat Simon and Garfunkel for my money. 'Bridge Over Troubled Waters'. Know that one? Or 'Mrs Robinson'? Now that was a song and a half... 'Here's to you Mrs Robinson, Jesus loves you more than you can know...' "

The officer broke off his singing only once they entered Linvall's apartment, for as soon as they opened the door a sight greeted him that he had not expected. Marcia stood there in front of the doorway completely naked.

Linvall looked at her disdainfully and kissed his teeth, Gussie simply stared wide-eyed and open-mouthed, the policewoman sneered and the policeman smiled.

So what's all this then?" the officer asked after a beat.

"I could ask you the same question," Marcia retorted quick as a flash.

"Now come now Miss...?"

"No!" Marcia shouted, "What are you doing in my home? Just get out! Alright?! Get out, or I'll call the police."

"Now don't give me that."

Marcia was in fighting mood and demanded that the uniformed officers should produce identification. She claimed that she lived in the house and not Linvall and that they should throw him out. The experienced policeman, with several years on the Force, inspected the loft. He had never seen an apartment so large, but wherever he looked he saw no sign of ladies' toiletries there. The officers eventually managed to assist Marcia from the loft. Linvall saw the look of fire in her eyes and knew that this was far from over. Later that evening, she drove Lacquan around to his 'uncle' and left him with Linvall to look after. She was going away for a long needed holiday break.

RUDE GAL DEH 'BOUT

I returned to work after my sojourn as a full-time baby father at home, to find that the bookshop had been run smoothly in my absence. I spent most of the day checking up on stock and phoning Pauline's number at brief intervals. There was still no answer, so I took the long way home so that I could pass by her yard. I looked up at her top floor flat and saw a window open. Finally, I thought, she was at home.

I let myself in with the latch key and was immediately hit by the strong fishy aroma that wafted in from the kitchen. Pauline met me at the kitchen door with a spoon in her hand.

"Oh, it's you," she said absentmindedly, giving little away.

I got a shock when I saw her. I had forgotten what she looked like without a pregnant belly. It had been a fortnight since I heard the radio message announcing to the whole of South London that I was a father and already she had slimmed down. If anything the little extra weight she still carried made her look even more appealing, in the gold lame cat suit she was dressed in, with a black jean batty rider sitting superfluously around her waist.

She was a sexy woman. I took one look and remembered that that was exactly how I got into this trouble in the first place, at the buppy party the year before, when before I knew it we were rolling between the sheets.

"Congratulations," I said, kissing her on the cheek. "A boy as well, you know how much I love that. So where's the yout'?"

"He's asleep in the cot in my bedroom. But don't wake him. He needs his beauty sleep."

I walked over to the bedroom, my heart pounding with every step, as I was about to meet my new son for the first time. He was a tiny baby. Even tinier than Jacob. He was soundly asleep, a teeny weeny thumb in his mouth for comfort. I knew straight away he was my son; even asleep that tiny lop-sided Lindo grin was there, but more than that, he was my exact spitting-image. I nearly fell about laughing when he wrinkled his nose the way I sometimes do, but instead I fell on my knees and wept like a baby. I was truly unworthy of this bounty of wealth The Father had bestowed upon me.

I was sobbing silently, the baby in my arms still asleep, when Pauline entered the bedroom.

"Be careful with him. What are you doing, are you crying? Oh Johnny," she said tenderly, "underneath all that tough exterior you're a real emotional sweetie, aren't you? It was emotional for me in the maternity ward also. Oh I wish you had been there, Johnny, because I could have done with your support."

"I didn't know when it happened did I, not until I heard your radio request on Valentine's Day and anyway, where have you been in the last two weeks? I've been phoning here all the time and I've been coming by. You just disappeared off the face of the earth with my son. Where the hell have you been?"

"I went up to Birmingham to see my mother. The boy is her grandchild as well, you know. So we stayed up there for a while so that I could recuperate and do some exercises and get down to my normal size. We only just got back. I needed time out, Johnny. To think about things, what I was going to do about the baby, about us, about my job, everything."

"Why didn't you leave a message at The Book Shack? At least to let me know."

"If you were so concerned about it Johnny, you would have given me your home number, not your work number. When they told me you had taken leave, I knew it was no use asking for your home number; you've got your staff well-trained there. And I didn't think it was worth leaving a message if you were away. I mean, the baby couldn't wait for you to call me back, he came when he had to come, there was no advance warning. Don't worry, I knew I could handle giving birth to a child without a 'new' man around to hold my hand as I was doing it." She looked me up and down. "You've lost weight, Johnny. Had a lot on your mind have you?" She couldn't resist an ironic smile as she asked it.

"Don't worry, I will look after my responsibility," I said rocking my son gently. "Don't worry about a thing, the kid will be well looked after. I can stand up here and say that proudly."

Pauline had the knack of guessing my intentions exactly. I could see her face chewing over each word I had just said, turning them over one by one, upside down, inside out and around and around for any hidden meanings. She reached her conclusion.

134

"So you're going to leave me aren't you?"

I avoided her gaze by turning my back on her as I rocked the baby gently.

"You are aren't you, Johnny?" her voice got louder: "You're going to leave me."

I could feel the anger rising behind me, boiling, spilling over. I thought it best to turn and face it.

"Me ask you a question!" she screamed, "I want an answer!!"

She looked at me with hate in her eyes. "I'm thirty-years-old, Johnny and I'm not getting any younger. I'm too old to carry on being the 'other woman' for anybody. And now I've left my job because of the baby, we have to talk about how I'm going to manage financially."

"Nobody's asking you to be the 'other woman', I just intend to carry on living with my woman that's all. I can't make any more commitment to you than that I will be a righteous baby father. Like I've said, I'll be around to give a helping hand."

Pauline looked at me bitterly. "You live in a fantasy world Johnny. You told me to have the kid, so I didn't dash 'way the belly. I carried your son for nine months and gave birth to him, while you were outta street having fun, and this is how you repay me for my efforts? I'm not just talking about sticking around and giving a hand. My mother can come down from Birmingham to give a hand and I have plenty friends who can drop around and give a hand. That's not what the kid's father is supposed to be doing. It's a fifty-fifty business I'm talking about. We should share the same joys and suffering. You need to be here, with your kid, twenty-four seven. Otherwise your pickney is going to turn his back on you one day. He will grow up honouring and respecting only his mother, because she's the one who raised him. Kids aren't blind you know. They can see how their life stays without you. Be careful how you stay Johnny, else one day you'll try and say proudly, 'ah my pickney dat', and the boy will look on you as if you were a stranger. If you spit in the sky it will fall in your eye. The most important way to provide for your child is to be a father to him."

Pauline succeeded in making me feel guilty. I laid my little son down in his cot, he needed that sleep if he was going to grow up to be big and strong. I turned to Pauline, I had no choice but to sit and try and reason some kind of accommodation. The ackee and saltfish was steaming in the pot and she asked me if I wanted a plate. To be sure, with so

135

much spice in the air, my stomach had begun to rumble.

"But fix me a drink first." Exhausted, I collapsed on the living room sofa and glanced out of the window at the trees outside. The first signs of an early spring were visible. Trees had come alive again with leaves and buds. Thinking on the beauty of nature's regeneration had a soothing, calming effect on me and I mellowed, sipping on the ice-cold glass of white wine and feeling fine. I went into the bedroom and used the phone in there.

"Winnie? It's me, Daddy. Just tell your mama I won't be home for dinner. I'm going out for a drink with some of the lads, yeah? Good. I'll be home about eleven-thirty. Nice."

I felt like a social worker, but I had promised to change my ways and the call fulfiled my obligation. Mama was always talking about how I had to fight the temptation of women. She thinks having more than one woman is easy. That's what she doesn't know, how could she? "It's hard work, Mama," I had told her more than once. "You think it's easy having to satisfy all these lonely women out there who haven't got a man? I have to be a lover to them, a friend, a husband, a confidant, a psychologist and a social worker. It's hard work, mama, and I ain't getting a penny for it. The government should pay me, because I'm doing this country a favour. If it wasn't for me and other men like me, the place would be overrun with hungry women who weren't getting their share and they'd be out on the streets swinging their machetes because we know a hungry woman is an angry woman."

When I checked it still, Pauline didn't have a leg to stand on because she knew I was going out with Lesley from time and that she was 'the other woman'. She should just write the whole thing down as experience and carry on with her life and let me carry on with mine. She's not the first baby mother on her own out there and although it's not an ideal situation to be in, she certainly won't be the last person it happens to.

"Have you decided what you're going to call the boy?" I asked as Pauline walked in from the kitchen, trying the saltfish on the edge of a wooden spoon for taste.

"I like the sound of 'J' so I was thinking Joseph or Jude."

"Jude? What kinda name's that?"

"Jude, you know Judas. Joseph was my first choice, but depending on how his father turns out, Judas might be more appropriate."

I looked at her, my eyes burning.

"You can't call a yout' Judas. That is the name of an evil man."

136

"Not necessarily, you know. There were two Judas' in the Bible. Only one of them sold Christ for thirty pieces of silver."

"It don't matter, he's the more famous one. You call a child Judas and everybody's going to think his surname's Iscariot. You can't do that. How do you think the child is going to feel when he goes to school?"

"I'll call him Jude instead then."

"Be serious woman. Jude, Judas it's the still the same thing, man. It's out of the question."

"Wait a minute, Johnny. You're suddenly talking like you're the one who carried the child for nine months and then went through the painful experiences of child birth. You weren't even there."

"It wasn't my fault, I didn't know you had gone into labour."

"No, because everything went so quickly. But that's not the point, you should have been around twenty-four-sevens. Your woman is about to have a child, you're supposed to be with her, in her bed, in her yard around the clock. Because you never know what you might miss. Anyway, going back to my point, I went through the painful experience of childbirth, not you. And do you know how painful it is Johnny? Can you imagine it? I think I have the right to call my child whatever I like after that and depending on how the father behaves, I might call him Judas."

I kept quiet, she held all the cards and I had no choice but to behave myself for the present.

"Mmmm, I've got that feeling again, Johnny," Pauline said licking her lips and placing the wooden spoon down on a newspaper. "Come over here and light my fire, Johnny. Come to me and run your fingers through my hair, darling," she purred, slipping a hand into the waist of her batty riders. "Stroke my hair, you know what I mean?"

I knew what she meant alright and she didn't mean the hair on her head. I looked her up and down hungrily. I wouldn't have minded sleeping with her one more time. She looked too nice to waste, her hair and make-up styled to entice me. She came and sat down on my lap with an arm around my shoulders.

"I know what you're thinking about right now," she teased. "You better come and get it quick, because you know another man could easily take your place, Johnny, and then too late will be your cry," she warned in a baby voice and wagging her finger at me as if she was talking to a child.

"Maybe we should eat first." I said as I eased her off my

lap and poured myself another glass of wine. Pauline went into the kitchen to serve up the dinner. The food smelled so good I could taste it. Surprisingly, it was the first time she had ever cooked for me. That may have influenced my decision to stay with Pauline that night. My nose followed her into the kitchen, just in time to see her splashing something from a dark brown bottle on top of my plate of ackee.

I grabbed her hand and took the bottle from her. The label was marked 'Oil of Love.'

"What kind of foo-foo is this? What the hell is this you're putting in my food?"

Pauline smiled a dark, sinister smile and looked me straight in the eyes.

"It's called 'Oil of Love'."

"Yeah I can read that, but what is it?"

"I got it from the local obeah woman. She says it will help to get me my man. I've got faith in her. I don't want you going back to your baby mother, Johnny... "

I couldn't believe it. Furious, I tipped the rest of the piss-coloured liquid into the sink and washed it down with hot water. My plate of ackee followed it.

"I'm not going to eat at this house again!" I cried, storming out.

"Don't go, Johnny don't go. I'm sorry!" she cried hanging on to my arm with all her strength.

I raised my hand to beat her down. She deserved a good slap, but something held me back. It was Mama's voice:

"If you have to raise up your hand to your woman, you're a bwoy. You're not a man, you're a BWOY!" Her words flashed through my mind as they always did in my moments of crisis. "If you and your woman don't get on you leave her. How many women think in the heat of an argument to box the man? With the man it's the first reaction. No argument on this earth can justify a man boxing up his woman. You wouldn't want your mother to know that you're boxing up your woman, would you?"

Mama had always been my conscience. I should have listened to her in the first place, she had warned me many times that if I went to the house of a woman who I didn't know too good and she was cooking for me, I should always make sure I stayed in the kitchen. I thought I knew Pauline, but I had just learned why I must always be vigilant. I calmed myself and shrugged Pauline away.

"Go on, walk out the door and say 'everything done'!" she screamed. "Go on, forsake your kid's life before it's begun!" I simply continued walking towards the door.

"Walk out of that door Johnny and don't bother coming back, you hear me! You can forget about seeing your son..."

I stopped dead in my tracks and looked at her sharp in the eyes.

"You shouldn't use the kid as a hostage," I warned. She had a victorious smile on her face. She knew what my weakness was. She had called my bluff and won. I had no choice but to sit back down on the sofa and obey.

"There's one thing you can do for me tonight," she said loosening my top shirt button. "I'm not gonna let you go until you do me right. Make love to me one time before you leave."

I looked at her hard. It was tempting, but I was determined to maintain my resolve. The only thing that bothered me was Pauline's tendency to use the kid as bait. Pauline stared me out, there was only one question in her mind and that was whether we were going to end up making love on the kitchen table or the living room floor. I was trying hard to resist the temptation.

'RUFF RESPECT

Everybody talks about 'respect due' nowadays. Wherever you go, people are quick to stretch out a clenched fist and say 'respect' without ever giving the respect due to those unsung heroes who devote their lives daily to the credit of the nation. Johnny 'Dollar' Lindo was a man of the future. He realised the need for a Saturday school in the area as an educational support to what the state had to offer the youths of south-east London. The Book Shack was the ideal place to have the school, it had the space in the back rooms and it was an unofficial meeting place for the community. The lives of young black youths in England were far too important to leave to the fate of the state educational system. As well as help on the curriculum in subjects like mathematics and physics, The Book Shack's Saturday school offered its pupils the necessary information to deal with the world outside. Classes were free and not only did the parents see a marked improvement in their children's school work, but it actually seemed like they enjoyed going.

Saturday school taught its pupils that contrary to popular belief, respect was not due to each and anybody, but was a thing you earned. It taught them to respect each other, that no one can take away what you know, and it tried to steer them away from bad company.

Johnny's view was that the kids nowadays were too lawless and they thought that the most knowledge you needed was to know who was the baddest or who smoked the most cigarettes. He tried to impress on his charges that in this world, unless you have a strong education, you aren't going anywhere.

The Book Shack's Saturday school didn't get any government funding and Johnny relied on charity to run it. He would steamroll anybody he met with a degree into coming and giving a class free of charge and reminded them of their duty to "give back to the community" which made it difficult for them to resist the challenge. Today he had recruited Gussie and Linvall to give a class on 'business' and 'photography' respectively.

The class of a dozen or so youths were only half paying attention to the talk. Other mini-conferences were going on as

Johnny addressed the class. He let it ride. Despite poor school grades, these youngsters, each dressed in the current ragga styles, were some of his brightest students. A couple of them came from as far away as Tottenham and Wood Green to attend The Book Shack's Saturday school where Johnny assured them that mathematics was the key to solving many of life's mysteries. But first he had to explain what mathematics was.

"Most people find mathematics difficult because they teach you what 2+2 makes without telling you why it must necessarily be four. Leroy, why do you think that 2+2 must always and necessarily equal four? None of the students were listening as they were studying the details of a leaflet that was being passed around.

"Lloyd, pass it over man. If it's of such big interest and more important than mathematics, I'd like to see it as well."

The tall youth with the chewing gum in his mouth walked over to Johnny and handed the leaflet over. Johnny studied it. It was a leaflet by a white leftist group, calling on mass action after the recent murder of a black teenager by a gang of white youths in South East London. The leaflet used the "by any means necessary" language of Malcolm X and a couple of black fists touching each other in respectful greeting to attract a black youth target audience to a demonstration that day, to the bus stop where the youth was stabbed.

Johnny continued his lecture on mathematics.

"So at the basis of mathematics is what they call 'logic'. Without logic, mathematics is meaningless and without logic life itself might be in jeopardy."

The youths were still not paying attention. They wanted to know what Johnny thought of the leaflet.

"There's nothing to say. I've seen it all before; different leaflet, but same words."

"Well we feel like we need to leave school early today, Teach, and go over there and show some support."

"Look Lloydie, your mother sent you to Saturday school this morning, not to some demonstration, and you're staying here until we done."

"Teach, that's not how me and most of the youths here feel, really and truly. Now, I don't mean you no disrespect..."

"If you don't mean me no disrespect Lloydie, sit down."

The boy sat down sullenly, unconvinced, but Johnny refused to allow his pupils to be the canon fodder for some left wing group. If anything, the black community had to embrace the protection of its youth from violence as top on its agenda.Gussie stood up to give his lecture on economics.

"...Tell the whole country about how unhappy you are about the way that youth got killed, by boycotting the white man's shop and you'll see how fast he pays attention. That's the power of economics. Most definitely. So from now on, when you're buying your yam and banana and your pear and mango, buy it from a black man. I know a lot of people say that black businesses rip them off. If a black man rips you off, a white man will rip you off the same way. So support black businesses. When you come to take your driving licences, remember that there are a whole heap of black driving schools around and if you have a little bad experience with one black business..."

Gussie ended his lecture to a thunderous applause of vocal gun shots. But still Lloydie wasn't convinced.

"Yeah, but all those things take time and organisation. We haven't got that. We've got to act now because youths are getting killed out there. What are we going to do about that? I've got cousins in Plumstead who are afraid to go out on the streets; a little eight-year-old cousin and the other one's five and they're too afraid to go to school in case the same thing happens to them."

Johnny paused. There was only one answer, however much he wanted these kids to avoid trouble.

"The only way you can stop those things happening to you is to always be prepared. Don't walk around with your head in the skies. Always be aware of who you are and what you are at all times and that the situation you're in can turn dangerous at any time. You must always be vigilant. Don't go and get drunk in a pub because those things can lead to disaster. Do what you have to do to stay alive. Your parents would rather visit you in jail than in a cemetery."

CAN'T KEEP A GOOD MAN DOWN

LEO — 'Nuff respect, lion. You're the don and today is your day. you have to curb expenditure even though a person close to you is depressed and you feel it's up to you to cheer them up. Do what you want and be with people of your wavelength. Make your day, or too late will be your cry.

"Do you pretend with her too?" Beres asked nodding towards Grace. Sonia simply looked away stone-faced. This wasn't the time or place to get into it with her estranged husband. They were standing in the office of her solicitors, Messrs Bailey, Hobbs and Lincoln Solicitors. Lara was there, Grace and Caroline also. Beres was collecting his daughter for a pre-arranged day out. All such requests had now to be conducted through the solicitors' office.

They stood in a long silence, looking away from each other. Sonia smoked a cigarette and absently tapped her lighter on the table. Beres was reminded of the many sleepless nights he had spent contemplating his downfall due to another woman's love. Sonia had had her cake and eaten it, now it was his turn to get a taste.

The formalities over, Beres, Caroline and Lara climbed into the large Mercedes he had borrowed from Dan Oliver's for the day. "So where are we going, Daddy?" Lara asked excitedly.

"Manners Lara, aren't you going to introduce yourself? This is my friend Caroline. Caroline this young lady who has forgotten her manners is my daughter Lara."

"Hello Lara," Caroline said cheerfully.

"Hello. Are you my daddy's new girlfriend?"

Beres and Caroline laughed. He was grateful that she had agreed to accompany him on his big day out with his daughter. He could do with her support for what he had in mind. Caroline and Beres had seen a lot of each other over the last two weeks, one might even say they were dating. He had regained his confidence with her and certainly Beres had begun to find that Caroline was all he desired in a woman: intelligent, attractive and good to be with. What's more, she seemed to feel the same way about him also. She was a

143

woman he could live in harmony with.

Beres gunned the car southwards, cruising the motorway at 90mph.

"Where are we going, Daddy?" Lara asked again excitedly.

"Think about it Lara, where do you want to go to more than anything, where have you been nagging me to take you for the last year?"

"Eurodisney!!" she exclaimed unable to control her excitement. "Oh Daddy, are we going to Eurodisney? Please say, 'yes' Daddy, please say 'yes'."

"I've got no choice but to say, 'yes' in that case." Beres said with a smile.

He had planned the trip meticulously. With the little time he had been allocated with his daughter he wanted to make sure that every second counted. He had Lara for the weekend and the trip to Paris seemed less far now the Channel Tunnel was in operation. He knew how happy his daughter would be going to Eurodisney. If he could get a week's access on her birthday, he'd take her to Disneyworld in Florida or Dinseyland in California. Then she'd really have a nice time.

The Hotel La Vista in Paris was a good base from which Beres had planned they would make their foray into Eurodisney country. It was a four-star hotel overlooking the Seine and Beres had booked the Penthouse Suite on the top floor with two inter-connecting rooms — one for Lara and the larger one for Beres and Caroline. Lara fell asleep almost immediately after the long journey. She had big dreams to dream about her forthcoming meeting with Mickey Mouse. Beres and Caroline had the night to themselves. There would be many opportunities for making love, but tonight with the lights of Paris glistening on the street below them, they wanted to talk.

"This is what I've always dreamt about," Caroline began, "stealing away with a knight in shining armour to Paris for a weekend. You don't know how happy you've made me."

She hugged him tight. A fire raged deep down in Beres' soul; the same fire that had raged when he first met Sonia all those years ago. Could it be that he was falling in love again?

Caroline placed his hand just below her breast. Beres could almost touch her heart beating.

"I know you can feel my vibes tonight."

"Yeah," Beres answered coolly. "Everything is right; the vibes are right, the place is right and the people is right. If life could be like this all the time, wouldn't it be perfect? You know what my dream is? I've been thinking about it all the way from London. Why don't we do a runner? You me and Lara. We don't have to go back to London. Why don't we just take the car and drive it all the way down to Ghana. I know some people there. We could live there. We could sell the car and live like kings off the proceeds. We could live as man and wife and no amount of British law would be able to take Lara from us. What do you say, Caroline?"

"You are joking aren't you?" She looked at him worried, but his expression said that he was serious. "Please, Beres. You know I couldn't do that. I run a business in London, you have your home there and you have your life there. I like you a lot. I even think I love you. But I don't want to run off with you, Beres."

"What do you want to do with me then?" Beres asked.

"I don't know just now. Oh I suppose I want to make love to you, I want you to make love to me and I want us to be close. My dream is that I'll find the right man to marry some day and you're a good possibility."

Beres shrugged his shoulders. It was a crazy dream, he agreed. If he wasn't going to get his daughter back through the courts, he would wait until she was eleven when she'd be able to choose between him and Sonia and he was sure she'd make the right choice. Meanwhile, if Caroline would make him forget how much he felt for Sonia she was worth every penny this weekend had cost.

145

R-E-S-P-E-C-T

It was Saturday evening, Chantelle and I had been to the early evening showing of a new Spike Lee movie at the Odeon Leicester Square and I invited her back to my place in Brixton to meet my parents after. As we made our way to the car park, Chantelle talked eagerly about how the black American director just couldn't portray women.

"His women characters always have the naff lines to speak and you can hear it's a man's words. He needs to get some strong, black women in there helping him write his scripts."

Chantelle looked dazzling, dressed in a black designer evening dress that looked more like a flimsy nightie. It wouldn't have bothered me if she had dressed in rags, she was my woman and I yearned to treat her right. She was the woman I wanted to spend the rest of my life with.

"Personally," I said, "I thought the film was alright. Okay, the usual 'I must try and satisfy everybody' scenario, but it was alright as entertainment."

"Well, I get frustrated with Spike. I've seen every one of his films and even though I liked *She's Gotta Have It* the best, it was a total male fantasy and some of the lines had me cringing."

I was driving my new BMW 3-Series which I had got on a good deal through Beres. As it was a warm evening I pushed the button which caused the roof of the car to peel its way backwards with a mechanical whirr and pushed the engine into gear. I checked my watch. It was quarter to nine. The car purred its way easily through the light evening traffic.

"Oh you don't know how much I enjoy being driven in a convertible on a cool spring evening." Chantelle said sexily as she leaned her head gently back against the seat rest.

"All for you, Chantelle," I smiled. "All for you." I looked at my watch again. I liked being with her so much that I spent my days looking forward to our evenings together. I didn't know what it was but every time I thought about her my heart would start speeding tripple time, I became weak in the knees, hardly able to speak. I had tried time after time to resist my feelings, but I didn't have the fight left in me to oppose it; the fight to continue my life of roaming. I was tired of running around and I wasn't getting any younger. As we drove, I wanted to put her close to me and whisper sweet things in her ear. I was on fire.

"I've got something really important to ask you," I said as I eased the car into Piccadilly Circus and then shut off the ignition in the middle of the junction..

Chantelle looked puzzled. "That's no problem, go ahead."

"Well that's the question," I said pointing skywards behind her.

She turned around. By now an orchestra of car horns were blasting the night air with dischord, their driver's irate. Chantelle read the electric message board that overlooked the square from roof height. The words: 'CHANTELLE WILL YOU MARRY ME?' were amblazoned across it. Meanwhile, Piccadilly Circus had jammed into traffic chaos. "Will you marry me? Will you marry me?" I mouthed deafened by the noise.

'Yes', she nodded, 'yes, yes, yes, yes'. I grabbed her and embraced, her, hugged her. Just then, I saw two policemen approaching my car to investigate the disturbance. I let Chantelle go gently and switched the ignition on hurriedly. I caught sight of the two pursuing policemen in my rear view mirror as I sped off towards Trafalgar Square.

"That was the best surprise any man has given me!" Chantelle said, unbuckling her belt and hugging me tight as we crossed Westminster Bridge. "When did you manage to do it? It must have been expensive."

"Well, it was worth it. It took a bit of planning, but it was worth it. So when shall we have the wedding?"

"I'm afraid you're not quite home and dry yet."

"What do you mean?"

"I'm flattered by all the attention you've been paying me and after seeing her name up in lights any woman would be yours. I will marry you, on condition that you pass a little test."

"What? Test!?" I thought I had heard wrongly. "We don't need that Chantelle, I love you with all my heart and would marry you a hundred times over."

"Oh, it's nothing to worry about," she said casually and produced a weather-beaten notebook from her handbag. "It's just three simple questions. I'm sure you'll have no problem getting the right answers."

I was bemused but had no choice but to humour her. "Go ahead and ask."

"What birth sign are you?"

147

"Virgo," he answered firmly. "Virgo the virgin."

"Right Virgo," she thumbed the pages of her notebook. "And how old are you?"

"Thirty-four"

"Thirty-four year old Virgo, let me see now... Leo, virgo. Right virgo twenty-six, virgo twenty-seven, virgo twenty-eight, thirty, thirty-four." She thumbed her way further. "Here we are. Okay. Three simple questions, don't be nervous. First question, what would you say the secret to a successful marriage is? Is it: a, staying faithful, b, keeping your partner happy or c, honouring and obeying your spouse?"

I thought about the question for a moment. This little game confused me. Chantelle was a fun-loving woman, good in every respect and aspect, but it sounded like a trick question and I wasn't sure whether she was serious about the test or not. But I was serious about the marriage proposal so I played ball.

"The main thing is to keep your woman smiling, believe me. You keep your woman smiling in a marriage and nothing can go wrong."

"So that's 'b' I take it?" Chantelle ticked off the appropriate slot and continued with the questioning. "List these three virtues in order of priority in your life, 'ambition', 'faithfulness', 'charity'."

I wasn't really thinking about what I truly believed when I answered. I understood this little game to be about how you treat your woman, so I answered accordingly. "Faithfulness to my woman is always paramount. So faithfulness is always first and then ambition, for however charitable you want to be, you have to be successful first, take care of your own house and then put everybody else's house in order if you can."

"So faithfulness, ambition and then charity?" She ticked away in her notebook as we cruised through Kennington with the cool breeze in our hair.

"So how am I doing?"

"We'll see. Here's the final question, so think carefully before you answer. In order of priority who are the greatest black heroes: Malcolm X, Martin Luther King or Marcus Garvey?"

Damn! Another trick question. What was she trying to get at now? I thought about it long and hard, as I steered the car into Brixton Road.

"Well really and truly, for me it's always got to be Garvey

148

first, because he was the grandfather, you know. Everybody followed after him. And then Malcolm X. If I was around in the fifties and sixties, it would have probably been Martin Luther King, but from what we know today, it's gotta be Malcolm because when you check it, people today are listening to the voice of Malcolm long before they're listening to Martin Luther King. And its from learning about Malcolm that a lot of people then get involved and start reading up about Martin Luther King, Kwame Nkrumah, Jomo Kenyatta."

"Okay, tell me now, what did I get?"

"I'll just add up your points," Chantelle said. After a moment she smiled. "You'll be pleased to know you scraped through."

I smiled proudly and gunned the accelerator.

BEST DRESSED CHICKEN IN TOWN

Linvall found it hard to believe how fast his son had grown in the three months since he last saw him. Lacquan had abandoned his childhood habit of sucking his thumb and had become a tall, handsome, athletic-looking youth. He had grown up fast and had become street-wise with an attitude and dressed like a baby gangster in baggy patched jeans and wearing a hooded sweatshirt over a black Raiders baseball cap which covered most of his face. Lacquan didn't just look nice, but knew his roots and culture as well. "Well Malcolm X used the 'X' in his name because his real name was Little," he answered confidently when Linvall questioned him, "but he said that it was a slave name and it wasn't his real name and because he didn't know what his real name was in Africa, he decided that 'X' was better than a slave name."

Linvall had rarely known a prouder moment in his life. His son spoke with the confidence of youths many years his senior and it was hard to understand why his school results were so bad.

That Marcia had simply dumped the kid on him while she disappeared on holiday didn't surprise Linvall. She had always been contrary and it was this more than anything that had made it difficult to continue their relationship. If he told her something serious, she would make a joke of it and when he was laughing she was deadly serious. The cuss and quarrel that resulted probably killed their relationship. When they went shopping together it would take a whole morning for her to buy anything. She would try on dresses, blouses and socks — everything. Pinks, blues and yellows she would try out the whole shop, but nothing was quite right. It was either "it nuh look right", or it was too big or too short. If Linvall said 'try the dark one', she'd say she preferred the bright. Sometimes they'd be in a shop all day and end up buying a pair of tights.

"I want to be a rapper when I leave school," Lacquan mused as he polished off the remains of the chocolate cake Linvall had sent him to Tesco's to buy for dessert. He had raided his uncle's tape collection of all its rap and ragga cassettes and now had Snoop Doggy Dogg blasting at full volume through the huge loudspeakers positioned at opposite ends of the large studio area. He enjoyed coming to his uncle's loft, because there was much more room in there than in the flat he lived in with his mother. Mostly he enjoyed using the loft as a gym to practice karate kicks.

"A rapper? So tell me 'Quan, you know what those rappers are talking about when they're talking about crack?"

"Oh Uncle, everyone knows about crack. I even know some crack heads."

"No, 'Quan, you don't really know about crack. You only think you do. Let me tell you something, crack is a drug... it's bad for you." Lacquan slapped his hand to his forehead in mock amazement to say, 'as if I didn't know that'. Linvall carried on regardless. "It changes your personality, you know, the way you are. You heard about Doctor Jekyll and Mister Hyde? Well that's a crack-head for you. I've taken photographs of some great singers and great people, who if it wasn't for the crack would be rich and famous right now. But crack destroyed them, you know what I'm saying?. And sometimes it's not their fault, sometimes they just wanted one hit from it. They thought, 'bwoy I can control it'. But you can't control it, dem t'ings control people. And you know what the worst thing is, 'Quan? It's that there's so much crack around nowadays that youts like you only have a tiny chance to stand up strong and resist it. If I was a man who had youts, I wouldn't really want my youts to grow up in a crack world... And don't follow nobody who takes acid neither. Acid makes you insane. You wake up thinking your mother's a stranger, and start mixing up Monday with Tuesday, Wednesday and Thursday and you'll walk in the rain and think that it's sunny. Stay away from those drugs.

"I still want to be a rapper," said Lacquan. "I don't have to chat about crack, do I?"

"Well I wish you the best of luck in life. But rapper or no rapper, you're not going to become anything if your school work doesn't start improving."

"I don't need all that," Lacquan said with all the wisdom of a ten-year-old and continued munching away. "Those teachers don't teach you anything at school. They're boring. I don't need to go to school, all I need is a deejay, a dancer and some dope lyrics."

Linvall listened, bemused. His baby sat at the table opposite him, except Lacquan wasn't his baby anymore. His child had his looks and his mannerisms, but Lacquan didn't carry his surname and in the absence of a father, Lacquan had turned to Ice Cube and Buju to make sense of the world he found himself in. Linvall was ashamed. As much as he enjoyed their music, it was his duty to give his child all the necessary information he would need to be a credit to the nation. He wanted to feel the joy of fatherhood, the joy of holding Lacquan, squeezing him and hugging him. But it was much too late for that. Lacquan was already too old at ten years of age for all that. Linvall didn't have any business claiming credit for the youth, except that Lacquan was part of him. When he looked at him he saw himself at the same age. Each day of Lacquan's life had been like a slap in the face, each birthday reminding him, 'your son is one year older and you don't know where he is or how he's doing' and now he was feeling it. Linvall had thought about it long and hard and decided it was time to get his act together with regard to his son. He had to tell the truth no matter what it cost. Unless Lacquan knew who he really was he would never have an influence on the child's life. The risk that he would grow up spoilt and wild was too great to take a chance.

"You're my father aren't you, Uncle Linvall?" Lacquan said suddenly. Linvall spluttered, he thought he hadn't heard right.

"What?"

"I said I know you're not really my uncle, you're my father."

Linvall sat paralysed. His indecision had ended but not as he expected it to. How had the boy known?

"I've always known. As far as I can remember."Lacquan spoke slowly and deliberately, avoiding Linvall's eyes. "I can't remember when I guessed. Mama told me my father wasn't around and the only person I met like me was you. And some other little things made me guess as well."

Linvall felt exposed. The cards were on the table. He got up and embraced his son tight as he had always wanted to. Emotional as ever he couldn't stop himself from sobbing silently. They had plenty to say to each other and sat talking into the early hours as they had never talked before. "I tried my best to prove my love to you," Linvall explained pulling the cork on an expensive bottle of red wine to celebrate and went to the refrigerator for a glass of coke. Lacquan insisted that he could handle the wine and convinced his father to pour him a glass. Linvall explained the details of his son's birth and the seperation from Marcia. Lacquan told of the hate he had held for his father for not being around when other children brought their fathers to school, hate for him not

152

having been around to defend him when he needed it or to take him to football matches. Lately though, his hatred had subsided and he had got used to being a child without a father. His son's frank admission of his feelings brought more tears to Linvall's eyes. He promised Lacquan that things would be different from now on. That they would do all those things that he had missed out on. He would be a real father to his child. In fact, he intended to start immediately. .

"How comes you've been messing up at school and getting in trouble with the police?"

Lacquan was visibly surprised to see his father's tone change from one of reconciliation to one of stern fatherhood. He gave a lame excuse. It wasn't him, it was the friends he was hanging around with. It wasn't his fault if they were always getting in trouble.

"That's all bullshit. You understand? I don't care what all the other kids are doing, I'm only concerned with what you're doing. Now that I'm officially your father, you're going to have to learn a few simple rules. First, I'm your father and I brought you into this world and I can take you out just as easily. Second, you will go to school and learn for whatever reasons. I don't need to give you any reason, you understand? And if you continue messing up, you'll have me on your case. We'll be seeing a lot of each other from now on." He had made up his mind to make time for his son every evening. "I'll want to know what you did every day of school, yesterday, today and tomorrow. You understand? I know there's no reason for you to even think of coming second place in any subject. Your friends have got the same brains as you, no different. So there's no reason why you shouldn't be top in every subject. Lacquan, this ain't no joke. When you come home from school, you'll do your homework and then I'll give you some more homework on top of it so you won't have any time to be getting in trouble with your friends."

Lacquan sneered at his father with an attitude, which said that after all these years he wasn't convinced. Linvall thought otherwise. He would see his son every evening, if only briefly. Now that Lacquan knew the truth Marcia wouldn't have the heart to stop him. He would also send Lacquan to the Book Shack's Saturday school in Peckham for some extra lessons. He wasn't taking no chances. He had arrived in his son's life in the nick of time.

If Lacquan had inherited any traits from his mother, it was his fussiness when buying clothes. Linvall was out shopping with him in Oxford Street. He had decided that his son should

153

get the opportunity to smarten up his act and as well as the dozen pairs of baggy jeans — each with their own individual patchwork — that he possessed, he needed clothes that would make him feel grown up. "You're going to start secondary school in September," Linvall told him. "And I'm going to make sure that you go to a school where they still wear school uniform, so you better get used to wearing suits."

They went from one store to another for hours, without buying anything. Linvall had his Barclaycard with him, so expense was no problem, but Lacquan just couldn't make up his mind. He had seen several pairs of jeans and training shoes that he would rather have, but when it came to formal attire it seemed like Linvall would have to decide for him. It had been like that all day. They had been to Floyd's barber shop in Brixton first. Lacquan refused to have his hair cut by anyone but Floyd's most creative barber; a slim youth with a triple gold crown by the name of Bobby Valentino. Father and son had argued over how many tramlines Bobby would cut into Lacquan's hair.

"I've got to have five," the boy insisted. "One for Marcus, one for Nathan, one for my mum an one for Leroy." In the end he settled for the one line his father allowed.

"It suits you perfectly." Linvall said proudly as his son stepped out of the changing room in Next For Kids wearing a nice grey suit.

"But it's such a horrible colour," Lacquan protested. "Everybody's going to laugh at me. Can't I have the striped jacket instead?" He pointed to a blue and white sports blazer.

"You're having this one, 'Quan," his father insisted unimpressed. "It's a good suit and your mother will like it."

"You mean *you* like it, Daddy. Why don't you wear it?"

"You will wear this suit. Do you hear me? You'll wear this suit for your mother when she returns and you'll put on your best smile and look your best."

"Why do you hate me?"

"Don't be silly." Linvall grimaced. Lacquan could have done with a good old-fashioned spanking years ago to knock some of the feistiness out of him.

Laden with shopping bags, they went in search of a couple of milkshakes from the hamburger bar. A black cab screeched to a halt alongside them as they crossed to the north side of Oxford Street. Lucy Fry leaned out of the cab and called out.

"Linvall darling. I've been calling you all day, where've you been? Look, I've spoken to one of my contacts on the tabloids and she told me that the heat's off us. Apparently our story is old news by now and there won't be any reason for photographers to snoop about."

It was only then that she realised that Linvall wasn't alone. Linvall saw her realisation as she glanced at Lacquan standing beside him. A week ago he might have bluffed her and said that Lacquan was his nephew, even if she suspected their likeness to be a close call, but he was through denying his son. Who didn't like it could lump it. He waited for her to ask.

"Who's that?" she asked suspiciously. "You've been seeing somebody else behind my back haven't you? I can smell it."

"It's my son."

By now the taxi driver had become impatient.

"Look lady," he called out, "do we have to hold up the traffic or can we get a move on?!"

"Oh shut up!" Lucy snapped, "You are being paid, aren't you?" She turned to Linvall. "Son? You told me... you bastard! You bastard, Linvall. You bastard!! I told you, I told you from the beginning, no kids! That's all I asked of you. You bastard! I don't want to see you again. Okay drive on, driver." As the taxi pulled away, Lucy leant out of the window and spat out with venom, "And don't think you're getting that presenter's job either, you bastard!"

"So is that your woman?" Lacquan asked his father with a cheeky smile.

"You're too fast!" Linvall chided, slapping the back of his son's baseball-capped head playfully. "Stop sticking your nose in big people's business."

SHAME AND SCANDAL

My parents were spending a quiet night, in watching TV together. I introduced Chantelle. Mama was charming and embraced Chantelle warmly, kissing her on the cheek.

"I knew you must be special, my dear, because Gussie has been talking about you all day, non-stop and that's the first time I've seen him like that. It's Chantelle this and Chantelle that. You must have some special magic on him."

I was embarassed, but proud. Papa got up to acknowledge her and gave me a look that said, 'I hope you're taking my advice about marriage seriously'.

"Mum, Dad," I began nervously, "I want you to be the first to know that Chantelle has accepted my proposal to her and we're going to get married."

"Oh my dears," Mama exclaimed, gripped by a sense of maternal pride. "I was hoping that this would be good news. I am so happy for you both. I'm sure that you'll be very happy together."

"This calls for a celebration," Papa said proposing a champagne toast.

"To Chantelle... what a beautiful name, to Chantelle and Augustus. May you live happily ever after." The Old Man was in ebullient mood, he couldn't keep his eyes off her, charmed by her as his son was.

"You're forgetting your manners, Augustus," he said stiffly. "Are you not going to tell us anything about your bride-to-be?"

"I'll leave that to Chantelle," I said going over to the cabinet for the bottle of champagne.

"Well what can I tell you?" she said confidently, "I'm thirty years old, I work as an associate producer at a film company in Mayfair and uhm... what else can I tell you?"

"And she knows how to make a man very happy," I added.

"So Chantelle Breakspeare," the Old Man continued, "where are your family from? Jamaica?"

"Chantelle explained that she was born in London also but that her mother was originally from Clarendon. Mama said she didn't mind who I married, but she had always hoped it would be a Jamaican anyway. I was so happy, I wanted

Chantelle to stay for the night, but I thought it unwise with my parents there. After all, it was strictly speaking their home.

I returned from driving Chantelle home to North London in the early hours. Mama had gone to bed, but the Old Man was sitting in front of the gas-heated 'log-fire', the sound of some late-night easy listening radio music playing softly on the stereo.

"I don't want you to marry that woman," he said firmly a few minutes after I entered.

"What?!" I couldn't believe what I was hearing.

"I don't want you to marry her," he repeated walking over to the window and peering behind the curtains out onto the darkened streets.

"What the hell has brought this on? Why don't you like her?"

"I just think you're asking for trouble with that woman. A whole heap of trouble."

"You've got to do better than that you know, Papa."

"Look, I know she's very beautiful and I'm sure you're in love. I just don't think she would make a good wife. She seems like she's not ready to start a family and I don't want you planting your feet on such a slippery platform."

I was angry, boiling up inside, but kept quiet.

"I think you could do better, a lot better," he said matter-of-factly.

"Find yourself a woman, but find a woman that is extra special in some way."

"This woman is extra special to me... I won't ever get tired of her. I want to share my life with her. I can't say what I feel for her in words, but take whatever you've felt in love and multiply it tenfold, fifteen, twentyfold. That's how I feel Papa."

"I said, find yourself someone better. Think about it, son, the business is yours if you take my advice."

"I don't care about the business," I said finally. "You always get your own way, Papa, but not this time. You see I really do love her. And I'm going to marry her. Fire me if you want to."

I turned to walk away, but Papa caught me on the shoulder and spun me around. I looked straight into his eyes. There was a lot of pain there as they recalled the memories of yesteryear.

"You can't marry her!" Papa blurted, "You can't marry her!"

157

"Why Papa, why?!"

"Because she's your sister, but your mother doesn't know it."

The news struck me like a mallet blow to the head and I had to lean against the sofa to steady myself.

"What are you talking about?" I asked shaking my head in disbelief.

"Look, you can't say anything to your mother... understand? She would be too upset. It all happened a long time ago, you were only a kid..." Papa's eyes rolled around in his head as his mind wandered back, unlocking the darkest closets in his memory. He avoided my eyes as he told his story, ashamed of what he had to say.

"It's strange, the moment she entered, I felt I had seen her face before. It took me a while to place it, but her smile, those big eyes, her mannerisms... they're almost exactly the same... unbelievable. Anyway, it was nearly thirty one years ago now. I had got a job working on a stretch of the M1 near Birmingham; hard work for little money and spending sometimes weeks away from my family in London. That's how it was in those days, you went where the work was and tried your best to find lodgings or else you'd end up in hostels along with hundreds of other men. Anyway, I met a woman up there. We met at a dance I was invited to. I suppose I was lonely, I had been up there for a couple of months and I suppose I was a soft target. When I first met her — Rita was her name — I really only wanted companionship. I wanted someone to go out to the pictures with, someone to have as a friend up there. But she liked me also and anyway, one thing led to another. We had been seeing each other for a couple of months when she discovered that she was pregnant. It was such a shock for me, I don't know why I didn't think of it before, but it was then that I first realised what the consequences of my behaviour could be. I had just not thought about it happening. But I knew immediately that I couldn't leave my family, nor did I want to lose my family. The next day, I went to the foreman and picked up my pay cheque and employment cards and took the train back to London without leaving a trace of myself." He paused with a look on his face that showed that he now found his actions incredulous. "I had all but forgotten about that side of my life until your bride to be stepped in."

He finished speaking. I sat silently. There was nothing to say.

BREAK UP TO MAKE UP

Linvall became a family man and lived in a cosy little house in the countryside with his wife and two children, maybe three... His relationship with his son had blossomed over the last few days and Lacquan had mentioned how much he would like to live with his father in the loft. "I won't be much trouble," he said. And that's when Linvall started thinking. He shook himself out of his daydream, he had allowed his imagination to run away with him.

Breaking up is hard to do, but making up is harder. Linvall had spent the week loafing instead of working. He hadn't done a single photo shoot in the last fortnight, but he had other things on his mind. He knew what he wanted to happen, but he knew also that Marcia was a hot-blooded woman who was hard to please. He had to catch her while her guard was down.

For every action there is a reaction. Marcia returned from her much needed break. She had been to the Lake District with an old friend and looked refreshed and ready to handle whatever else the world threw at her. She was pleased to see how fine Lacquan looked in his new gentleman's style. Linvall had obviously been a positive influence.

"I told him I was his father," Linvall confessed hesitantly. Marcia turned her head slowly and fastened a steel gaze on her baby father. Linvall braced himself for an onslaught of abuse. Marcia had warned him that if he ever revealed his real identity to Lacquan, she would never allow him to see the boy again. But Marcia didn't explode.

"So how did he take it?"

"He already knew?"

"What?!"

"Yes, I was surprised as well. That boy is sharper than you think, you know."

Linvall filled her in on his decision to spend more time with Lacquan. Marcia agreed.

"Let me make it clear, Linvall. I'm not forgetting that you declined to pay a full and active part in your child's life from the outset. And I'm not going to let you forget it either. That's something you're going to have to live with for the rest of your life. I brought that boy up myself, with my blood, sweat and tears. I carried him for nine months without you, I sat up at nights with him when he was ill and doctored him without you, I clothed him and fed him and sent him to school without your help, wiped his nose for him and prayed for his future, you were never around. And you can't claim any credit for him now, because I'm not asking you for anything. I'm simply showing you that your son needs a man in his life. That's all. And I don't believe you when you say that you've turned a new leaf; you haven't proved anything to anyone yet."

Linvall's heart pounded with excitement. While Marcia's declaration may have given notice to a lesser man to pack his bags and go, Linvall knew his baby mother well and realised that her lack of anger at being told about his actions showed a softening on her overall position with regards to him. There was a long shot possibility that he could yet realise: his recent dream of forming a family unit with Marcia. It was a million to one shot but to Linvall it seemed like the chance of a lifetime. He promised that his new parental responsibilities would take effect immediately and to Marcia's surprise even offered to go around to her flat over the next few days and do any little DIY jobs that needed doing.

Linvall couldn't remember ever ceasing to love Marcia. They had split up, but that was her decision, it wasn't because they had stopped loving each other. And though he was then unprepared for a serious relationship, he was good and ready now. It wasn't going to be easy, he knew that. They were both stubborn characters and their egos sometimes collided. He was angry when she stripped in front of Gussie and the police officers, but he saw the funny side of it now and just put it down to her stubborness. Anyway, there were little things about him that drove her crazy also. She was tidy, yet he was untidy. It drove her crazy when he scattered things about. He thought she was nitpicking and inflexible. But she always had time to listen to his problems and to give him a hug whenever he needed it. He needed a hug more than ever now and his woman by his side to help him survive in this country.

The bits of DIY turned into a major renovation of the flat. Linvall was around at Marcia's early the next morning and every other day over the next week. He started with the stripping and then hanging of wallpaper and then went on to do some painting and other decorating needs as well as general cleaning and window cleaning. He wanted to do the things that Marcia couldn't do, to show her that she, as well as Lacquan, needed a man around.

Linvall was around early also on the weekend. On Saturday morning Marcia greeted him in her nightie. He read the twinkle in her eye wrongly however, because she led him past the bedroom and into the kitchen. The washing machine needed plumbing in. She even started talking about sex as he worked, sex and men and how she was so tired of the men she was meeting nowadays. Linvall felt like he was in with a chance and suggested that they could make themselves more comfortable once he was finished with the plumbing. Marcia simply kissed her teeth and walked out. Linvall ended up replacing the kitchen untis before he was finished. The flat looked like new and Marcia showed her appreciation by giving him a brief hug. She did invite him to stay for dinner however. It was a long time since Linvall had tasted a good plate of curried goat. He was up for seconds in no time and then thirds. Marcia ended up shooing him out of the kitchen with a wooden spoon. Lacquan saw that his father needed to talk to his mother alone and surprised Marcia by declaring himself ready for bed without her having to chase him as she usually did. Linvall sat relaxed, feeling comfortable on the leather settee, the goodness of traditional cooking energising in his stomach. His baby mother sat beside him. Not next to him, but beside him. As the night progressed she rested her hand against his chest. The music was sweet and the lights were low. Linvall couldn't have asked for more. They could both feel what was going down, but Marcia maintained her posture, reluctant to shift her position. They flicked through an old photo album.

"Do you remember when we fell in love?" she asked. "You were young and innocent. I was young and foolish and had a nice smile and nice legs."

"Yes!" Reminiscing brought sweet memories to Linvall. "You've always had nice legs," he complimented her.

"Remember when this one was taken?" he pointed out a pic in the photo album. "No, you wouldn't because you weren't there. You weren't there for my eighteenth birthday and you gave some foolishness about your car wouldn't start as an excuse. But still I continued to love you. Wasted my best years on you. If I could only turn back the clock... Remember when we used to sit on those benches after college? I gave my life to you, Linvall and learned that in love there's no real guarantee. I wasn't asking for much when I met you, I wasn't looking for a pretty boy or a rich man, just someone who would honour and respect me. That wasn't too much to ask, was it? And when I was pregnant, you were always quick to

161

say 'take care of our baby growing inside of you sweetheart'. Sweet, sweet words as I got bigger and bigger and happier and happier until the day I said we should move in together because we needed to share the job of bringing up the baby. When you refused me flatly I knew you didn't honour me and when you couldn't understand why I didn't want to be a baby mother bringing up the child alone, "like so many other women," I knew you didn't respect me. It took me years to get over you, Linvall but I eventually got tired of tears and since then my life's been a lot better."

"Sorry," was all Linvall could say, but that wasn't going to be enough to make Marcia love him again. No matter how clearly she explained the situation to him, she couldn't shift Linvall's belief that she could possibly fall for him again. They just had to find a way to live together. They needed to sit down and level with one another. He suggested that to clear the bad air, they should each write down everything about the other which drove them mad. She joked that she would need a trailer load of paper to write down her complaints "and that's with tiny writing!" Linvall was serious, but Marcia wasn't. "It's too late for all that sort of thing anyway," she concluded.

It was while he was going over the times table with Lacquan after school one afternoon that it dawned on Linvall that he hadn't ever really tried reaching out to Marcia, never attempted to climb on a rainbow to get her. He had worked hard in the last week and had begun to wonder whether it was all in vain. All he had got for his efforts were a few smiles and cups of tea. He needed one last grand gesture.

"What do you think your mum wants more than anything?" he asked his son.

"Well, she was telling me last night that she wanted you to ask her to marry you, but she said she's not going to wait forever."

The answer had been staring him right in the face and he couldn't see it. He looked at his watch, it was five-thirty. There wasn't much time. He was determined to do it tonight.

"Lacquan, I've got to go out in a hurry. I won't be long. I don't want you leaving your books until you've learned that thirteen times table. I'll test you on it when I get back." he grabbed his jacket and crash helmet and rushed out.

Gussie had just closed The Mighty Diamond up after another bumper business day. But when he saw his friend waving frantically in the window he opened up.

"You've got to help me out, Gussie. I want to buy the most

expensive diamond wedding ring you've got in the shop. Money no object."

"Do you know how much the most expensive ring is?" Gussie asked.

"How much?"

Gussie walked his friend over to the display shelf. Well, this is the about the finest we've got and it costs £8,000."

"I'll take it," Linvall said without hesitation. "There's just one problem, I haven't got the money just now."

"That's no probelm, Linvall. I'll reserve it in the safe for you until you're ready. And of course don't forget to claim your five percent 'buddy reduction'," he winked with a smile.

"No, there is a problem, Gus. I have to have the ring today and pay you later."

Gussie smiled a business man's cynical smile. "No can do, I'm afraid. Company rules." He drew Linvall's attention to the 'Please do not ask for credit because our refusals are intended to offend' sign above the counter.

"Gus, come on man. My life depends on taking that wedding ring home tonight."

"Well my life depends on stopping you from taking it home until you've paid for it. Come on Linvall man, you know better than that. It's my old man's business, not mine. He makes the rules. Anyway, who are you going to marry who's so important that she can't wait for a ring?"

Linvall had deliberately avoided mentioning his baby mother's name, but he was a desperate man clutching at straws.

"Marcia."

"Marcia?! Marcia?!! You have got to be kidding me!" Gussie exclaimed, his eyeballs popping in disbelief. "After all that woman's done to you, you still haven't learned?"

Linvall said it was his funeral. How could he get the ring home tonight? Gussie had to come up with a way. Gussie walked over to the shop window."

"Well, your Harley looks nice. What would you say it was worth, eight, nine grand?"

Linvall saw his motorcycling days flash before him; all the good times he had had posing on the Harley, pulling women, riding out into the country. He was happiest when he was on his bike and had only considered selling it to ward off an impending financial drought. The real test would be if he could bear to sell it for Marcia.

"Come off it, it's worth ten or twelve grand more like it." Oh what the heck, Linvall thought, as he hammered another nail into his bachelor days.

"I've always wanted to ride a bike," Gussie shouted at Linvall, his pillion passenger, as he throttled the Harley over Blackfriars Bridge. Linvall was hanging on for dear life. Gussie had insisted on taking his first riding lesson by driving the bike's former owner back to South London. Unfortunately for Linvall, he always carried an extra helmet. At least he had the ring in his pocket. It had cost him his motorcycle, but it would be worth it if it did the trick."

Linvall looked at Marcia through cloudy eyes and got down on his knees. He was chocking up inside, praying that her feelings for him could be revived. If she'd only give his love one more try. One more try, that's all he was asking.

"Marcia, I know we've been through some rough times over the years and that I've put you through things you never deserved to suffer. I can understand if you're still angry at me but remember that every saint was once a sinner and every sinner could yet be a saint. I want to do it right this time, Marcia. This time, let's get married. I'm asking you to put all that behind you, let the past bury the past and marry me for the future and this time, I promise, I'll dedicate my life to you."

He dipped into his breast pocket and pulled out the ring he had bought earlier and held it in front of her. Marcia's eyes clouded also and eventually she burst out crying.

"Oh you silly fool," she said embracing him tightly. "You're hopeless, you know that? Twelve years. That must be one of the longest times a woman has had to wait for a proposal. Of course I'll marry you. If it means that you'll be a father to your child and you'll give me that little bit of respect and loving that I ask for, I'll marry you several times over."

They kissed and embraced like young lovers and the angels played sweet soul music in their ears.

MURDER SHE WROTE

It was late when I reached home but I could see from the light in the bedroom, that Lesley was up waiting for me, an ominous sign.

"Tell me, Johnny, was it worth it?," she asked casually, looking up from the book she was reading in bed.

"What?"

"Was it good? You've been sleeping with her havent you? I can smell it on you. You slept with her and then came waltzing over here tonight — sweet talking her and breathing heavily one minute and then saying, 'I'm leaving', the next?"

"Oh for goodness sake, Lesley... What are you talking about?"

"You know the thing that disappoints me the most, is that all my friends and family laughed at me and said Johnny's not worth it, but I didn't listen to them. When you fell down, I was there to pick you up and keep you close to my bosom, next to my heart. You let me down, Johnny, you let me down."

"Oh come on, Lesley," I soothed, walking over and putting an arm around her. "It's all over. I made a mistake, but it's all over. It's you I really want and I've said that. I've told Pauline it's all over. My only problem is that I want to be a father to my child — to all my children, so I have to go over there every now and then."

But Lesley wasn't listening. She just stared ahead with a blank expression on her face.

"You've been taking everything I do for you for granted. But all that is over, Johnny."

I searched her eyes closely for further clarification. I had always feared that I may lose Lesley one day, but I was determined that this wasn't going to be the day; but if I didn't win her back completely, 'too late' would be my cry.

"It's you I want, Lesley," I repeated. "What I feel for you is so real and so strong I couldn't walk away even if I wanted to."

"Don't you think I have the same urges as you? When men were checking me and I had urges to be with them, I sat down and thought about it and decided my family came first."

I had to admit that it had always been a boost to my

165

confidence to know that I could trust my woman completely in any situation. It's the sweetest thing when a man checks your woman and you know he can't take her. Even if he applied science, he still couldn't cause her to leave you. A man needs the confidence to know his woman won't diss the programme when he's not around.

Lesley's mother came over early in the morning. Winnie was at school and I was on my way to The Book Shack to open up, but she pushed me back inside the house. Said she had to speak to me. She didn't mince her words. She called her daughter into the living room and told her to chuck me out immediately and if Lesley didn't, she said she would personally.

"Why should she do that? I'm the best friend she's got."

"Chuck him out, girl! No excuses! No second chance, just chuck him out on his ear!" she insisted.

"Look Mama," I said reasonably, "me and Lesley are going to live together regardless of who don't like it or who like it. Me don't tell nobody how to live them life so don't come and tell me how to live mine."

"All I know is that you is giving Lesley stress," Mrs McFarlane pressed on. "For years yuh been giving her stress and it's time that it stop! I think you should do the honourable thing and just pack up your bag and go!"

"Please," I protested, appealing for calm, "don't scandalise my name."

"Johnny" she spelled it out slowly and clearly, " I want you to leave Lesley and when I say leave ... I mean LEAVE! I don't want to see you back here after two weeks or two months or two years. I mean LEAVE FOR GOOD!! You're just dragging each other down! You're a nice boy Johnny, you've got manners, you're not rude... But I still want you to leave."

"Mum, me and Lesley came to that conclusion also — at first... and we thought about it and we decided we're going to stay together. It's taken me a long time to grow up y'know and I'm 34 now, I've matured and what we have been through in the past weeks has helped me to mature."

"Yuh no mature!" her unsympathetic answer rang in my ears. "I come here and tidy up this place and when I gone and come back I see glasses in the sink and everything needs cleaning. I always have to walk behind and pick up the pieces after you. Yuh nuh mature!"

"Mum, I understand that you've just come out of a relationship that never went too well and you don't want the same thing for your daughter, but I am going to look after

166

her. We're going to make it work this time."

"Johnny, I say fe LEAVE! And don't come back. You can look after your children and come and visit them, but LEAVE!"

"Mum, you say I'm not mature, but remember the other day when you tell me to buy carpet fe Winnie's room...?"

"I shouldn't have to tell you to buy carpet!"

"You never have to tell me to buy it, because I was the one who threw the old carpet out in the first place, so obviously I was going to replace it... I'm only asking if you remember the day when you tell me..."

"Yes, yes, yes I remember. What's it got to do with anything?"

"Good. Well when me and Lesley went to go and buy the carpet I saw a piece that would fit in Winnie's room. Lesley said, 'Johnny, you're always in a hurry'. I said 'Let's take it. If it don't fit, I'll bring it back.' She said, 'You're too rush-rush.' I said, 'Okay'. Now there was a carpet that would fit twice Winnie's room. Lesley said 'No, no. You're too impatient.' So now you come here and see that there's no carpet and you say 'obviously the fool boy wotless', not knowing what really happened. You see how people don't see the whole situation but they think they've got the full picture and start to pass judgement on it?"

"So how are you going to support your other children? It's at least three children you have now by at least two different women."

"What are you talking about *at least*? That's all the children I have. You don't think I can count?" I said.

"I want to know if you're going to promise to support your child. You want the baby, but you can't have him without paying."

"Trust me, I'll be paying for my youts, all ah dem"

Mrs McFarlane kissed her teeth to show that she was unimpressed. "How can I trust you, when you're out ah street when your woman needs loving, but you don't give her none. All you give her is pure distress." She turned to her daughter, "You see, I always tell you, if a man love you, he will do the decent thing and marry you."

"You see mum, you don't know that do you? I bought a ring two years ago y'know. I said 'let's get married right away,' but Lesley turned me down every minute when me mention it. Isn't that right, Lesley?"

Lesley looked up at me disdainfully. She seemed to be decided; her head having been turned against me by her mother. When she spoke, her voice was slow, tired and deliberate.

"Johnny, I want you out of here, today now. I don't mind you coming by to see the kids, but not too often. Every now and then so that you can play your part in bringing them up, but that's all. I don't want to talk about it, we've talked enough and I've got nothing more to say to you. Just pack your bags and leave."

I begged her to reconsider but she continued to be firm and resolute, "I want nothing to do with you anymore."

Men, like women, get the hint eventually and I started thinking about where I was going to spend the night. "Don't worry," I said, "I'm going. My mama always said never stay where you're not wanted." I went to the wardrobe and took out a white terelyne shirt, a recently dry-cleaned dark-blue suit and a pair of solid gent's shoes. "Don't worry about me," I said on my return to the living room, with as much irony as I could muster, "I'm a big man, I can take care of myself. I'll come back at the weekend for the rest of my stuff."

"I want everything out today!"Lesley demanded unreasonably.

"How am I going to manage that?" I protested. "I've got to get to work now, to open up the shop."

Just then the phone rang. I looked at Lesley and she looked at me and we both went to pick it up. Mrs McFarlane got there before us however.

"It's for you," she sneered and pointed the receiver in my direction. "Some woman screaming that I should tell you that your pickney don't have any food to eat and no clothes to wear and you should come..."

I grabbed the phone in a hurry. It was Pauline, I couldn't believe it; sounding hysterical and screaming down the line at me.

"How did you get this number?"

She simply pressed 'redial' on her phone, she explained cockily. 'Damn!' I thought. She demanded maintenance money from me, said she needed to go out raving that night and a lot of other nonsense or she would report me to the Child Support Agency.

"How's the yout?" I asked anxiously.

"Well if you want to see him, it will cost you fifty pounds," she said.

Suddenly the line went dead, I spun around and saw Lesley standing with the phone jack in her hand.

"Put it back in!" I commanded.

"If you want to call your fancy woman, you can do it at the phone box across the road."

I would have cussed Lesley straight away, but with her mother standing right behind her and the look on her face telling me that our love was history, I decided otherwise and went across the road to make the call.

Pauline was still in a hysterical mood when I called back, threatening that I would not see my baby again if I didn't pay her 'x' amount of cash straight away. I was worried. When she was in that kind of mood, I was afraid she might buck up on a machete, because I wouldn't put it past her to use it. I didn't get a chance to speak for long, as a commotion had developed in front of Lesley's house. Passers-by had started gathering on the pavement outside, cheering and whistling loudly. I looked closer, Lesley was flinging my books out of the window and into the street, closely supervised by her mother. I cursed loudly to myself, something like "bloody bitch!" before hanging up and rushing across the road.

My books were all over the place and others were flying out of the upstairs window fast. The bystanders laughed out loud when they realised that I was the intended victim. I had no way of hiding my embarassment however, because Lesley had locked the front door from the inside. She was a crafty one.

"Please Lesley, don't disgrace us like this!" I reasoned, but the books continued flying out.

"Do you tell her the same things you tell me when you fall on top of her at night?!" she shouted. "Do you? Or do you just make her feel like she's a good piece of 'gimme-some-tonight but I don't know if I'll be around tomorrow'? I don't want you in my house again Johnny and I don't want your things here. And count on me for nothing!"

I began the arduous task of gathering the books. I was so angry and determined to make her pay. This was too embarassing; even if she wanted me back I wouldn't have her.

"Don't blame me Lesley, don't blame me the day your son turns around and asks why his father isn't around and you have to tell him the truth, that you kicked his father out and he turns around and cusses you for it because all he ever wanted in his childhood was a father like the other kids. One day he'll be old enough and he'll cuss you and you just remember what I'm saying at that time."

The male bystanders nodded their heads in agreement. Baby fathers right across the capital could empathise with me. The female bystanders laughed in a unified chorus.

169

"It's too bad you can't understand nothing but what you read in those books!" one of them chided.

I knew my distress wasn't over when I made my way to the bank to withdraw a hundred pounds because I hoped the money would buy me time while I tried to calm Pauline down. I would have been wiser to cut my losses for the day.

The first thing I discovered was that the locks to her flat had been changed. My keys were now redundant. I flung them away and rang the bell. A big, burly, African muscleman with a pin-head and no shirt on his torso, opened the door with a broad smile from ear to ear. Despite his bulk, his childish, slightly moronic face revealed a kid who couldn't have been more than seventeen years of age and he looked at me as if I was yesterday's man. Pauline stood behind him, a triumphant smile half-obscured by the African's pectorals.

I made my way in. African glanced back at Pauline for approval and she nodded her head.

"So you've got yourself a new boyfriend." I said emphasising the 'boy' as I stepped into the living room. Pauline followed with her African, leading him over to the sofa.

"Yeah, I've learned that love is not as important as the material things in life. I've decided to take you to court for the maintenence. I'm going for it."

She sat on African's lap and gave him a deep, long, soulful kiss, ignoring my presence. I had a hundred pounds in my pocket, but the woman was too feisty.

"Look, all I want to do is see that my yout' is alright and then I'll leave you and your boyfriend alone," I said, making a move towards the bedroom.

"He's not here," Pauline said quickly. "My mother came down from Birmingham; I've sent the boy up with her. I don't want you to see him before all this is sorted out in court."

Pauline had her legs wrapped around that boy's body. She put those hot, wet lips on his mouth then pulled his head down to her breasts, urging him to bite and whispering about how good it was. The boy obeyed her every command and ran his hands along her thighs, breathing in her ear, his eyes rolling in his head as he groped for the wonderland between her legs. Pauline, her head thrown back, looked over at me with that mischievous look in her face. I told her straight that I hadn't got any money, so it would be no use playing me for a boops. I could almost taste her mouth on African's big, hairless chest.

"You're not going to get a penny from me. Not one penny."

"I'm afraid it's not up to you," she said smiling. "They'll get it from you whether you like it or not. This is the government you're dealing with here you know."

"Well, I'll chip from my address so I'm harder to track down."

I've already registered your name at the family section of the country court and I'll give you the letter personally, even if you rip it up."

She wouldn't ease off the pressure, not before she had finished twisting up my insides and chewing every ounce of pride and modesty from me and spitting it out again. She began talking in cliches like, "Money talks and bullshit walks a marathon..." — talking like my baby was her mealticket for life — "I don't ever have to work again," she rejoiced. I tried to reason with her sensibly, but it was no use. She was behaving like a child, like one of those millions of children having children in this time. I was startled by the sound of my baby crying in the bedroom. I glared at Pauline, she had lied. She looked up from African's lap and simply shrugged her shoulders. I had only taken a couple of steps towards the bedroom, when what felt like a ton of bricks smashed down on each of my shoulders and sent me crashing backwards into the wall. I came down with a thud, dazed and with a blazing fire raging up my spine.

"Watch yourself," African said in a thick, Jamaican patois, "else you'll bite off more than you can chew."

I looked up at him puzzled, but decided that this was indeed one of those many times when brawn was mightier than brain. I left the flat resolved that if Pauline wasn't prepared to bring my youth up the way I wanted her to, I wasn't going to contribute a penny to his maintenance. He who pays the piper, calls the tune.

"Close the door on your way out!" Pauline called after, as she resumed her love games.

171

Ordinarily Gussie would not hesitate to take his problem to his mother. Millie Pottinger had always been a pillar of support in her children's lives and always had a positive word of encouragement when they needed it. When all else failed, Mama was always there. This was one problem however that it took Gussie a week to get the courage to offload on her. Eventually he got tired of saying there was nothing wrong when she asked him why he was looking so glum these days.

"I'm not going to marry Chantelle."

"Why not?" Millie asked confused. "I thought you were both agreed."

"Well Papa told me not to tell you, but she's my sister." Gussie didn't relish giving his mother the blow by blow account of her husband's thirty year old infidelity, but he had no choice and watched her closely as he filled her in. Millie stood expressionless, thoughtful, her mind flashing back many years.........

It was years ago, back in Jamaica. She was sixteen and a virgin. She hadn't even been kissed. When you're the preacher's daughter in a little old seaport town on the east coast of Jamaica just after the war, only the most courageous boys would offer to carry your books home. And if they were the roughest boys around, your father would definitely not approve. Toyan was different from the others. He was tall, handsome, intelligent and charming. Even though he hung out on the street corners looking tough with his rough friends, his eyes would melt when he saw Millicent and her school mates walking leisurely from school. Giggling mischievously her friends would abandon her the moment they saw Toyan approaching, raising his hat from his head with a broad grin. Millicent was shy. Her strict religious upbringing had taught her to deny, reject, abhor her natural feelings towards the opposite sex; at least until she was married in the eyes of God. But being with Toyan was how she had always imagined heaven to be: calm, serene, peaceful. With him she discovered a part of herself that she had never known — that she could love life, joy and happiness. She was an adventurer and wanted to climb the highest mountain, just for the fun of it and she wanted to swim an ocean and visit people in foreign lands and learn their cultures, learn their histories, music, literature. She wanted to see Africa, to visit the pyramids and cross the Sahara on a camel. She wanted to visit India, Australia, Japan. Just because they were there. And lying with Toyan on a secluded beach every day after school, her dreams seemed possible. He taught her to swim and he took her high up into the hills from where they could look down on their town and see the fishermen putting out to sea, hunting for their daily catch.

"One day Millie," Toyan promised, "one day I'll take you to all the places you want to go, Paris, Rome, England, Africa, New York and all dem places. Nuh worry yuhself."

Millie told him that she believed he would. Believed, that one day they would both see those places together. Millie loved him truly, but even she couldn't believe it when Toyan, as bold as day, knocked on the door of her father's house. He told Pastor Grant about how much he loved his daughter and how he was hoping to ask her for her hand in marriage, but he wanted to do it the proper way to get the father's blessing first. Pastor Grant called the police, in a fury, and ordered them to remove the intruder from his home. But Toyan didn't give up that easily. Even though Pastor Grant took to collecting his daughter from school and walking her the short way home from school, Toyan would walk a few paces behind them on their journey, just to catch the odd smile from his loved one — the preacher's daughter. He even started attending church, sitting in the front row where he could get a good view of Millie, to the fury of the Pastor who was powerless to stop him, and his daughter's accomodating smiles back. The whole thing was becoming a scandal. Eventually Millie's father relented — or so the young romantics hoped — when Toyan was invited to the Grant house for supper.

"So you want to marry my daughter?" the Pastor enquired.

"Yes sah! I want to marry your daughter, take good care of her, treat her well and bring up a family with her, sah!" Toyan flashed Millie a confident smile across the table.

"Well alright," said Pastor Grant who was older and wiser. "Tell me, how do you intend to support my daughter exactly? You have job? You have money?"

"No sah, but you know how it go, we'll work out sump'n."

"I beg your pardon, Sir, but you have to 'work out sump'n' *before* you marry my daughter. I'm sure you'll agree with me young man that my daughter deserves the very best of the very best. Here is my house, it's not much and indeed we may even call it humble. But it is the bare minimum my daughter is used to. I've given this matter a lot of thought young man. Everybody in this parish knows me as a fair man, so I'll tell you what I'll do... Even though I expressly don't want you to marry my daughter, I will give you a chance to prove just how much you love her. If you can come back here with enough money in your bank account to match mine, fair enough, I'll give you both my blessing. Until then, my duty is to make sure that my daughter is provided for as best as possible and at present I can provide for her much better than you. That's a fair deal isn't it?" the Pastor turned to his daughter for approval. Millie couldn't deny that her father was being reasonable. So strong was her love and admiration for her young suitor that she believed no task too great for him. She was sure he could do it and promised to wait for him as long as it took. Toyan accepted the challenge. He announced his plans to travel to Kingston the next to day, "to seek my fortune."

Despite his assurances that he would be "back shortly", Millie soon realised that Toyan's sojourn to 'town' was not going to be brief. She didn't know how long it took to seek one's fortune, but people in the village were always talking about money floating on the streets of Kingston. The weeks turned to months nevertheless. After six months Toyan wrote her his first and only letter. Though clumsily written, it gave a chronological account of everything he had done since leaving the village. His mother's sister had kindly given him a place to stay, on the floor in a room with her six sons. Her husband had helped him get a job at the sanitation works where he worked burning the tons of rubbish that were collected daily from the streets of Kingston. It was hard work and the pay was appalling. He hadn't managed to save much money yet, but he was confident that he would return to claim his bride the moment he had enough money together.

The months then became years. Three years in fact. Millie heard a rumour from one of the boys hanging out on the street corner that Toyan had "gone ah foreign", but otherwise it was as if he had disappeared off the face of the earth. Millie — who had become a school teacher in the local school — still held a torch for her departed suitor and trusted that her heart was with him just as his was with her every minute of the day. On the quiet days when she had time to reflect on the short time they had had together, she was filled with joy and a sense of pride.

Lloyd George Pottinger brought a breath of fresh air to the youth of Port Maria. He came to town with a purpose and lots of ambition. Beside him the local youth seemed clumsier and slower, for he was sharp, well spoken and polished. He had travelled across country from Old Harbour to set up a carpentry business in Port Maria. It didn't take him long to establish himself and he quickly got a reputation for being a master craftsman of furniture who was dilligent and prepared to work through the night to finish an order in time. It didn't take the young ladies of the town long to see that here was a man who was a good catch for any woman. Winnie got her chance to admire this young man with the Midas touch when he came to church on Sundays, always elegantly dressed and courteous. It didn't take him long to notice her also. From the pulpit, Pastor Grant eventually noticed the coyly exchanged glances between his daughter and the fine, young carpenter. He was pleased and wasted no time in inviting Lloyd for supper.

The meal was a sober affair, before which the Pastor invited the guest to say grace. Both Millie and her father were impressed by the fluency and poise with which Lloyd asked the Father to bless their meal.

"So what are your plans?" Pastor Grant asked him as they relaxed by discussing each other's favourite passages from the Bible. "Do you intend to stay in Port Maria or will not the limited confines of this small fishing port be too limiting for a young man with your ambition?"

"Sir, even as we speak, I am making plans to leave Jamaica for work. That's where the future lies for my generation. In England, there is work for everybody and there are opportunities that we won't see in Jamaica for another twenty years. The only reason I haven't gone yet is because I don't want to leave before I've saved enough money to give myself a good start in life."

"That's very sensible," Pastor Grant said, impressed. "I've heard of so many people who have gone to England, only to find that life was a struggle over there also. With a bit of money behind you you ought to be able to set yourself up nicely."

Pastor Grant and his guest talked for hours in the living room, with his daughter sitting listening with interest.

"So, are you a married man?" Pastor Grant asked.

"No sir, unfortunately I have not had an opportunity to share my life with a woman as yet, but I assure you that I intend to make that a priority before I leave to England."

Not long after, the Pastor declared himself exhausted after a long day and made his way to his bedroom, uncustomarily encouraging his daughter to entertain their guest in the proper manner.

Thoughts of Toyan had, over the years, slipped further and further from Millie's short term memory. That evening Lloyd Pottinger's charm helped to banish them on a more permanent basis. Lloyd told her of his plans, his visions and his dreams and the way he talked you really believed him capable of achieving anything he wanted to. Winnie stayed awake all night, dreaming of the most eligible bachelor in Port Maria.

Pastor Grant was pleased when Lloyd asked for his permission to ask his daughter's hand in marriage. He blessed the young carpenter's request with as much pride as any father could and when he saw that his daughter was also happy, he embraced Lloyd immediately as a future son.

Lloyd proved to be a dream fiance. He was gentle, tolerant and willing to pamper Millie more than she had ever been. He bought her little presents, dresses and books mostly. He vowed that when they were married, everything he owned would be hers. He didn't speak much about his upbringing in Old Harbour, except to say that as an orphan, the first word he learned was 'survival'. Now he wanted to have children whom he could give the love he had never had.

Their wedding was the largest the little village had seen. No expense was spared and not only did the Pastor give away his daughter, he also officiated. There was food for everyone and the atmosphere was merry. A trio of local musicians serenaded the happy couple until Lloyd carried his bride home to her new home in his house. There was a lump of sadness in Pastor Grant's throat as he saw his daughter leave, for he knew that in another month his daughter would be gone forever, with her husband, to a land far away.

The next morning as Millie shopped in the market for that evening's meal — in her new and respected role as Mrs Lloyd Pottinger — she was confronted by a tall, handsome gentleman dressed from head to toe in a bleached white hat, suit and shoes. He raised his hat off to her with a warm smile. It took her only a moment to recognise Toyan, newly returned from Florida — where he had saved a small fortune cutting cane as an H2 worker. He had only just arrived in Port Maria and was on his way to show the Pastor his bank account.

"You didn't write to me for two and a half years. Toyan, I waited for you as long as I could," Millie cried sorrowfully. Toyan could see from the way she avoided his gaze that he had been beaten only by time and not by her passions for him.

"So you're telling me you're married?" he asked cautiously, in his recently acquired American accent.

"Yes, yes, I'm married!" Millie exclaimed. "If only you had come yesterday."

After a long pause, Toyan insisted that she join him the next day on the secluded beach of their earlier youth. He would bring a picnic and they would talk about old times. Millie's heart was pumping furiously, and confused. She wanted to see Toyan so much and because her husband spent most of his time in the workshop, she would have ample time to slip away unnoticed. And even though she didn't know what a picnic was exactly, she didn't want to miss the opportunity of tasting any slices of the American social pie Toyan may have brought with him.

They spent the next afternoon sitting on their beach, filling each other in on the years they had missed together and talking about the old days. Toyan had got an opportunity to sail to Florida on a steam ship and jumped at the chance. Though conditions in the canefields of Florida were much harder than his spell at the sanitation works, the money that could be earned was sometimes three times as much as he earned in Jamaica. After just his first season as a cane cutter, he was able to save enough money to buy a grammophone system and a number of the popular New Orleans rhythm and blues-style records. He had then started running house parties for the Jamaican community over there who had little in the form of entertainment aimed specifically at them. After two years he had made enough money to come back to Jamaica and buy himself a house and set up a business. He was going to build a recording studio in Kingston, he said. And he was going to record the new Jamaican music that people were already calling 'ska'.

They drank from the French wine that Toyan had bought in Miami and brought to the picnic. He even allowed her to puff from one of his American cigarettes. As she listened to his plans, Millie's heart told her that Toyan had kept his promise and that he would now live the exciting life that they had always talked about with another woman. Her dreams of England faded. There was a clear tinge of regret in her voice as she told Toyan about the type of man her new husband was. She was sure that Toyan was being generous when he

177

said her husband sounded "a'right". She agreed to meet up with her childhood sweetheart at the same time for the next three Friday afternoons before she left for England. She realised such innocent liaisons could be interpreted scandalously, but she knew that she would never live a peaceful life with Lloyd in England unless she succeeded in exorcising the ghost of Toyan from her affections. He had rented the grand old plantation on the hill overlooking the village for the weeks he intended to rest in Port Maria before going on to Kingston, but it would have been even more scandalous were they to meet there.

The next few weeks were even more confusing for Millie. Her husband had set himself on a single-minded course to amasss as much money as possible to take with them to England, so he worked tirelessly at his workshop at the other end of the village, even if it meant burning the midnight oil. And while he worked he had no time for loving and didn't seem to have time to stop and talk whenever his wife brought him his meals. Meanwhile, on their Friday afternoons together, Toyan seemed to be the very essence of charm. he seemed to be interested in nothing but talking about Millie. He had matured into a suave and sophisticated young man with a worldly knowledge that few of his contemporaries in the village possessed. And he was an honourbale man who never once tried to compromise his former sweetheart.

On the Thursday night, two days before they were due to sail on the HMS Windrush, Millie was busy baking a surprise cake for her husband. She had felt guilty about her intentions to see Toyan for a last time on Lloyd's birthday and wanted to make up for it. The cake ready, she waited until just before midnight to carry it through the darkened main street of the village to the workshop on the other side. Already a few yards from the workshiop she could hear the stifled moans of sexual intercourse. She almost dropped the cake as she raced towards the workshop and pulled open the door. She found her husband lying naked atop a newly-varnished table, locked in a tight embrace with one of the village girls. He looked up and only just managed to duck as his birthday cake came hurtling towards him.

The next day, Millie exorcised the ghost of Toyan from her heart finally. She went before their appointed time at the beach to the old plantaion house and gave a perplexed Toyan that which was rightfully his after three years of waiting. Too many plans had been made not to follow Lloyd to England, but this afternoon, she would make unrestricted, uninhibited carefree love with her first love.

"Don't worry," Millie said finally, "go ahead and marry
Chantelle anyway."

"Mama, I can't do that, it would be incest. For one thing it's
against the law and for another...."

"Go ahead and marry her," Millie repeated. "You're not
your father's son, but your father doesn't know it."

Everyone agreed that the wedding at the end of August
was the best they had ever been to. Some of the guests had
previously been to a double wedding, but nobody present
could remember a triple wedding. Linvall waited proudly as
Marcia walked down the aisle, Gus smiled proudly as
Chantelle approached him and Beres beamed as Caroline
made her way slowly beside her co-brides. Johnny was best
man for them all and had three rings in three different
waistcoat pockets. The pastor told the congregation of his
pride in seeing six young people coming to the house of the
Lord to testify their love for their partners and the whole
congregation said an "Amen!"

The reception afterwards was in the ballroom of a well
known hotel on Park Lane. It went remarkable smoothly for
such an impressively large affair.

Caroline and Beres spent most of the wedding night in
their bridal suite, holding each other's naked bodies tight as
they looked out across the dark expanse of Hyde Park over to
the bright lights of Knightsbridge in the distance and dreamt
of their future together. Caroline wanted three kids one after
the other. And she vowed to love Lara as her own child on the
occasions her husband was allowed access. Beres promised
that he would always be attentive to her every need and
always be there for her.

Gussie and Chantelle were rolling on the massive bed in
their bridal suite the moment they entered it. Gussie was
looking forward to the extra-special loving Chantelle had
promised him all week. He liked it hot and one look in her
eyes could tell him that she was smouldering.

"There's just one thing," Chantelle said nervously.

"Yes, what is it?" Gussie breathed heavily.

"I used to be a man," Chantelle replied.

The reception was a late night affair and carried on long

179

after the three couples had stolen away up to their bridal suites in the hotel. His best man role over, Johnny relaxed with a glass of wine and talked with Fat Willy who had come with his main squeeze. The Brixton Massive FC team manager noticed a hint of change in Johnny's words as they discussed the number of team players who had married over the last year. Johnny seemed to have sympathy with them and no longer talked of the importance of spreading his seed, but longed for the day when Lesley would forgive him and give him the opportunity to prove that he could make her happy and take care of his family. Now he was spouting a new wisdom. "Love is like a bird in a cage. When you're a bird in a cage, you have a comfortable life, because you're in the warmth," Johnny said. "And you're fed and you're protected. But when the bird in the cage sees a bird flying free in the air, it wishes it were like that, while the bird that is flying free in the sky looks down on the bird in the cage and thinks, 'well you've got the good life'. Each of them looks at the other's life and thinks that it is better. That's why people under fifty never make the right choice of partner. They don't know what they want. That's the advantage with the Asian system of arranged marriages. I've been reading up about it. They stay married to each other for ever. It's no use allowing the young to decide who they want to marry when they don't have any experience of it. You should leave all that to the older folk."

Fat Willy wasn't convinced by Johnny's new philosophical convictions. "So supposing your parents arranged for you to marry a really ugly woman," he asked, "and they thought she would do perfectly for you, would you still do it?"

Johnny answered without hesitation.

"Absolutely."

Willy laughed. Somehow he couldn't see Johnny walking down the aisle with Frankenstein's daughter or Queen Kong.

"No seriously, I would. If my parents felt this ugly woman had the right character, the right temparament to deal with me on a permanent basis, then why not? That doesn't mean that I wouldn't be out there on the street checking prettier women when those certain juices inside of me started moving about. One advantage with an ugly woman is that you don't have to watch over your shoulder all the time because no man in his right mind is ever going to check her."

Fat Willy still wasn't convinced, but accepted that every man does his thing a little way different.

It was so late you could almost call it early, but the wedding guests were still not ready to go home. The hotel staff had nothing to grumble about, they were getting paid by the hour; the longer it took, the longer they earned. The music was bubbling on a mellow lover's groove and everyone got in the mood holding their partners tight across the dancefloor. Johnny had been watching Lesley all night. Gussie had insisted on inviting her to the wedding and although they had exchanged glances earlier in church, they had given each other a wide berth. Seeing her dancing now, in the arms of a sharply dresssed, smooth dancer was twisting his insides. They were dancing close now, smoothly and effortlessly, to *their* tune. It couldn't have escaped Lesley that this was the same revival tune they had danced to on Valentine's night at the Diamond Rooms when they first met all those years ago. Johnny couldn't take anymore and made his way across the dancefloor and tapped Lesley's dancing partner on the shoulder. He was reluctant to give up his dance, but Johnny was insistent and short of causing a scene, the man had to bow out gracefully. Lesley turned her head away from Johnny as they danced. She didn't say a word. She didn't need to. Johnny was happy to let the record speak for them both and as their hips rolled together as one, he learned what one dance could do. Lesley however, was not easily forgiving. She managed to release herself from Johnny's gentle grip before the deejay mixed into the next tune and walked off the dancefloor towards the exit doors. Johnny couldn't just stand there looking stupid and made after her as if they were both calmly walking off for a breath of fresh air. He caught up with her just outside the exit.

"Lesley, hold up now. I just want to talk. Come on, stop acting that way. Just talk to me, nuh."

Lesley stopped and turned towards him.

"Johnny, don't come and make out like everything's fine. I told you I didn't want anything to do with you anymore. She continued walking unsteadily at a pace a little too quick for her high heeled shoes. Johnny had to sprint to catch up with her.

"Okay, okay. I'm a bastard, yeah, you're right. But look at me Lesley, look how maaga I am. I haven't been able to eat, because I threw away the most important thing in my life, the thing that gives me my air to breathe, I threw away our love. But give me a break Lesley, I've suffered enough and I've learned a good lesson. So give me a break Lesley, if not for me, for the kids. I want to be a father to my children."

Johnny knew that the kids were Lesley's weak point and he was exploiting them, but he had no choice. If he had one more chance, he would see to it that he was the best father a child could hope for. Fat Willy and his baby mother stopped on their way out to offer their opinion.

"Come on Lesley, give Johnny a break, wha' do you man? We all know that you gave birth to the youths," Fat Willy mediated, "but at the same time if it wasn't for the seed that Johnny planted inside you there wouldn't be no pickney, so ease off the pressure and let him see his youths. Ah wha' do you?"

"But at the same time," Willy's baby mother added, "if he's not prepared to be there for you one hundred percent, don't take him back."

Johnny looked pleadingly into Lesley's eyes

"Come on Lesley, let's go together to Carnival tomorrow, the whole family: you, me, Winnie and Jacob. Let's have a family day out at the Carnival. Okay, I know it's done at 7.00pm, but after a few years we're used to that now. Let's make the most of it."

"No, Carnival ain't what it used to be," Lesley said eventually, a far away look in her eyes and a tinge of sadness in her voice, as she lamented the passing of the good old days. "They're complaining the crowd is too big. But the way I check it, every year they are blocking up more and more roads where the crowd could ah gwan."

"Let's hope we can see some changes next year," Johnny added as he walked Lesley slowly towards her car. That they were on speaking terms was as much as he could have hoped for. Johnny waved Lesley goodbye as she sped homewards. Morning was breaking and birds were singing in acknowledgement. Despite the chilly wind, it looked like it was going to be a beautiful day.

In his honeymoon suite, Gussie remained paralysed. The look in Chantelle's eyes told him she was serious, yet his brain refused to register her confession as such. Faced with most men's worst nightmare, he fell into a state of shock, unable to make sense out of nonsense.

182